Midlife Magical

Mystery Tour

WITCH WAY SERIES

Shelley Dorey

DEDICATION

Once again, to my sister. Wanna go on road trip?

Contents

One

Kara

The last time I saw Maren was eight months ago. Considering how small Auburn is, that was kind of weird. Auburn's a town that's a forty-minute drive from the "big city" Syracuse. A couple of banks, a movie theater, a few gas stations—sort of small. We have a Burger King and McDonald's, but no Wendy's or KFC, you know? Now we do have a Denny's, and that's where I work. You'd think Maren and I would see each other a lot more, right? Well, we don't.

It wasn't like there was some big rift between us. Nope, we'd just been caught up living our own lives, following two very different paths. In lots of ways, it was like we lived in two different worlds.

Yeah, the last time I'd seen her was at her annual Christmas party. Josh and I had endured it, making small talk with people who would never acknowledge, let alone see me, if we crossed paths on the street. Her friends and clients existed in a world that was totally alien to mine.

But today... I swiped a tear from my eye, blinking fast to see the road in the blur of trees and pasture. Today I needed to see my sister. Aside from my son, Josh, she was all I had left in the world. And no way was I going to confide the results of my medical tests to my kid. He had his life before him, just starting college in Syracuse.

It would be hard to tell Maren and hard for her to hear, but...damn it! She was family. Someone I could cry with and rail at the world! This was so unfair. But then when had life ever been fair where I was concerned?

"In half a mile, turn right onto Oakridge Road. Your destination will be on your left."

The GPS yanked me out of my thoughts and I took a deep breath. Shit! I was almost there? Sad to say, but I'd never been out to see her latest project. At least twice a year she and Wayne bought some dump to renovate and flip, so no wonder I needed the GPS. It was hard to keep track of her home address. In addition to flipping houses, the two of them made great money doing real estate deals as Auburn became the bedroom community of the big city. The office was more Wayne's domain; Maren preferred working on their latest house.

I noticed a plume of dark smoke spiraling up into the blue September sky. As I drove, it grew bigger, so much so that I could smell it in my car. It was early for people to be burning leaves. And leaves don't make pitch-black smoke.

"In fifty feet, turn right onto Oakridge Road," the GPS instructed.

"Yeah, yeah." I flipped the turn signal and peered out the windshield at the smoke billowing high above the trees to my left.

"Your destination is on the left."

As I wheeled the Honda down a tree-lined driveway, my attention was drawn to the flaming pyre in the center of the lawn. Blurred in the shimmering heat waves was a wild-haired woman, scooping up stuff and hurling it into the fire. Oh my God—she looked like some kind of witch in a Halloween special!

I stopped the car, staring hard at the woman before scrambling out of the Honda. Holy shit! That was Maren. What the hell was she doing? She was in some kind of frenzy, darting to a heap of refuse, arms flailing as she slammed objects onto the pyre.

"Take that, you bastard!" Screeching, she hurled more into the fire.

I flew across the lawn towards her. It was only when I was ten feet away that I could see the pile of garbage consisted of clothes. An entire man's wardrobe was strewn on the grass in separate piles. One was suits, button-down shirts, and a bundle of neckties. Another was casual wear— golf shirts, Dockers, jeans, shorts, and concert T-shirts. Despite the leaping flames, there was still a mass of clothing waiting to be tossed in. And alongside the clothing was a selection of sports equipment for the middle-aged man: tennis rackets, squash rackets, rarely used hockey sticks, a set of skis, and of course, the mandatory set of golf clubs.

If it wasn't for the fire, you would think my sister was setting up a garage sale. Yeah, she was the organized one. Even as she shrieked, she shook out his polo shirts before flinging them at the flames. She was so intent on burning a pair of dark pants that she never turned around to even acknowledge I was there.

"Maren! What're you doing?" A dumb question. As I rushed to her side, she spun around to face me. Narrow eyes glared at me while stringy locks of brunette hair framed her soot-smudged cheeks. She reached for another striped golf shirt, shook it out of its folds, and flung it into the flames.

"What's it look like, Kara? I'm burning every stitch that lying, cheating bastard owns!" A shower of orange sparks shot out from the fire and she waved them away. "He's lucky he left when he did, or I'd throw him in there too! Him and the two-bit whore he's running around with!"

My mouth fell open as I gawked at her. Hearing that Wayne was cheating wasn't news to me, of course. They almost broke up when Wayne had his "seven-year itch," as Maren called it years ago. She forgave him for it, but I never did.

Seeing Maren, consumed by rage, burning his clothes, left me speechless. This was my sister? The calm and rational woman I'd grown up with had totally left the building. Instead, this was a woman full of fury, frantically destroying her bastard husband's wardrobe.

"He dropped his bombshell this morning! Over coffee, if you can believe that!" Spittle flew from her mouth, and she wiped it away with the back of a paint-stained hand. "He came home from work and told me he's leaving me. For Suzanne Barber, of all people! Sellin' houses wasn't the only thing that little slut was doing at the office. And all the while he's screwing her, I'm busting my ass getting this dump ready for the market."

"Oh my God. Suzanne Barber? He's leaving you for her?" My eyebrows raised as I shook my head. Unbelievable. Of course, I knew who she was. Auburn is a small town. I'd seen her coming out of their real estate office, and I'd even seen her at Denny's, although I lucked out and never had to serve her. She was a thirty something, skinny blonde with a rack that she got from her doctor, not her mother. Rumor had it she had been a stripper in Rochester before settling in Auburn a couple of years ago. I don't know if it's true or not, but I wouldn't be surprised. I really didn't know all that much about her, other than the sneaky smile that never made it up to her eyes.

"Yeah, Suzanne Barber! If I wasn't so pissed off, I'd be insulted that he left me for her." She glared past me. "Hand me the five iron, Kara. What better way to stir this fire than with his favorite club? Ha! There's a double bogey for ya, Wayne!"

I turned to see the golf bag next to the pile of clothes and grabbed the club. Handing it to her, I cautioned, "Here!

Don't burn yourself, okay?" This whole scene was unbelievable. Wayne, leaving my sister. And Maren? I had never seen her this out of control or angry. Her lips pulled back in a taut grimace as she pitched a pair of plaid pants into the blaze. It was good to see her finally fight back, but truthfully, she looked more than a little unhinged.

"Maybe we should go in the house and get a drink. I think you could use one, Mare. We'll talk and try to figure this out." I went to clasp her arm, but she brushed my hand away.

"No! I'm not leaving until every scrap of clothes he owns is burned to ash! That and his precious golf clubs!" Her gaze smoldered when she scowled at the house. "Maybe, I'll set fire to that dump too. See how he likes that! He thinks he can just up and leave me after almost twenty-five years and two kids, to go 'live his life.'" She did air quotes."Well, he's got another think coming! I'll destroy him and everything he has!"

A cold ball of dread crystallized in my stomach watching her twisted features and hearing the venom in her voice. This wasn't good. Maren was losing it. It was the threat of burning the house that was the final straw. Maren liked her financial security. That was the reason she worked so hard and put up with Wayne all these years. Aside from that cheating episode, he was a self-involved asshole.

She stuck with him out of a sense of loyalty and security for her and her children. But her kids had flown the nest, leaving her with an ass-hat husband.

"Maren. Burn his clothes, if you want. Hell, he deserves that." I bent and scooped up an armful of shirts, socks, and, yuck…his underwear, and dumped them into the flames. When I turned to her, she grinned, but I wasn't through. "You can't burn the house, Mare. You could go to prison for that, and it won't be covered by insurance. The clothes are one thing, understandable to anyone. But not the house. You'd play right into Wayne's hands if you did that. He'd get you locked up, if not committed. He wants you out of his life so he can be with that woman. He also wants the business and all you two worked for. Do you really want to give that to him so easily?"

Her forehead furrowed. For a few moments, she was quiet, staring into the flames. "No. I will not make this easy for him. He's going to pay."

Her jaw tightened as she looked over at the house. "Plumbing contractors are supposed to come out tomorrow to put in new fixtures. That isn't going to happen— not now! And no way am I climbing any more ladders to paint another ceiling in that dump!"

I heard the conviction in her voice, but I didn't trust that she'd feel that way later. What if this rage came back to her in the middle of the night? "I think you need to stay with me tonight. Get away from this place for a while. We'll talk and figure out your next step. You don't want to stay here and destroy anything else. It'll come back and bite you in the ass, if you do."

She looked over at me, and tears glistened in her eyes. "You're right. I need to get away from here, even if it's just for one night. One night to get drunk and cry on your shoulder." She covered her face with her hands. "Shit. I have to call the kids. How am I going to tell them? This is going to break their hearts. How can I be civil, talking about their father?"

I stepped into her and gave her a long hug. "You're going to be all right, Mare. Your kids will be too. Trust me, we'll get through this. If anyone is going to regret anything, it's going to be Weasel Wayne. We'll get you a good lawyer to make Wayne pay for all the cheating and for doing this to you."

For a long time, I just held her, stroking her back as she cried. I'd come out to tell her my own horrible news and found her at the darkest moment of her life. Poor Maren. I needed to take care of her and get her through this mess. That's what older sisters are for, aren't they?

My own problems could wait.

***

An hour later, with the fire thoroughly drenched by the garden hose, and her overnight bag packed, the two of us drove down the main street heading to my apartment. It was another blessing that my son had left for college the week before, leaving his bedroom free for Maren. It wasn't much of a place—two bedrooms with a kitchen and living room above a florist's shop, but it had served Josh and me well, especially on my earnings as a waitress.

I interrupted Maren's litany of verbal abuse aimed at Wayne when I wheeled into the parking lot of my go-to corner store to buy milk. I drank black coffee, but Maren had always liked tons of milk in hers. "I'll just be a minute. Do you need anything?"

"Pick up a bottle of rye if you don't have any at home." She fished in her pocketbook. "Here. Make it Crown Royal, if they have it." She handed me a fifty-dollar bill.

"No way! Put your money away. I've got this!" I walked across the lot to the store, mentally calculating the balance in my bank account. I was pretty sure I could cover her whiskey without going into overdraft. If not, so what? I'd pick up an extra shift if I had to. She needed this to get her through the night and help her sleep.

When I went inside, Abe looked up from his newspaper at his usual spot behind the counter. "Hey, Kara! How you doing? You heard from that boy of yours?"

I smiled at the old man who, also like me, put in long hours working. "Doing fine, Abe. Josh texted me earlier today. He had his first day of class yesterday. So far, so good." I made my way to the back of the store where shelves of liquor were watched over by a camera set in the ceiling. I cringed when I saw the price of the rye. No wonder he had security back here! I grabbed it anyway. Next, the milk.

As Abe scanned my purchases, he asked, "Check your Powerball ticket, Kara?"

"Sure. I think I single-handedly keep the state in the

black, buying these things." I rolled my eyes but scooped the ticket from the side pocket in my purse before grabbing my debit card.

"Ya gotta be in it to win it," he said as he stepped over to the ticket scanners.

It was the same response I'd heard at least a million times between Abe and me over the years. What the hell? It was just four dollars, not going to break the bank—four dollars spent on dreams of traveling the country, free as a bird. I watched him insert the ticket into the machine as I tapped my card on the counter. I was about to turn to check on Maren sitting by herself in the car, when the machine chirped its message.

"You're a winner! Woo hoo!"

"See? What'd I tell…"

When his voice trailed off, I looked at Abe and saw his eyes practically bulging from the sockets, staring at the machine.

"What? What'd I win?" The quip about it being just seven dollars or a free ticket, died on my tongue. The air left my chest, watching Abe blink and then do a double take. "Tell me, Abe!"

His hand went to his forehead as he bent forward. "Oh my God. Kara! You matched five numbers!"

"Five numbers?" Holy shit! That meant millions! My knees went weak, and I clasped the edge of the counter. How much?

"There's other winners, Kara. But it says here that you won three hundred and fifty thousand bucks!" He scraped his fingers through his thinning hair. "Congratulations! It couldn't happen to a nicer person!"

Okay, call me greedy. But he'd burst my bubble that I wasn't a millionaire. Still…three hundred and fifty thousand smackeroos!

I was rich!

Two

Maren, a week later...

My gaze darted to the door opening in my lawyer's office and I did a double take. An outrageously handsome man, over six feet tall with an athlete's body, stepped out. Oh. My. Goodness. There was no way this guy lived in Auburn. I would never forget that face or the way his well fitted suit adorned his physique, the rich fabric draping perfectly; like an athlete at an awards dinner. Although his tousled blond hair and the lopsided smile were boyishly charming, the dark-rimmed eyeglasses and steady gaze in his eyes showed a quiet confidence that was magnetic. He stopped short, and a broad smile lit his face as he strode over to me. My heart skipped a beat as I sat glued to my chair.

"Maren? Maren West!" Extending his hand, he continued, "I wondered if it was you when Alex handed your case off to me. Maren Porter? I should have known it was you. Of course you'd be married, now a Porter." He rubbed the side of his face. "Wow, Maren; you still look like you're in college; you haven't changed a bit."

I took his hand, peering up at him. Who the hell was this? He acted like I should know him! Where was Alex Johnson, the elderly lawyer I was supposed to meet?

"I'm sorry?" I let it hang there, hoping he'd tell me his name and how I knew him. His other hand rose to clasp both of ours while he gazed into my eyes.

"Derek Scott! We went to school together. I left here when I went to college. Gosh! That was over twenty years ago. I recently moved back to Auburn. Don't tell me you don't remember me." His head tilted and he smirked. "I guess I never made that big an impression. But you...well, you were pretty popular in high school."

I leaned in, peering closely at his face and eyes. No way was this, Derek! The Derek Scott I remembered was a chubby kid who practically lived at the library. Although, thinking back, that was probably a refuge from Tom Evans and his gang always picking on him. Derek Scott! No wonder I didn't recognize him! This guy could have stepped off the cover of Esquire magazine.

"Derek! Oh my God! I'm so sorry I didn't recognize you. You've...you've changed." That was a serious understatement. He'd morphed into some kind of Greek god.

The secretary cleared her throat, signaling that we were disturbing her work. I glanced over and saw her adjust her monitor to block us from view.

Derek's eyebrows rose and he pulled a face, like a kid caught with his hand in the cookie jar. "Come into my office and tell me how I can help you, Maren." He glanced over at the secretary. "I'll be in consult. Hold my calls, please."

She rolled her eyes a little, and now with a bit of a smile, said, "Duh. What else do you think I'd do? Now get to work, would you?"

"Yes, ma'am." He threw her a salute. He looked over at

me. "Yeah, it's my name on the diploma, but Penelope actually runs the place." He flashed a grin that showed two perfect dimples in his cheeks.

My mind whirled as he herded me into the inner sanctum. What the hell had happened to the old Derek Scott that I knew? Looking around at the space, framed degrees lined one wall, while a large window was behind his desk. Derek stepped to the first of two tan leather chairs, pulling it out for me to be seated before taking his place on the other side of the desk.

For a few moments, I was actually flustered, setting my purse down and straightening my skirt over my knees. Look, I've taken more than my share of meetings, both as the host or the visitor, working on every sort of real estate deal you can imagine. I knew my way around office dynamics like nobody's business. I've had very, very successful Donald Trump wannabes try to steamroll me. I've had slick operators try to charm me and learned quite well how to handle myself in a meeting and usually come out ahead.

Yeah, a real tough cookie in a boardroom…and a complete doormat on the home front.

But this time… it was bad enough to be there seeking legal counsel, but to have the assigned lawyer be someone I knew from high school? And did he have to be so damned hot?

Derek must have sensed how awkward I felt when he spoke. "Yes, we've been out of touch, haven't we? Well, I've been practicing law for almost twenty years. I don't mean to toot my own horn, but I win the majority of my cases. A lot of things have changed since high school. Which brings me to…why you're here." He placed his elbows on the desk, leaning forward with a friendly smile. "You didn't kill someone, did you? Rob a bank or blackmail an enemy?"

It had the effect he'd intended when a chuckle burst from my throat. "You didn't mention arson, Derek. You might have me on that one." When his eyebrows arched, I raised my hand. "No arson. Thought about it though."

"When you made the appointment, you said it was a 'family law' matter."

I nodded.

He sat back in his seat. "That's a little cagey." When I didn't reply right away, he added, "You're not here to update your will, are you?"

I shrugged. "It's a small town. I didn't want the details to get out."

He looked around the office. "Just us here now, Maren. Is this what I think it is?" He looked at my left hand.

"I'm just wearing this for show, for now," I said, holding up my wedding ring.

He closed his eyes briefly and sighed. "I'm sorry."

"I'm here to start divorce proceedings. My husband, Wayne, informed me that he's leaving me for someone he hired for our real estate office. This, after already cheating on me once that I forgave, while we raised our two kids. I need to ensure that I get every penny in the settlement that I'm entitled to. But of course, I'd be happier if I got the lion's share."

"Okay, the arson? You were just kidding, right?" His smile faded as he peered at me.

"Not really." Maybe I shouldn't have grinned but I couldn't help it. "I burned every tacky tie, every sleazy shirt, his pants, and tidy whities!" I was on a roll. "It was a glorious bonfire! I only wished Kara had brought marshmallows when she showed up. All at the house we were renovating to flip."

Seeing his eyes open wider and his mouth fall open yanked me back to reality. "Is the fire going to go against me?" But truthfully, I'd do it all over again. It had been so worth it. Derek's reaction, after his initial shock—shaking his head and then chuckling—only added to my satisfaction.

"In light of the circumstances, I think I can soft pedal that. You were angry and in a state of shock, although I'd advise you to stay away from matches, at least till this is settled." He sat back and opened the file folder on his desk. "Okay then. I'm going to need a financial statement from you and a copy of your tax return. We'll request one from your husband as well."

He handed me a printed form, which I scanned with a glance. It could have easily been created by a bank, standard questions about assets and liabilities. It hit me with a cold finality. This was it. My marriage of almost twenty-five years now amounted to just numbers on a page. It was kind of pathetic.

"Okay, you say this isn't the first instance of Wayne's adultery. I'd like details of whatever you remember, especially if you can corroborate it with witnesses. We might not have to use it if both of you can come to an uncontested agreement, but it can't hurt to have it if he decides to play hardball. Do you think that's likely?"

For a few moments, I sat there silently thinking. It wasn't a question of whether Wayne would fight me. I knew he would try to grab every penny. My cheeks warmed thinking what a fool I'd been to put up with his bullshit for so long. The times I'd seen him flirting with anything in a skirt and then the "affair." What a fool I'd been to turn a blind eye.

But no time to get maudlin. "Wayne is unscrupulous. He's shown that time and time again over the years we've been together, both in business and on a personal level. He'll fight me tooth and nail, Derek. One other consideration is my son, Jordan. He's attending the University of Texas in his first year. We need to ensure that Wayne continues financial support for that. Our daughter, Amy, is out on her own, married with a baby."

"Oh my. You don't look old enough to be a grandmother." His eyes met mine. "It sounds like it wasn't easy for you. Don't worry. I've handled guys like Wayne before. I was going to advise uncontested divorce, but in this case, I'd say we level adultery at him. That threat, especially in a small town where he does business, might be more powerful. Leverage, y'know."

For the first time, I let myself relax into the chair. I liked the way Derek's mind worked, playing the angles. For the next half hour, I related the incident of infidelity while Derek wrote notes. He explained the whole legal process and outlined different contingencies and what to expect.

Finally, he finished with his notes and sat back in his chair. "I'll contact you once I've heard back from his attorney. In the meantime, you have some work to do with the financial statement and your marital history. Offhand, I think your chances of securing sixty percent of all assets, as well as spousal support, and support for your son are pretty good."

It was music to my ears. I'd thought I had a good case, but hearing him say it…well, a weight had definitely been lifted from my shoulders. I wasn't going to end up wondering about my next meal. Even so, his next comments surprised me.

"I've had some personal experience with divorce as well, Maren. My marriage ended a year ago, in similar circumstances. Helen met someone at work and, voila, here I am! Since there were no children or ties to keep me in Atlanta, I decided to move back to Auburn. It's a simpler life and where I grew up." He sat back, and when he looked at me, there was a smile on his face.

Did he just look me over? Was he looking at me? I mean, I know he was looking at me—who the hell else would he be looking at? But was he *looking* at me?

Managing to keep my voice steady, I replied, "I'm sorry to hear you went through this too." How I was able to keep my voice even while my mind had flipped into overdrive was anyone's guess. Oh my God! He was single? Maybe…

Stop it, Maren! I gave myself an inward shake. I had to get through this divorce before I got tangled up with someone else, even a guy as hot as Derek. I'd been with Wayne for waaay too long, compromising and putting up with his BS to make things work.

But this is the twenty-first century now. Maybe the rules

are different?

"How's your sister, Kara? She's still in Auburn, right?"

"Yeah, she's still here."

He nodded. "Good. Good. Being with family is important, especially now."

"Yeah, for sure. I've been staying with her the last week." As I got up, I pictured Kara setting off that morning to look at a used RV. I hadn't seen her that happy since Josh was born.

I glanced away from him for a second. "She came into some money and is trying to talk me into going on a cross-country road trip with her. But even if I wasn't involved with these divorce proceedings, I'm not sure I'd go with her. We'd probably drive each other nuts."

"Why not go? Sure, you're sisters and bound to bicker, but you two could have a good time together. I remember you gals got along pretty good back when we were kids, right?" I nodded, looking at him as he continued, "And having your big sister to cover your back is a real blessing, you know. Lots of women in your situation have to face this on their own. Divorce is a huge emotional adjustment. Take it from me. It's not easy, even when the divorce is amicable like mine was. Divorce is life changing, and takes time to get used to."

This was the last thing I thought I'd hear from him—advising me to go on a trip with Kara. And the fact that he was single and...okay, I'd been out of the dating game a looong time, and maybe I was rusty on reading signals, but I'd gotten the impression that he was maybe just a little interested in me. Which would explain the sinking feeling in my gut when he'd encouraged me to go on this trip with my sister. Was I really that out of it? Not that I was ready to date or anything.

I shook my head. "I'm fine. Really! I'd rather be here to make sure Wayne doesn't clean me out of house and home in this divorce."

"I hate to break this to you, Maren, but divorces are

often drawn-out affairs, taking months. Don't let these proceedings stop you from taking a vacation. After you provide me with details of your finances, it's going to be a series of back-and-forths between me and his lawyer. We can stay in touch, maybe do online meetings. I've got your back as far as the divorce settlement is concerned."

He put his hands palms down on his desk. "Wayne dropped this on you out of nowhere. Don't let him rob you of your chance for having some fun with your sister. I'm no shrink, but I think you need a break from all this, at least for a couple weeks."

His words about Wayne robbing me of fun struck a chord. I worked seven days a week, both helping in the office as well as coordinating with contractors on the properties we'd bought. That wasn't even accounting for the hours of hands-on work, painting and sanding. Even parties we gave were mostly to help support our business. And forget about southern vacations, hanging around a pool by myself reading, while Wayne went golfing. In twenty four years of marriage, we only went twice. Everything Derek had said was true, but I'd worked too hard to risk everything taking a vacation with my flighty sister.

I wasn't like Kara. This was Kara's dream, not mine, to do the cross-country road trip. But at the next thought, my gut sank lower. The same thing about being robbed of fun applied to my sister. She'd raised a child on her own, stuck in a dead-end and exhausting job. Even if she had bought and paid for that lifestyle with her choices, she could afford her dream vacation now with the lottery winnings. Would she take that trip on her own? And would it be just as much fun for her on her own?

I smiled. "I'll give this trip some thought, Derek. I'll have those papers to you in another day or so. Thanks for meeting with me." I began to gather myself.

"Hang on," he said, pushing a form across the desk. "You need to sign this letter of engagement, and we'll need a check as a retainer."

"Oh. Of course." I flipped my purse open and took out my checkbook. "How much?"

"Normally, it's twenty-five thousand, but let's start with fifteen, okay? If I need more, I'll let you know."

Fifteen thousand dollars? That son of a bitch, Wayne! I could cover it, no problem; my checking account was linked to my investment account which was healthy enough. But I had to spend FIFTEEN THOUSAND DOLLARS to pay for Wayne dumping me?

Nodding—never show surprise in a meeting, was a skill I developed years ago—I filled out the check and stood up. I slid the document across and looked it over. I'd read and signed tons of engagement forms with lawyers over the years.

But this time I put my purse on Derek's desk, opening it wide. I dropped my checkbook back in and put the check on the center of his desk.

Standing straight up, I pulled my wedding ring off my finger, dropped it in my purse, and signed the form. With a sharp nod to Derek, I said thank you, and left his office.

I didn't start to cry until I got to my car.

Three

Kara, that same afternoon...

Straining on my tiptoes to peer out the kitchen window showed only my car parked below. I glanced at the clock. It was after four. Shouldn't Maren be back from the lawyer's? Rubbing my hands together, I practically floated across the room, picturing the RV I'd just bought.

Oh God! It was amazing! Of the four I'd looked at over the last couple of days, this was the only one with twin beds in the back, perfect for Maren and me! A Phoenix Cruiser. Even the name was perfect! Maren would be smoked when she saw its kitchen with all the bells and whistles she was used to. A kitchen sink with a spray hose, a microwave—duh!—but the pièce de résistance was the propane stovetop and oven! Okay, a small oven, but big enough for two cookie sheets, big enough to roast a small—very small—turkey even! The dining area had ample space, and after dinner, I could picture the two of us watching a movie on the big screen while sitting together on the cozy leather sofa. I'd even suffer through the murder mysteries she was so fond of, if it meant we could be together on this trip. Okay, she wasn't going to be thrilled with the tiny bathroom, but everything else was incredible. Oh, the sights we'd see!

I forced myself to take a seat, sitting quietly on the sofa waiting for her. Since I'd left the dealership, I'd rehearsed what I was going to say to convince her to go with me. It wasn't just for me though.

Maren needed to get away from Auburn for a while. She was wound tighter than a spool of thread. I'd heard her during the night, getting up and making something to eat even though she tried to be quiet. When Maren snacked late at night, it meant she was stressed. I'd seen her do it in high school before big exams. This whole divorce crap was taking its toll on her. It didn't help that she felt the need to be so damned diplomatic, talking to her kids about it. Even though he was their father, he was also a cheating, lying bastard, lower than shark shit. Facts were facts.

Finally, I heard a car's engine and the bang of the car door shutting. I popped up from the sofa and raced to the window again. There she was, walking away from her black Suburban. My hand shook as I grabbed a glass, then some ice cubes, before pouring whiskey for her. I was pulling out all the stops to make my case. She had to go with me.

The apartment door opened and she called out, "Kara? You won't believe who…" She smiled when she saw me with the whiskey glass extended. "Okaaay, this is scary. You're greeting me at the door with a drink? What'd you do?" Shrugging her jacket off, she then took the tumbler from me, all the while watching me with suspicious eyes.

It took every ounce of self-control not to blurt it out. And self-control wasn't something that I'd ever been blessed with. But letting her talk was more important. Plus, it might help soften her up when I told her about the RV. "How did it go with the lawyer? Does Mr. Johnson think you've got a good case?"

She smiled before taking a long sip of the drink. I followed her from the entry, watching her slip her heels off before settling on the sofa, putting her feet on the coffee table. "Not Mr. Johnson. Do you remember Derek Scott from high school? He's back in town and now works for Alex Johnson. He's my lawyer!"

Maren was a couple of years behind me in school, so at first it was hard to picture the kids in her grades. Not to mention that had been more than thirty years ago! It wasn't like he'd even stuck around so that I could picture him coming into Denny's either.

Her polished fingernail drummed on the glass as she waited. Finally, she came out with a clue. "Chubby kid with blond hair in a brush cut, always in the big sweatshirts to hide his stomach. He was soft spoken, but it never failed, he always had the right answer when the teacher called on him. Big Star Wars knapsack?"

Star Wars. Yeah! The penny dropped, and I knew immediately who she was talking about. "He had a red Raleigh Bomber! I remember his bike because I always wanted that one!" More memories tumbled into my head. "He was always bullied. I remember him tearing down the street on the bike to get away. He used to hang around on our block a lot, usually near our house. Dad asked him one time if he was lost."

"That's him!" She laughed. "He's nothing like that now; let me tell you! He lost the weight and turned into a gym rat, judging by how ripped he is. And his face..." Uh-oh...Maren had that face she saved for the Backstreet Boys—Nick Carter, especially. She went on, "He's pretty good looking now. He also thinks I've got a solid case to the extent that I might get sixty percent of everything. He said hi to you, by the way."

My eyes opened wider. "Sixty percent? Awesome! I'd say that's cause for celebration, Mare! My treat! Let's go out for dinner. Maybe Tomasso's for Italian, or would you rather do steak at the Flaming Pit?" This was also part of my plan, as both restaurants were near the dealership where my new RV was parked.

"Italian, I think. So how was your day?" The way she said it, drawing out "day" told me she suspected I'd been up to no good.

My stomach did a flip-flop now that the moment had arrived. I took a deep breath, trying to keep my voice steady when I answered her. "Good. I looked at a couple of motor homes. You know, the Class 'C' that's just a bit bigger than your normal pickup truck."

"And?"

I scrambled into the spot next to her, grabbing her hand excitedly. "I bought one! Oh Mare, you've got to see it to believe it! Actually, it's on the block next to Tomasso's. Right on the way! Wait till Amy sees us pulling up to her place so you can visit and see your new granddaughter. It's perfect! I know her place is small, but with the camper, we can sleep there and still be able to visit her during the day. How sweet is that!"

Her hand sluffed mine away when she raised it. "Hold on! I never said yes to going on this trip with you. Much as it would be fun and wonderful to visit my granddaughter, I need to be here, Kara. For the divorce and all. Actually, I was going to go home tonight. It's time to get back to normal again. Well, as normal as I can manage at this point."

My heart fell into the cushions of the sofa. "Maren, it's just for a month or so. And I'm covering the costs. We can go down to South Carolina to see Amy and then swing over to Texas so you can visit with Jordan. It's not just you who needs a break. Your kids need you too, y'know."

Not to mention my own needs. It had been years since Maren and I had spent real time together. And considering how short my timeline was, this was it for me. But playing that card—the sick-sister card—wasn't even on the table. I'd never lay that on her, especially now when she was stressed with the divorce.

She finished her drink and stood up. "If you asked me to

do this next year, I'd probably agree. But right now..." She shook her head. "There's too much riding to just leave on a vacation, Kara. I don't trust Wayne. My lawyer says he's pretty good, but Wayne's going to hire the best as well. I need to be here to confer with Derek."

I fought the lump in my throat watching her go into the kitchen area to rinse out her glass. This trip meant everything to me because it was pretty much the only chance I'd have to take it. Ever. I dropped my head. No way I was going to drop "sick...well dying actually, sister" on her—she'd just been dumped after years and years of marriage.

The more I thought about it, the more I could see her point. She was scared, damn it; it was fear keeping her here. Fear that if she wasn't here coordinating everything, Wayne would win and she'd be broke. Maybe she was right. If I convinced her to leave and he did win the lion's share, I'd never forgive myself.

It wouldn't be the first time I'd made a bad call.

I stood up and slipped my poncho on. "Okay. This is your decision. But we'll still stop at the dealership so I can show you the rig. Who knows? You might fall in love with it and change your mind?"

"Rig? Wow, listen to you. You're even starting to talk like one of these nomad RV'ers." She slipped her heels back on and headed for the door. "You go on this trip, Kara. It's your dream, and you certainly don't need me to hold your hand to do it."

Actually I really might, but I kept my mouth shut for a change. As I followed her from the apartment, I murmured, "You're right." But inside, my heart hurt. I didn't really need her—I hoped—but I sure as hell wanted her to come with me. Maybe I'd made a mistake. Maybe I'd been too hasty in buying the RV. This dream trip of mine suddenly lost a lot of its luster.

***

She wheeled the Suburban into the parking lot next to Tomasso's. "I'm starving. We can see your new camper after we eat. That way we can take our time and you can show me all the features. How's that sound?"

Not like I had a choice, now that we were parked. I forced a smile. "Sure. Sounds good."

Walking in the door I inhaled through my nose. The smell of garlic and toasty bread made my mouth water, while the vibrant reds and blues of glass in Tiffany lamps above leather-covered booths caught my eye. The maîtred' came over and greeted us warmly, holding two leather bound menus.

Maren smiled at the young man. "We'll take a booth near the window if you have one open." She plucked at my sleeve, signaling for me to follow.

I'd kind of zoned out, remembering only now that I should have taken my meds earlier. In all the excitement of the RV, it had totally slipped my mind. Oh well. I'd take it as soon as I got home. When we were seated, Maren ordered a whiskey for herself and a draft beer for me.

As soon as he left, she leaned across the table. "Maybe I'll stay at your place tonight and go home in the morning. It might be better to face that dump in the light of day. I might still get the contractors in. If it's finished, we'll get more money for it when it sells. Much as I hate doing anything that will benefit Wayne, it's in my interest too. I've got to be practical and set my emotions aside even if it's hard to do."

There was something about the way she moved, kind of jerky and the forced cheer in her tone that struck a wrong chord in me. She was working hard to give the appearance that she was fine, but that image was brittle, like a porcelain doll. It was in the strained tendons in her neck and her too-wide smile.

I sat back, rubbing my hands across my tummy. "I think you may be putting more pressure on yourself going back there, Mare. Give it a few more days. Hell! Stay at my place as long as you want. It's all yours if and when I go on this trip. Don't wear yourself out. You have enough on your plate right now without working on that house."

"What do you mean 'if'?"

"Well, it was a great idea when I thought of the two of us going, but just me?" I shrugged. "I mean, I'm fine on my own...but I really wanted you to come."

She reached over and took my hand. "Kara...I can't! I just spent fifteen thousand dollars on a lawyer!"

"What?" Shit, I never even thought of that! Wait a minute. She could write a check for fifteen grand? Just like that? I sat back in my seat. Up until I hit Powerball, I was worried about spending forty bucks in a convenience store! I mean, I knew she was loaded, but I didn't know she was that loaded. I made a sick smile. "Maybe we should have Derek pick up tonight's tab, huh?"

She snorted. "You wish. Lawyers are the most tightfisted people on earth. No way."

Our waiter showed up with our drinks, carefully setting them on the table before pausing to take our orders. But we hadn't even looked at the menus yet.

"Can you give us a moment?" He nodded at me,and then smiling, turned away.

That was when all hell broke loose.

Four

Maren

I picked up the menu to scan it, but movement at the entry caught my eye. Shit! Wayne and his homewrecker had just walked in and were sidled close together waiting to be seated.

He looked rumply. His shirt was taut across his growing stomach; his tie was loosened (he never wore a loosened tie in public), and the pants of his suit needed him to tighten his belt a notch or two.

My mouth dropped when it hit me. He had just thrown his clothes on! Those two just had a romp in the office, I'd bet my life on it!

Just as the thought hit me, Wayne looked up and straight at me. As always, his eyes were watchful and assessing; he called it his "sizing-up" look ever since we made our first home purchase together. He had the uncanny ability to know a seller's bottom price at a glance. With just a quick take of someone, he was able to see their weak spots and their strong points.

His face turned to stone as we held each other's gaze from across the dining room.

I shifted my gaze for a second to his bimbo who was staring at the posted menu. I swear to God her lips moved as she read the freaking entrées. I couldn't help myself. I rolled my tongue under my lower lip, shaking my head slowly. He threw me under the bus for that?

My attention snapped back to Wayne as he made his way over to our table, his eyes narrow as he came at me. Uh-oh.

His beady blue eyes were slits in a face the shade of a ripe tomato. His suit jacket flapped open, framing the beer belly overhanging loose pants. My jaw clenched tight seeing that skanky Suzanne right behind him, muttering some inane and incoherent plea.

Screw him. Bring it on, you asshole.

"You bitch! You burned all my stuff!" He slammed his hands on the table, leaning in so close I could smell the cologne wafting off his sweaty mug. "I should have called the police on you! You oughta be locked up...you...you lunatic!"

"Get away from me, you lying piece of shit! You and your stripper girlfriend! You deserve each other. When I'm through with you—"

"Wayne, please. Let's just go." The blonde bimbo tugged on his sleeve, trying to get his attention. "We don't need this shit, not here. Don't make a scene, please." She couldn't even look me in the eye, keeping her gaze on him. Such a prize!

"Leave her alone." Kara had popped out of the booth and was toe to toe with him. "You heard your girlfriend. Just go, you slimy jerk!"

Wayne's girth combined with his anger had intimidated me in the past at times, but not today. My blood pounded hard in my ears as I stared at the guy who had betrayed me.

It was a good thing there wasn't any cutlery on the table or I might have shoved a fork in him. I kept my voice as steady as I could. "You're going to pay for what you've done, Wayne. To me and to our kids! I hired a lawyer today and I'll ruin you. I put up the bulk of the money to get it started. For what? So you and your simple twit can run it into the ground? Think again, needle dick!"

Two of the waiters and the maître d' showed up at the table, getting in between us, nudging Wayne back a few steps. Kara held her ground.

"Sir, I must ask you to leave," the maître d' said.

Wayne's head darted to the side, pointing his beefy finger at me. "You're insane! My lawyer's going to wipe the floor with you! Even the kids think you're losing it!"

The waiters managed to get him to the door as I sat there, staring. My heart was going warp speed, and I was practically huffing like a racehorse, trembling with rage. How dare he confront me like that! Causing a scene like he was some innocent victim, when this was all on him.

Kara sat back down and pushed in beside me on the bench seat. Her arm went around me. "Are you okay? We don't have to stay, Mare. We'll give him five minutes to be gone and then we'll leave too."

The waiter appeared at our table. "I am so sorry for that outburst. Can I get you another drink? It's on the house, of course."

Kara waved him off, muttering that we were probably going home. All the while, I sat stiff as a board, taking deep breaths as I willed myself to calm down. Was this the way it was going to be? I couldn't go out to a restaurant and enjoy a meal without running into that asshole? Bad enough to see him, but her too? Flaunting themselves all over town like they weren't the biggest liars and cheats to draw breath. This was too much.

My gaze fell to the table although nothing in front of me registered. Derek's words echoed in my head: You should go on that trip with Kara. He hadn't come right out and said it, but after hearing about me burning Wayne's clothes, he obviously thought I needed a break, if not a therapist. Maybe I did. A break, but certainly not a therapist. I just had a dump truck drop a load of life's shit on me, that's all.

I could handle this.

But I also needed to regroup.

Kara's words started to sink in, when she squeezed my shoulder. "I'll get us a pizza to go. You finish your drink, and then we'll go home, sweetie."

I shook my head, staring down at the tabletop. "No." I lifted my head to her. "The owners stood up for me just now, and I'm giving them my business."

"But—"

I rested my head on her shoulder. "And you had my back without a second thought. Honest, I thought you were going to slug him."

"Nah, he's too big. But he woulda' gotten a kick right in the nuts. A hard kick."

I let my voice get small. "Like Sean Watson in the third grade?"

She giggled. "Yup. He was pickin' on ya."

"I've never gotten into a real fight in my whole life."

"You're the businesswoman, hon. I've had to wrangle drunks on overnight shifts after closing time. I've been in a few dustups." Her hand stroked my shoulders. "Brains and brawn, that's the West sisters, huh?"

"You're a lot smarter than you give yourself credit for," I replied.

"And you're a hella lot tougher than you show the world, hon."

I let out a long sigh and sat back to look into her eyes. "After we eat, I think we should stop to see your new RV. I think maybe I should get away for a while and let this sink in. I need to see my kids. Derek thinks it might be a good idea too."

Kara's jaw dropped so far, I giggled. All she could say was "But…but…" with her eyes wide.

I nodded. "Women's prerogative; I changed my mind. Getting my head together away from this environment might be a good thing."

She grabbed me in the fiercest of hugs. "Thank you, Maren! Thank you! Thank you! Thank you!" she said over and over.

Yes, my big sister is the more effusive of us; it's always been that way. But this time, you'd think I just saved her life or something.

Five

Kara, two days later...

Y ou'd better slow down, Kara. The turn's just ahead."
Maren had a death grip on the dashboard, leaning so
far forward that the seatbelt strained, pressing into
her middle.

"Relax. I've got this." I glanced over at her and rolled my
eyes. She couldn't look more nervous with her bunched
eyebrows, peering at the road ahead. "Y'know, I practiced
driving this thing all day yesterday. It's only backing up and
making turns that's a bit different than driving a tank like
your SUV. And backing up isn't so bad with the rear
camera. You should try driving, so you'll see for yourself."

"No way. This is just so...so big! I have enough
problems with my Suburban, let alone this monster. I hate
to break it to you, Kara, but I'm afraid you're going to be
doing all the driving. I'll be navigator, which thankfully, the
GPS takes care of."

She pointed at a stop sign just ahead. "There! Turn right, and the first left is me. I hope no one's there, if you know what I mean. We'll make this snappy. Get in, get my clothes and out again."

"I was just here a few days ago, hon." She hid it well, but I could see by the pulsing muscle under her cheek that she was wire-tight. It made this trip all the more necessary to get her back to her usual self, not this ball of nerves that she'd become.

I stopped the rig and then edged out into the intersection, making a wide turn. Thirty-two feet of vehicle did take some getting used to, despite what I'd said earlier. I followed the road to her place and carefully turned in. Heading up her driveway, I noticed the charred spot on the lawn where she'd had her bonfire of Wayne's stuff. There weren't any other vehicles at the house, so we had it to ourselves.

"Let's get this over with." Maren unbuckled and slipped out the door of the truck. When I joined her in walking up the walkway, past newly planted shrubs and chrysanthemums, she continued, "I'll try to keep my suitcases to the bare minimum but I still need to pack for three seasons. It'll be warm in South Carolina and Texas but coming back, who knows how cold it's going to be. Just pray we don't have snow by then."

"If you forget anything, don't worry, I'm sure there'll be stores." When I stepped inside, the smell of fresh paint and a ladder in the center of the foyer greeted me. The walls showed scabs of plaster, patching cracks and nail holes in the tan surface. The carpet on the stairs leading to the second floor had seen better days, worn and in a dingy chocolate color. The whole place had a tired and forlorn feel to it.

Maren will never give this house the love it needs, and it knows it.

As I followed her up to her bedroom, I commented, "So you got the papers to your lawyer? And he knows you won't be around for a month or so?"

She glanced back at me, "He was thrilled to see me take this vacation with you. We'll be in touch with each other using video calls. If he needs a signature, he said he can handle that electronically. He's already made sure that Wayne can't clean out the bank or our investments. Derek knows what he's doing."

That was a relief. I plunked myself down on the king-sized bed, watching her get her suitcases from the walk-in closet and set them on an upholstered bench. "And the kids? Did you talk to Jordan? How are they handling this? You haven't said much about that."

She paused with her hand in the top drawer of the dresser. "It's funny. I thought they'd be devastated by us getting a divorce. But, aside from the initial shock, they're taking it okay, I guess. Jordan is more upset than Amy. But that's because he's more protective of me. He's worried that I'll be all alone in the world."

"What am I, chopped liver?" I said lightly. In my head I thought the opposite. 'Yeah Maren, I'll be lucky if I'm still alive by Christmas'. But I kept that nugget to myself. Stage 4 cancer's stage 4 cancer. The specialist I saw tried to put the best face on it, but I knew where I was heading. It wasn't terribly painful.

Yet. The meds I had were keeping the symptoms at bay.

Normally, I'd have spent hours online researching with the help of 'Doctor Google'...but this? No, I was doing all I could to remain blissfully ignorant once I was given my diagnosis and expected timetable. I had three, maybe as many as six decent months left before my body would be overwhelmed. I hadn't decided what I'd do then.

But I wasn't going to be a burden and put Josh or Maren through that shit.

Maren stared at me. "You okay?"

I nodded. "Yeah. Just a brain fart, I guess." I plastered a smile. "So is your son trying to fix you up already?" I teased. "The idea of you not having a man in your life bugs him, huh?"

"Well, you know Jordan; he's just being protective of his mom."

"Yeah, yeah." I waved at her. "There's a difference between being alone and being lonely, Mare."

She paused. "I guess I'll be finding out all about that, won't I?" She sighed, then set her lips firmly for a moment. "And I'll manage."

"Damn right you'll manage." I tilted my head. "And Amy? I suppose she's pretty caught up in her own life with a new baby." I tried to soft pedal it, but the truth was... Amy had always been the pragmatic one of the twins, a hard-nosed realist whose honesty skated a narrow line bordering on rudeness. Not my favorite of the two kids; Jordan had more empathy.

Maren's eyebrows rose and she let out a long breath. "I don't think she believes this is happening. She didn't come right out and say it but I think she's got it in her head that this is some kind of midlife crisis her father and I are having."

"Wayne's having the midlife crises, hon. You're picking up the pieces."

She shrugged. "When the divorce is final, she'll have to face facts. Or maybe she doesn't want to deal with this. I mean, she's got a new daughter to care for and her own marriage to worry about." She plopped on the bed next to me. "I know how she's feeling."

"What do you mean?"

She took a deep breath. "Well, we've had friends whose marriages broke up. And...when they did, I sort of pulled back from them. Particularly the woman." She fluttered her hands in the air. "I mean, I was all 'supportive' and 'understanding' at first. But, and now I'm ashamed to admit it, when the splits happened, I avoided them." She shook her head. "It was like she had some kind of disease I didn't want to catch."

I saw her chin tremble, and she added, "And now I

caught the disease. I'm ashamed of how I acted now that I see what's it like on the other side." She covered her face in her hands.

I put my arm around her. "It wasn't a disease, hon. They just went onto a different team."

Her head shot up and she looked at me, baffled. "Does it always have to be a sports thing with you?"

I laughed. "Maybe! ESPN's on at Denny's twenty-four seven!" I patted her hand. "They were your married friends, Mare. When they split up, they became your divorced friends. And that's a different thing. You were in the NFL together, and they went over to the NBA or something." I patted her hand again. "I don't fault you for dealing with their fallout the way you did."

Letting out a snort, I continued, "And as far as Amy...well..." I peered at Maren. "I take it you didn't go into a lot of details about Wayne and Suzanne?"

She stood up and resumed packing clothes silently for a few moments. Finally, she looked over at me. "I told them that their father has found someone new. I can't lie to them, Kara. They'll find out at some point when they meet Suzanne, what a money-grubbing skank she is. I'm not going to slag her. It just makes me sound bitter and mean. Wayne and his bimbo can loop the rope around their throats themselves. They don't need to drag me into it." She pointed a finger gun at me. "I'll slag those two to you all day, but not to my kids."

I decided to change the subject. "You didn't say anything about the logo I painted on the camper. 'Magical Mystery Tour'—I think it's pretty cool! That's us, Mare."

She pointed a gun finger at me again. "Just leave the magic mushrooms out of it, okay?"

"No magic mushrooms?"

"Kara!"

"Okay! I was just kidding! No dope, don't worry!" Truth be told, I hadn't gotten high in some time. Sure, drunk every once in a while, but not high. "We'll play this straight, don't worry. It's still going to be an adventure, and you're gonna have some fun for a change, sister."

For the first time, a smile lit her eyes. "I sure hope so."

***

When we were back at my place later that night, with my bags packed and in the camper, I took a seat on the sofa next to Maren. It was hard to contain my excitement!

I lifted my bottle of beer to clink it against her highball glass of whiskey. "A toast to the West sisters, two badass motoring Mamas! Look out world." I actually shimmied my shoulders, I was so pumped!

She bumped her glass against mine and smirked. "Not sure how badass we are. We'll look more like middle-aged hippies when people see the logo you painted. But the Beatles? That's before my time, but you are much older than me."

"Shut up! Two freaking years! And mid-forties is not middle-age, Mare!" I gave her a playful elbow in her side. "As for the Beatles—they were slightly ahead of my time, but their music was classic! The Stones, Eric Clapton, Dylan, Van Morrison! The old stuff was the best."

"What about Green Day, Nirvana, or R.E.M.? The nineties were pretty great too. But it's your camper, your choice I guess, even if you are wrong. I can see we're going to have some issues choosing our playlists." She pulled her phone out of her sweater pocket. "I already have my playlist set up." She stuck her tongue out at me.

Crap! I knew there was something I'd missed. But with getting the camper, practicing driving it, and letting the restaurant know I was officially done, it had slipped through the cracks. Oh well, I'd suffer through her faves the first day and then get my playlist set up. After that, it would be old rock 'n' roll.

Maren picked up the remote and clicked it on to Netflix, scrolling through the Murder Mystery lineup. Another crap! I'd seen enough mystery shows with her over the past week to last a lifetime. I snatched the controller from her hand, ignoring her groans as I scrolled until I came to the section on the screen that had "My List" showing.

"Come on!" She rolled her head back, groaning at the ceiling. "Don't tell me I have to watch one of your paranormal programs or some shit on vampires." She got up to freshen her drink. "How could we even be sisters? Sometimes, I swear you must have been switched at the hospital."

"Grab me a beer, will ya? This show is different! It's getting great reviews, Mare. It's all about aliens and UFO's visiting us. These sightings are by the military and scientists, so it's not just horseshit. They're real and they're here. Ever hear about Area 51? They captured an alien and his spacecraft."

She came back and handed me my drink. "Some people say they did. And people like you who eat this stuff up, buy into it. How much money did they make, doing that documentary? That's the part that's real, Kara. Not little green men from Mars—greenbacks in the bank."

When she settled on the sofa next to me, she picked up her phone again. "I'll get caught up on my email and messages. I'm sure I can multitask, considering what's on. I seriously don't understand how you can like this crap, but whatever. It's your turn to pick something to watch on TV."

"Hmph." I settled deeper into the cushions and hit play. Times like this, I missed my son. Josh had turned me onto the alien docs. He was much more open-minded than my pragmatic sister. Maybe I had been switched at the hospital. It was going to be an interesting trip, considering our different tastes.

Six

Kara, a few days later...

Jerking forward, my eyes popped open. Oh my God! Where were we? Why was I waking up behind the steering wheel? What happened? I'd been trying to find the Green Ridge State Park with Maren, when—

"Maren!"

My gaze flew to the passenger side. Maren jolted upright so fast, only the seat belt prevented her from slamming into the dashboard.

"NO!" Her piercing wail was immediately drowned out by my own shriek.

"Aaiieee!" The two of us—middle-aged, grown women and mothers of adult children—screamed like teenagers at a horror movie. Except this was real life and not Netflix. And I was anything but chill; we were both terrified.

My heart thundered in my chest so hard it hurt as we gaped at each other. The whites of Maren's eyes showed, while her hands flailed, batting the air in front of her.

Shit! Maren was in full-on panic mode. I had to do something to help her. Reaching for her shoulder, I forced a steady calm into my voice: "It's okay. You're fine, Maren. I'm here. Nothing's going to hurt you." I made a show of sucking a lungful of air in, urging her with my eyes to join me. "Take a deep breath, okay?"

For a moment she just stared at me as if seeing me for the first time. "C'mon, Maren. You're okay. We're in the RV. We're fine. Just breathe."

Her mouth snapped shut, and she swallowed hard, her hand flying to her neck. Her lips trembled with small moans escaping as she held my gaze like a trapped animal. When the two of us synchronized our breathing, a flash of what had happened the night before hit me like a Mack truck.

A blinding light! We'd been lost in the dark, driving these winding dirt roads in the park trying to find the main campsite. The nighttime forest lit up with a brilliant white light, coming from everywhere all at once! But there weren't shadows cast, like a searchlight would cause. Our entire surroundings radiated a blinding light like nothing I'd ever seen before! It happened suddenly, without warning. There'd been complete silence: no hum or bang. One moment we were creeping along a dirt road in the woods, and the next instant we were awash in a flood of white light!

That shock and terror were the last thing I remembered until this very moment.

"Kara? What the hell happened last night? Where are we?" After peering outside at the stand of trees, her gaze lowered to my chest and her forehead furrowed. "That's my shirt." She tugged at the front of the blue T-shirt she was wearing, staring down at it. "This is your shirt. How did I end up wearing your shirt, Kara?"

Oh my God. I gaped at the screen print of Stevie Nicks clutched in Maren's fingers. That was most definitely my shirt. Maren wouldn't be caught dead in anything that drudge-campy. She was more the Eddie Bauer casual chic type.

Shit, Kara! You're losing it! You've got to focus! How did our clothes get switched? What the hell had happened after that blasted light blinded us?

"Kara? What's going on? When I woke up, my heart was going a mile a minute. I had the worst dream, but I can't remember the details. Only that I was scared shitless." Her lips parted as she slowly shook her head. "Why would we fall sleep here in the cab and not back there in our beds? And why the hell would we exchange shirts?"

I'd felt the same terror waking up as she had. Hell, I was barely keeping it together even now. I stared across at her. "I don't remember anything past that bright light, Maren. Do you remember when that happened?"

She shook her head. "No. I don't remember a light. Something happened to us last night though. None of this makes any sense."

For a few moments, we both just sat there silently. Yeah, something strange was going on. Yet outside everything looked normal enough. Branches of pine and spruce swept the sides of a narrow dirt road. Above, sunlight flickered through the canopy of leaves. Was this Green Ridge State Park?

She gasped before her hand flew out, smacking my arm. "We were lost! I remember how pissed I was when the cell phones and the GPS cut out!" Grabbing her phone from the console, she turned her attention to it.

Oh my God! Yeah! I'd cursed that damned cell signal, failing us just when we needed it most. I grabbed my own cell phone from the mount on the dash. When the small screen booted up, my eyes opened wider, doing a double take.

Beside me, Maren murmured, "That can't be right. What the hell is wrong with this damn thing?" A side glance showed her teeth pressed into her lower lip while she flicked the button to reboot her phone.

My hands shook as I looked at my phone again. The day

showing on the screen was Friday, September seventeenth. But how could that be when yesterday was Monday? But the phone clearly showed Friday below the temperature reading of seventy-four degrees.

"That can't be right, Kara! Today is Friday?" Friday came out as a high-pitched screech from a face that was now paler than I'd ever seen my sister. "Friday? "

Scowling, I peered at my phone. "What happened to the last three days? How could this be true?" We'd spent the first night in that state park in New York and last night trying to find our spot in Green Ridge Park. We got lost but...

Oh God. The phone fell to my lap, and I peered out the front windshield, scanning the forest. Then it hit me. This was like something out of a movie.

A science-fiction movie. But for real!

Damn that Joe Rogan podcast and the documentary I'd watched! But I couldn't get the Navy pilot's story out of my head. He'd described the Tic-Tac-shaped spaceship and its impossible moves. And he wasn't alone in these reports. Instances of UFO's were waaay more frequent than most people thought.

So were encounters with alien life.

I turned to my sister, deliberating for all of a nanosecond on whether to tell her what I thought. "Maren? I think we had an encounter with aliens."

I gulped before adding, "I think we were abducted."

Seven

Maren

For a moment I could only stare at my airheaded sister. "That. Is. The. STUPIDEST thing I ever heard." Shaking my head, I continued, "Jesus H. Christ, you always go off to la-la land at the drop of a hat, Kara. Abducted by spacemen? C'mon!" It was that damned documentary she'd watched, eating this crap up with a spoon. She should have named this RV "Gullible's Travels."

"You don't think we were abducted, huh?" Kara reached over to pluck the front of my shirt. Well, technically, her shirt but..."How do you explain this, then?"

Damn it! She had a point that our clothes being switched was weird, but...aliens? Come. On. My jaw tightened before I snapped, "Oh, so now I gotta be Sherlock Holmes because you're going all Twilight Zone?" There had to be a logical explanation for the clothes. My arm swept to the enormous RV space behind us. "Look, we moved into your rolling tour bus just a day ago! I could have mistakenly put on—"

"It's the Magical Mystery Tour, Maren. I even painted it on the side." Her chin lifted and she sniffed. "At least get the name right."

Oh, for Pete's sake! I shushed her with a wave of my hand, continuing. "It's possible that we packed our T-shirts in the wrong drawer, and you grabbed mine and I grabbed yours. Maybe we're just noticing that now!" That had to be it! I had a lot on my mind, and Kara…well, it wouldn't be the first absentminded thing she'd done.

She looked down at the sweater covering her chest and grimaced. "I don't know. You know I wouldn't be caught dead in a sweater set and—"

"That's a Chadwick's sweater, Kara! It probably cost more than your whole wardrobe." To add insult to injury, she was criticizing my clothes?

But if we hadn't mixed them up this other morning—Wrong! That was three mornings ago!—then the only realistic explanation was that Kara was behind this. I mean there were just the two of us, and I sure as hell hadn't caused us to pass out and wake three days later. It had to be her, or I was totally losing it!

I scowled at her. "What'd you do? If this is your idea of a joke…" And then a memory bubbled to the surface, a time when we were teenagers. "Pot brownies! You slipped me some wacky tabacky, didn't you? Or was it something else this time? It wouldn't be the first time you did something like that because you thought it would be funny." I'd never forget stumbling into the kitchen, and eating ice cream with my fingers all the while she laughed her head off.

"Oh, for God's sake, Maren! That was over twenty-five years ago! I did it once when we were in high school!"

"You did it more than just once! Remember on Christmas break when you came home from your first and only year at college? The magic mushrooms? I slept for a full day!"

"Maren, I swear I didn't slip you anything." She crossed

her heart twice, looking at me with big blue eyes, trying to appear innocent.

But I wasn't buying it. How could I when it was the only thing that made sense! And considering her track record...

"I call bullshit. How could you do something like this to me?" I sat back in my seat and crossed my arms over my chest. Why had I ever trusted her, going on this trip? "I never thought your so-called road trip was a great idea to start with and this just proves it!" It was hard to say who I was angrier with, her for playing this stunt, or me for agreeing to this trip. "You've never changed, have you? You get a stupid idea and run with it without thinking!"

"Now, wait a minute! That's not fair. I didn't do anything!"

But I'd heard enough. This was totally out of line on her part, and I totally didn't need this added stress in my life. "Bullshit. Y'know what? I'm going home. This trip is over, Kara." What a fool I'd been to agree to this. How could she do this to me? I glared at her. "You have some nerve slipping me drugs at our age! Like getting dumped by my husband wasn't enough! This is your idea of a joke?"

"Maren! I didn't do anything!" Fisting her fingers in her long blonde hair, she practically shrieked, "On our mother's grave, I swear I didn't do that, Maren."

Oh my God! "Now you're bringing Mom into this, huh? You've got some damn nerve, Kara West." I shook my head and sighed. After what she'd done to Mom, hardly visiting her when she was dying in the hospital? Kara could have at least buried the hatchet between them for that. But no. Now she was swearing on Mom's name?

Kara would never change. She'd always been flighty, never even finishing nursing school even though she had the money and brains! This trip was another of her hare-brained schemes, like when she'd gotten into Amway, or lost money to try her hand at a craft business.

"I'm getting the hell out at the next town we come to. I'm renting a car...and I'm going home." Home. Such as it was. But it was better than getting drugged by my sister and waking up three days later! I was probably lucky to be alive!

There were tears in her eyes when she leaned over the console that separated us. "Maren...I didn't slip you anything! May Josh die a horrible death if I'm lying to you. But I swear on everything dear to me that I'm telling you the truth!"

For a few moments I peered at her. Slowly, it sank in.

She wasn't lying. To swear on Josh's life? He was her world. She was telling me the truth. Much as I wanted to believe this was all on her, I just couldn't. Which made this situation, losing three days and being scared shitless even more unsettling. "Then what the hell happened, Kara?" I whispered.

In a small voice she said, "I think it was aliens, sis."

Again, with the alien horseshit! "Bah! If not you, then somebody slipped us something! It's more likely that than a visit from ET, Kara!" How else could losing three days be explained? It had to be that we were drugged.

I thought of the day's drive, stopping for gas and something to eat. "That waitress with all the tats and the ring through her eyebrow? Would she have put something in my Coke? But why? What kind of psycho would do that to two middle-aged women?"

"That wasn't it, Maren. I remember her. True, she was kind of out there, but I don't think it was her." Kara tapped my thigh. "Look, we were asleep for three days, but are you thirsty or hungry? What about going to the bathroom? Shouldn't we be starving right now?"

I sat there trying to figure this out. No. I wasn't starving. I wasn't even jonesing for a cup of coffee, which was the first thing I always felt in the morning. And I didn't need to go to the bathroom. Wouldn't you feel any of these things if you were passed out for three days?

I knew where she was going with this, even if I couldn't logically explain it. "Look, there's no way I'm buying into anything involving aliens or any woo-woo crap. That's your jam, not mine."

But Kara wasn't listening. Her face was blank as she started patting her chest and then her thighs and arms. "What are you doing? Are you okay?"

"I'm checking myself!"

"For what?"

Ignoring me, she jumped up from her seat and, stripping her shirt off, headed to the back of the rig. I unbuckled the stupid seat belt and followed her. What was she checking for? Should I be doing a pat-down on myself? Christ! This was just getting weirder by the moment.

When I got to the bedroom, Kara was peeling off her jeans and sneakers. She opened the closet door and twisted from side to side, staring at her reflection in the mirror. Wearing just a bra and panties, she was a sight to behold, lifting her arms to check the underside and turning her feet out to inspect the insides of her legs.

Finally, I could stand it no more. "What the hell are you doing?"

"I told you already! I'm checking myself for injuries or…where they may have injected something into me." She glanced over at me. "You should too! Get out of those clothes and examine yourself."

"What the hell? Who injected you? If you say aliens, I swear I'm gonna smack you!" I folded my arms over my chest, rubbing the backs of my arms. No way was I gonna strip down and contort myself, gaping in the mirror like my nutty sister!

"Does my back look okay?" She turned away from me, giving me a bird's-eye view of her back. "Do you see any marks or anything odd?"

"Aside from the fact that you need to hit the gym more?" I leaned closer and pinched the underside of her arms, her "wings," as I liked to call that soft flap of skin. But really, it was probably the only bit of spare flesh on Kara. She was in pretty good shape for being forty-seven.

"Just check, okay? Humor me."

"Nope. No stitches or marks or anything—good grief!—now I'm sounding like you!" Argh! I threaded my fingers through my hair, staring at the floor and trying to keep my voice even. "It wasn't any aliens, Kara!"

"Sez you." The next thing she did was tug the top of her panties out and peer down at her crotch. "The missus is good, I think. Although, it's been so long since I had a date, let alone sex, I think I'd notice if I'd been probed down there." She grabbed her pants and shoved her legs into them. "Your turn, Mare."

"My turn?" THAT wasn't going to happen! I'd humored her but this had gone far enough.

"Yep. Strip, and let's check you out. We were out for three days, sis. Someone could have done something to us. In fact, I'd be surprised if they didn't." She stepped over, and her fingers gripped the bottom of the T-shirt.

"Kara!" I slapped her hands away. "No way! I'm good!" I turned away and headed for the front of the RV. But her worry about someone—a human—accosting us while we were out cold, played in my head. We were in the middle of nowhere, but who knew? I glanced around, inspecting the kitchen and living room areas. Everything looked the same as we'd left it. I checked the side door. Still locked. As were the doors to the cab part of the RV.

When I looked back at Kara, she was now dressed, leaning against the counter with a smug look on her face. "Look, Maren, the rig's the same way we left it yesterday…I mean, three days ago! So, if someone didn't break in, it has to be aliens. And don't forget that bright light or the fact our phones crapped out."

No way was I going to waste any more time arguing with her. She had this alien crap in her silly head and there was no reasoning with her. I wandered back from the cab, and looking around at everything, my gaze snagged on the smoke detector mounted on the ceiling.

"Is that just for smoke, or does it pick up carbon monoxide?" I sniffed a few times, staring at the blinking green light on the gadget above. Carbon monoxide would explain why we'd passed out. But wouldn't it also kill us? Maybe we didn't get a big enough dose for that.

Kara stepped over to me, looking up at the detector. "It's supposed to pick up both—smoke and carbon monoxide. But it's fine. There's no carbon monoxide leak in here."

I went to the back of the rig, still sniffing like a bloodhound, checking all the rooms. There wasn't any odor other than the air freshener mounted in the bathroom, but was there an actual odor to carbon monoxide? "Carbon monoxide, Kara! That's the only thing that makes sense! There has to be a leak somewhere and it knocked us out. You bought this RV used, right? Did you check that? Maybe that's why they sold it!" Aha! Now I had a reasonable explanation for what had happened. I knew there had to be one, unlike what Kara was trying to spin.

"For God's sake, Maren! You're grasping at straws here! Anything to find a logical explanation as to how we fell asleep like Rip Van Winkle, only to wake three days later! This RV came from a dealer! It was certified safe!" She pointed at the circular device mounted on the ceiling. "That thing works. That's how I know it wasn't carbon monoxide! I'm telling you, it was aliens."

"Now who's grasping at straws? Aliens!" Knowing Kara, when they told her everything was tickety-boo, she wouldn't question it. "I think we need to take this thing to a garage and have it tested! We're lucky to be alive."

This time, it was Kara who ignored me, brushing by and staring out the window above the sink and counter. She murmured, "No broken branches or signs of scorch marks in the trees. Of course, that doesn't mean much. With their advanced technology, anything's possible. We could have been beamed up like in Star Trek."

Okay, I'd totally had enough of her horseshit. I headed back to the cab and plunked myself down in the passenger seat. "Can we get out of here?" I caught a whiff of my armpits as I tugged the seat belt on. Pretty ripe. "I can't wait to have a shower, but I'll wait till we're back in civilization."

Kara slipped into the driver's seat. "No argument here. The sooner we leave this place, the better." She glanced over at me and grimaced. "Hope this thing starts after being out of commission for three days. What if they did something to it?"

Oh God. What the hell would we do? I barely breathed, watching her turn the key. The rumble of the engine was a welcome sound. Even so."I vote we drive this heap to a garage and get it checked out while we check into a hotel. I'd like a long, hot soak to get this grunge off."

As soon as Kara put the rig in gear, the GPS kicked in. "Recalibrating," was announced from the speakers.

I rolled the window down and sucked in a lungful of air. "Great. The stupid thing could have told us that three days ago! Instead, the useless thing zoned out."

Looking over at my pigheaded sister, I saw her leaning forward, steering the big rig down the dirt road. "Roll your window down, Kara. I don't need you passing out while you're behind the wheel."

I looked up at that damned GPS and gave it a swat. "You! You stupid thing! Recalibrate us the hell out of here and back to civilization! The next thing you know, Kara's going to tell me that Bigfoot is out there, tromping through the trees."

"Very funny." She pulled a face, grimacing at me.

I kept gulping fresh air, watching tall pines and maples flash by as we drove. Finally, the GPS chirped.

"Go straight for one mile and take the first right onto Falls View Lane. Your destination will be on the left."

She looked over at me and rolled her eyes. "Can you believe that? We could have walked, we were so close."

"Just get us out of here. The sooner we leave Green Ridge Forest, the better." What a freaking nightmare.

Eight

Kara

U nder normal circumstances it would have been a lot less than a ten-minute drive; I'm a bit of a lead foot, sue me. But on this day, I drove as carefully as the first day I'd gone solo behind the wheel. No way was I taking any chances. Who knew if we were going to get zapped by that bright light again?

Neither of us had much to say as I wended my way through the forest road. We were both lost in our own thoughts. For me, at least, it was more a case of recovering from shock. Three full days? I was still trying to wrap my head around it. Did we spend all that time sitting in the camper? Or had we been taken away someplace and examined, like it says in all those books and TV shows?

Oh shit! I yanked the van to the shoulder, threw it into park, jumped out of my seat, and hustled to the bathroom.

"What's wrong?" Maren called out to me, her voice screechy with fear.

"Gotta pee! Now!" I replied, hopping into the tiny

bathroom.

And that was the first lie I told my sister since we woke up.

I opened the tiny vanity door under the sink and reached all the way to the back, my hand searching for the bottle. I had another bottle squirreled away in my purse, but I didn't want Maren to see. I popped out two pills and swallowed them dry, my hands shaking. I had missed three days' worth of doses. What the hell was that going to do to me? I felt fine, but still, three days was not good. I tucked the bottle back in its hiding spot and returned to the driver's seat.

"That came out of nowhere," Maren said. She leaned over to look at me, biting her lower lip. "Please tell me it was only number one, okay? I don't want any explosive—"

I cut her off mid-sentence. "That's all it was! I should have peed before starting out, I guess!" Okay, my second lie, and it went over perfectly.

She shrugged. "I don't have any need to do anything...and it's been three days." She rubbed her tummy. "But now that I think about it, I could use something to eat."

Hearing her words, my own stomach rumbled. "Yeah, me too." I wheeled the RV back onto the road. A coffee and a plate of pancakes would go down well. Or a steak. Or burgers. I didn't care. I was hungry but not famished. Shouldn't I be starving after going without food for three days?

I looked over at her a few times, wondering what she was thinking. She'd been pissed thinking I'd drugged her—as if!—but it looked like she had solved the mystery by coming up with the carbon monoxide theory. To her way of thinking anyway. "So, do you still want to go home? I really wish you'd stay, Maren."

Her eyes were flinty when she looked over. "If you get this thing checked out at a garage for gas leaks, I'll stick it out. At least until we get to South Carolina to see Amy. We'll see after that how things are going."

My gut sank lower. There was nothing wrong with the CO_2 detector. But if it would shut her up and keep her on this trip, then I'd humor her. "Okay. First chance I get, I'll have this thing looked at."

Yet, considering we'd been taken by aliens, gone for three days, we were both okay. Aside from being somewhat hungry and a little thirsty, that is. It was a mystery why it'd happened, but we were physically fine. Mentally, that might be a crapshoot.

We drove steadily lower to the valley below. Laid out before us was a picture-perfect postcard of a small town by the Potomac River. I could see a couple of church steeples, a downtown business district lined with storefronts, a supermarket and tree-lined residential streets.

"It's a pretty sight," Maren said. She pointed over toward the flowing river. "There's got to be some kind of snack bar or diner over there. We can grab a bite and stretch our legs; what do you say?"

"Sounds like a plan."

"Let's hit the snack bar. I don't want to eat inside." She raised her arm and sniffed her armpit. "Yuck! I need a shower."

I pulled into a parking area that surrounded a combination diner and snack bar that had gas pumps next to it. Between it and the riverbank were a collection of picnic tables. Along the shore of the river there was a scattering of people getting in some post Labor Day swims. Some were younger families with little ones, and there were a few groups of teens who had probably cut class.

I looked over at Maren. "I wouldn't mind a shower myself, as well as brushing my teeth for ten minutes." Argh! What had those aliens done with us for three whole days? I mean, I was hungry and a little thirsty, but not anything like you'd expect after being out of it for three days!

I gave my head a shake. I couldn't think about that right now. Later, when Maren was busy in the shower, I'd look online for alien-abduction experiences. I'd also look to see what I could expect for missing three days of doses. Shit, I hope that didn't cut my once-in-a-lifetime road trip short! Also, it would be great if Maren took an extra-long shower. "You want to jump in the shower now?" I asked her. "We have enough fresh water and such."

Shaking her head, she replied, "I'll wait for a full-sized shower with unlimited hot water in a motel. Right now, I need to stretch my legs and breathe some fresh air. I'll just walk over to that picnic area and check out the river. From the looks of all those people over there, we're not the only ones stopping to enjoy this spot."

I glanced over to the parking lot where a few other RVs were parked, with families eating ice cream cones at wooden tables while young kids in swimsuits chased each other, working off pent-up energy. It was a typical American scene of families vacationing, enjoying the last of the warm weather before the chill of autumn set in.

"You go and find a table. I'll grab some burgers and fries after I top off the gas tank, okay?" Nowadays, I never let it get below a quarter of a tank. In my old life, I'd play Russian roulette with the "low fuel" light on my dash, but not anymore. I had tons of money in the bank now.

"Sounds good."

She hopped out, and I pulled over to the pumps.

As I filled up, I mulled over what the hell had happened.

What surprised me more than anything was just how...how normal everything seemed. We had been out cold for three full days, woke up, changed our clothes, and were now stopping for a lunch break.

We'd just been kidnapped by aliens, for God's sake! I shouldn't be doing something as mundane as gassing up and debating whether or not I wanted bacon on my cheeseburger! I ought to be...

What? I ought to be what?

Well, I should be phoning CNN, at least!

I laughed out loud so hard, the guy at the next pump over jerked his head to look at me.

"It's okay, I'm just remembering a comedy special," I said, giving him a shrug.

He rolled his eyes and went back to his car.

*Hello, CNN? This is Kara West. Me
and my sister were tootling around
Green Ridge State Forest, and we were
just abducted by Darth Vader for three
days.*
CLICK.
Hello? Hello?

Yeah. Right. "I'll have that bacon cheeseburger," I said aloud. I didn't even bother to see if someone overheard me talking to myself. Screw them. Let them disappear for three days and see how they acted, okay? I'll do mundane.

For now.

Even though I knew I was right about the alien thing, there was no way I'd push the issue with Maren. She'd been through enough already with Weasel Wayne announcing he was leaving her for another woman. I'd barely been able to convince her to take this cross-country jaunt as it was, without now pushing the alien theory.

The nozzle shut off with a clunk, and I glanced at the numbers on the fuel pump. Holy Toledo! A hundred and sixty-four dollars! I smiled. Just a month ago, a forty-dollar fill-up would have made my heart stop. That winning Powerball ticket changed everything.

After parking the RV near the restaurant, I glanced down the lot to where Maren was perched on top of a table, her legs dangling over the edge as she gazed at the river.

There was a scoop in the shoreline that created a swimming area that was roped off from the river's relentless flow. About a hundred feet farther out there were rocks jutting up, making small rapids in the waterway. The frothing water was a lovely backdrop. A red kayak with a teen in a helmet skimmed along before disappearing in a slight dip between rocks that bubbled with white foam before popping up on the other side.

When I stepped inside the diner, the cornucopia of smells—grease from the fryer, coffee brewing, gravy, and the sweetness of baked pies—filled my nose. It was like coming home, although my days of slinging hash were over, thank goodness. I took a seat at the long counter and grabbed a menu.

Ten minutes later, with a brown paper sack filled with coffee, two bacon cheeseburgers, and some muffins, I headed across the lot to join Maren. The sun was warm on my shoulders with just a hint of a breeze coming in from the water. The laughter and squeals of kids playing along the shore drowned out the clusters of parents chatting at picnic tables.

Perfectly normal, yet surreal after the mystery of the three lost days.

Suddenly a bloodcurdling shriek pierced the sultry air. I froze in place, watching a blonde-haired woman race down the sloping embankment to the swimming area. Her frantic screams of "Danny! Danny! Oh my God! Help!" tore through me.

A man scrambled past the woman, his legs churning up water as he raced to the rope barrier. Beyond the line floats, I caught a glimpse of an orange lifejacket and a young boy bobbing in the water, being swept farther out into the main current. The man—the boy's father, by the looks of it—dove under the barrier and reappeared, swimming hard to reach his son.

Oh my God! The kid was in the churning current, turning and bobbing as he became swept downriver toward jutting rocks and white water. The father was still a good distance back with little hope of reaching the tyke before he was bashed against the stones.

Nooooo!"

At Maren's wail, my gaze bolted to her, watching her race to the river, her hand extended before her. She was almost at a right angle to where the river swirled with rapids, where the boy was headed. Oh shit! She'd never make it if she jumped in to save the kid.

Just as I was about to scream at her to stop, the air wavered around her. Time slowed to a crawl. My mouth fell open as I peered at the scene before me—Maren pointing and the boy in the river.

It was beyond belief, but it happened. As God is my witness, a miracle!

The young boy flew out of the water and up into the air like he was shot from a cannon. When he was about ten feet up, he hovered there for a moment above the raging waters. Then like a kid's balloon at a birthday party, he floated twenty feet over and gently alighted on top of one of the rocks, downstream from the rushing rapids. The orange life jacket was a cushioned bump on the dark stone. The boy's head turned and he screeched, "Daddeeeee!"

He was safe, but... Oh my God! How had that happened? That was impossible! He'd been airborne, floating over to that rock. I stood stockstill, gaping at the scene.

His father reached him! The man clung to the stone, with the young boy safely on top of it. And help was on the way to get them out of the swirling waters. A small boat with two guys in it, one steering at the rear while the one in front held a red safety buoy and rope, headed to retrieve the father and son. I breathed a sigh of relief. Thank God.

Movement at the periphery of my sight snagged my attention. It was Maren. She stepped back from the shoreline and looked at me. Her eyes were glassy, and a smile began to form on her lips. "Kara..." she called. "Did ya..." Her eyes rolled up in her head showing just the whites, and she folded, landing on the grass. What the hell—

"Maren!"

I dropped the bag of food, and my feet flew to her. Squatting down, I gripped her shoulders while checking for her breathing. "Maren!" Oh my God! Was she okay?

Her eyelids fluttered, and I let out a whoosh of relief. Her gold-flecked brown eyes creaked open and a smile flickered on her lips. "He's okay. The kid…he's safe, right?"

"Yeah! But what about you? Are you okay?" My heart kicked into overdrive as I scanned her face and head.

She stared at me silently for a few moments before pushing herself up to a sitting position, peering at the river. "I think so. Yeah, I'm good."

"What the hell happened?" My hand shook before I cupped her cheek and swiped a stray lock of her dark hair behind her ear. Her face had paled and her skin was cool. "You fainted? I've never seen you faint—"

"I did that, Kara! I saved that boy." Her hand gripped my arm tightly and her eyes became wide. "It was the strangest feeling. Like a jolt of electricity in my hand, but…it wasn't painful."

She looked out at the river again and her voice became whispery. "I got him on that rock before he was swept through the rapids. I did that. I know I did."

Pulling back a bit, my gaze did a closer inventory of her head and scalp. Had she hit herself when she fell? What the hell was she talking about? She hadn't even gone into the water.

But then I pictured the boy bursting up from the water and floating—floating!—over to safety to rest like a soap bubble on the rock. My eyes opened wider, staring at my sister. Was that what she thought? That strange thing that happened, the boy airborne and safely set on that rock was her doing? The whole thing had been crazy. I would never have believed it if I hadn't seen it with my two eyes. And now Maren was claiming she had something to do with it? With that?

Oh my God! What the hell was going on with my sister? She claimed I was nuts because of the aliens, but now she thought she did some kind of Yoda shit? This was Maren? My no-nonsense, logical sister claiming that somehow she magically saved that boy?

She clutched at my arm. "I was desperate for that kid to be safe, Kara! There was no way that the father was going to get him in time. And even when I raced to help, I couldn't have swum there fast enough to help the boy. But then it happened..." Her gaze shifted to the side, silently lost in her own thoughts.

I shook my head, staring hard at my sister. "Look, what I saw was unbelievable. Crazy even, but it did happen. Somehow that boy lifted out of the water and then was set down on that rock, enough so that he was out of danger. You think that somehow you caused—"

"No!" Her hands left me and she gazed down at them, rolling them over to peer at her palms. "I don't think it, Kara. I know it! Don't ask me how, but as sure as I'm sitting here, something weird happened with my hands. That strange jolt of electricity in my hands reached out to help that kid. I knew if he could reach that rock, he'd be safe."

My gaze shifted to my sister's slender fingers and the soft pink of her palms. They looked normal enough. So was she having some kind of psychotic breakdown? Oh God. She'd even passed out for a few seconds!

The next thought caused an icy spike to shoot through my chest. Did it have something to do with those aliens? Did they do something to screw with her mind? Was she losing it?

She kept talking in that soft, wonder struck voice, which was also kind of worrying.

Where was her normal, take-no-prisoners logic? For more than twenty years, Maren was always all business. Her years and years of wheeling and dealing with property developments had turned her into a straight-shooting capitalist, always getting to the bottom line with no nonsense.

Now? Holy shit, now she was as spacey and disoriented as me after a few joints. What had happened to her? It had to be from those aliens!

Her voice was almost melodic, whispering with wonder.

"Can you see the energy field around my hands, Kara? They're glowing, man! I can see a pale-blue halo floating over them that shimmers and flows in waves." She waved her hands delicately like some Hawaiian dancer. Watching her hands float back and forth, a weird smile played on her lips.

Oh shit. The way she was acting and her voice. It was like I had given her magic mushrooms! But I swear on my mother's grave, I didn't. She was zoning out, gazing at her fingers? Crap! What had those aliens done to her?

She grabbed my wrist and turned her attention to my hand. "There's an energy field around you too. It's kind of orange, but it's faint." Her eyes drifted shut, and she kind of went woozy, swaying a little from side to side. "That took a lot out of me. I feel like I could sleep for days."

"Maybe I should get you to a doctor. Do you think you've got enough energy to get to the rig? I'm not sure that—"

She swatted my arm and laughed. "I'm fine. Tired and hungry, but I feel great. Hell! I saved that kid's life. I hope you bought me a hero sandwich." She giggled and then pushed herself up off the ground, holding onto my arm with her other hand.

Holy shit! If I didn't know better, I'd swear she was stoned out of her gourd. She even had the munchies, giggling and weaving a bit. The whole way, walking back across the grass to the parking lot, she kept fluttering her fingers and smiling at them.

The sack of take-out food and coffee was just up ahead, lying right where I dropped it. When we came to it, I was about to reach down to see if any of it could be salvaged, when her hand pressed against my stomach, stopping me.

"Let me. I can do this." Her other hand drifted out, hovering over the grease-stained paper bag. She stared at the sack with narrow eyes, crooking her fingers.

"Do what?"

"Look!"

My gaze lowered to our lunch. The bag jolted up from the pavement and rocketed into her hand. Just. Like. That.

Followed by my jaw almost hitting the ground. What the hell? I blinked, staring at the bag of food clutched in her hand. Did I actually just see that bag shoot up from the ground and into her hand? Now I was the one losing it! What kind of parallel universe was this?

"See? I did it! I knew I could do that and I did." She swayed to the side, and I immediately yanked her into me, reaching around her waist to steady her.

Holy shit! What the hell was going on? I'd seen that with my own eyes! The bag jetted from the ground into her hand just like she said. She'd done that with just her will. But it had taken a piece out of her to do it.

Supporting her with my body, I steered us to the door of the RV. When we reached it, she turned her head, gazing at me with wide-eyed wonder.

"I did that, Kara. I saved that kid."

Nine

Kara

I watched Maren like a hawk as she sat at the table eating her burger. Actually, more like devouring. She snarfed through that bacon cheeseburger like it was a quick snack, and with grease still running down her chin, she polished off the last piece of the blueberry muffin. She washed it down with a giant slurp of coffee that dribbled down in two rivulets from the corners of her mouth.

"So good..." she murmured, then sitting back on her seat, she let out the mother of all belches.

Maren belched. She never, ever, ever passed anything so much as the tiniest burp in her entire life! I swear to God, if she started farting, I'd totally lose my shit. Who is this person?

Not to mention that my brain was still short-circuited from her making that bag of food lift into the air. There was no doubt that she'd done something to get that boy safely onto the rock. But how? How did she suddenly have this kind of weird power?

Shit. Paranormal power! She was able to really, really move stuff with just her mind!

It was because of those aliens! It had to be. We'd been abducted for three days, and somehow she'd come out the other end with some kind of superpower. She could use her hands and wish something to move and it did!

I watched her grab a few napkins and swipe at the mixture of burger grease and coffee glistening on her chin. She let out another belch and sat back. For my prissy sister to act this way was bewildering. This was the woman who always carried not one, but two bottles of hand sanitizers in her purse and ate pizza with a knife and fork.

"That was good. I'm heading to the bedroom; I have to lie down now." Maren started to get up, but I reached over to stop her.

"Wait. Just give me a few minutes to talk to you before you pass out, okay? Plus, I'm not comfortable with you in the back while I'm driving. I should keep an eye on you, in case you have a concussion or something." No way was I letting her out of my sight. And if she had a concussion, should she even be sleeping? Wasn't that a no-no after hitting your head?

She threaded her fingers through her mane of chestnut curls, staring down at the table. "Look, I'm not sure how this is happening. Frankly, I feel totally out of it, like maybe I'm dreaming or something, even though I know I'm not. It's scary"—her eyes met mine—"and yet it's cool as anything."

"Cool doesn't begin to describe it." My forehead tightened as I gaped at her. The color was coming back into her cheeks, and other than being sleepy, she looked fine. Yet was she? She's had just used...what was that word? Telekinesis!

Telekinesis! How could she be so blasé about this? If that had happened to me, I'd be running around trying to move everything I saw with my mind. I'd be doing cartwheels, screaming at the sky from the sheer awesomeness of it!

I leaned over the table and took her hand in mine. "This is huge, Maren! You just did two acts of telekinesis. You moved that boy out of danger, and then you scooped up our lunch with just your mind."

She held her hand up, waving her fingers. "No. It was primarily these babies, Kara. I felt the electrical charge flowing out my fingertips. But yeah, this is…it's incredible."

"But why you? You don't even believe in anything paranormal. I'm the one who eats up any movie or book on this stuff. I watched all four seasons of Stranger Things, and every episode of Supernatural that's out."

She smirked. "And every documentary and YouTube vid."

"Yeah! So, if we were abducted by aliens, why was it you that was affected like this? Why not me?"

Her only answer was a shrug of her shoulders.

It was so unfair! What I wouldn't give to be able to do what she just did. I'd use it for good, but also wouldn't it be nice to just levitate something you wanted rather than having to leave a comfy sofa and go get it? As I stared at her sitting there so calmly, her eyelids getting heavy as she gazed at the table, I couldn't help feeling a little resentful. She didn't even believe we'd been abducted by aliens, yet she was the one to benefit?

Not fair. Not fair at all!

"Now do you believe that we were abducted, Maren? How else would you get this psychic power? You never had it before, and it sure as hell doesn't run in our family! No fortune tellers or magicians on either side. Yet the aliens gave you this woo-woo gift."

"Yeah, well, I'm still not buying that explanation as to how we lost those three days. I still want you to get the exhaust checked on this beast. But"—she stifled a yawn—"I don't need to check into a motel. I'm so tired, there's no way any mechanic clanging around with this thing would wake me. I just need to lay down for an hour or ten."

"No. I can't let you out of my sight, Maren. You can adjust the passenger seat and nap there, so I can keep tabs on you. Frankly, I'm worried. Maybe we need to put this trip on hold till I know you're going to be okay."

I scooped up the burger wrapping and the empty cardboard coffee containers. Should I take her home and get her examined by her doctor? There might be something wrong inside her head from what those aliens did.

Even though this cross-country road trip had been my dream for as long as I could remember, my sister's health was more important. It was bad enough that I had my own health issues without jeopardizing Maren's. That was another reason I wished that weird side effect of the alien thing had happened to me, not her. If it was life-threatening, I had little to lose. Not that I was going to get into that with my sister. Not yet anyway. "Maybe we should head back to Auburn."

"No, don't do that, Kara! I'm fine. We need to take this trip. Even though I wasn't sure about it when you first suggested it, I feel different now. This is important. I think our luck has changed. If nothing else, this tele-thingamajig proves it!"

She got up and started toward the front of the RV. "I'll ride shotgun." With a snort, she added, "Too bad I didn't have this ability when I torched Wayne's clothes. I could have tele-thinged him right into the center of the blaze."

I smiled as I followed her to the front. "It would have made painting your last house a breeze, that's for sure. Although I'm not sure setting Weasel Wayne on fire would have been good. Not that he didn't deserve it, but you'd end up in jail, and that would totally ruin our trip."

"Good point." She settled into the captain's chair and made it as horizontal as it would go. As she settled in, she gazed over at me. "Don't worry about me, Kara. If I need to get to the doctor, I'll let you know. But I've just got a strong feeling that things are okay with me. I want to do this trip and see where it takes us. 'K?"

I was silent for a few beats, watching her. She could be as stubborn as me sometimes; it was in our genes. She said she was okay, so I'd have to go with that. It didn't mean I wasn't going to keep a close eye on her. Finally, I answered, "Fine. But if you—"

"Yeah, yeah." She closed her eyes, effectively ending the discussion.

We weren't even out of the parking lot before her snoring began.

It was hours later that I parked the rig in Hampton Views RV campground.

The miles had flown by in a blur as I lost myself in all that had happened. And what was up ahead for us when the world learned about Maren's new telekinesis ability. She was a real-life hero—hell, superhero! It wasn't just me who had seen that little kid lifted from the swirling waters to safety. There'd been a few people with cell phones filming the whole thing. Maren would be famous when it all came out how she'd done it. I even had my answers all lined up for when Jimmy Fallon asked me how it felt to be the sister of a superhero.

My friends at Denny's would be gobsmacked when they saw me and Maren being interviewed not just by Jimmy on The Tonight Show…we'd do 'em all! Ellen, Oprah…maybe even Car Pool Karaoke with James Cordon!

"Come fly with meeee…" I sang quietly. Yeah, we could do that song. Or that oldie…"Up, Up and Awayyy In My Beautiful Balloon…"

A chill went through me. We could get high with Joe Rogan! Just like Elon Musk did!

We were going to be household names—the West Sisters from Auburn, New York. Not bad for a waitress and a house flipper.

I glanced over at Maren who was still out cold in the passenger seat, her head tilted back while her mouth had fallen open, softly snoring. Seeing the fine lines on her forehead melt away with sleep, she looked more like she was thirty-five instead of forty-five. She took after Dad with his almond complexion and wavy dark hair, while I'd inherited Mom's pale Nordic features. No one would ever mistake me for being in my thirties anymore. Pushing fifty in a few years, I felt every second of it.

I sighed as I unbuckled the seat belt. It looked like I was going to have to do the hookups in the campsite on my own. Why wake her? After all that had happened, she probably needed her rest. Besides, this was more my thing, wanting to travel in an RV. It would be easier to hook up the water, electricity, and sewer lines by myself.

After grabbing my notepad of instructions from the drawer, I stopped dead in my tracks when it hit me.

Maybe I got that gift too!

I wanted to smack myself in the head for taking so long to come around to this. I put the notepad on the dining table and took a step back, staring at it.

Okay notepad…move!

Nothin'. Damn. Wait. Maren, pointed at that kid and the bag of burgers. I stuck out my hand, pointing at it. Now, move!

Damn. Nothin' again. I stepped up to it. Maybe I needed to be closer or something. I put my hand over it, just an inch above. "Move, dammit!"

The stupid pad just lay there on the tabletop, practically laughing at me with its instructions on how to drain the freaking sewage tank, scrawled on the pages!

"OOOohh!" I mumbled at it. "Not even a page riffling?" I hissed at it. This was so damn unfair!

I stared at my hands so hard, my eyes crossed. No aura either, dammit.

"Fine!" I muttered and swept the damn pad off the table.

Now in a full-blown snit, I powered down most of the electrical appliances before heading out the side door to start the hookups. The screen door slammed behind me. If I woke Maren up, too damn bad. She could levitate herself to the back bedroom area for all I cared.

The closest neighbor was two sites away, a behemoth of an RV that totally owned the campsite it occupied. It could have easily been a tour bus for an up-and-coming band; it was the size of a school bus.

A black couple, well into retirement age, sat in lawn chairs under the awning of the giant rig. They looked over at me when I let the door slam behind me. The wife gave me a friendly wave before folding her hands in her ample lap. With the oversized sunhat, the bright yellow blouse, and blue Capris, she embodied contentment. Whereas she was full size, her husband was the opposite; his dark arms were like spindles poking out of a plaid sports shirt when he set the book he was reading aside. He rose from the chair, gave me a smile, hiked his pants almost to his shoulders and came over.

"Howdy, neighbor!" When the elderly gent was a few feet away, he smiled and extended his hand. "I'm Howie Winston, and that fine woman over there is my wife, Laura."

"Kara West. Pleased to meet you, Howie." Casting a glance at the cab of my rig, I volunteered, "My sister, Maren, is inside, asleep."

My hint hit home when his voice lowered, his gaze taking in my RV. "Nice setup. My wife and I started with the Phoenix. You can't beat it for a smooth ride and the craftsmanship."

I made a bit of a sulk. Sue me. I was still miffed at that stupid memo pad not levitating. "Compared to your rig, this secondhand RV isn't much more than a glorified cargo van."

He snorted. "Not with that extra bunk space over the driver area. And you get an extra foot or two on the sides." He patted the side of my rig and said in a low voice, "Don't take it personal, Mr. Phoenix. You're a great class C, not like those glorified vans that are class B's. This young lady owes ya an apology." He eyed me sideways.

"You make a habit out of talking to RVs, Howie?" I asked. Meeting an old guy who talks to cars wouldn't even score on the weird scale of stuff that happened to me today.

He shrugged. "Doesn't hurt. You look after your rig, and your rig'll look after you, right?"

I can't believe I did it, but I did. I stepped up next to my rig and patted its side. "Sorry for the van crack; you're a lot more than that." Damn thing cost a hella lot more than a van, even secondhand.

"Atta girl," Howie murmured. He stepped back and took in the sides of my RV. "We sure loved our Phoenix! We had a lot of good times in it, that's for sure. Drove it to Alaska one summer, coming back along the West Coast."

"Alaska?" My eyebrows raised high and I chuckled. "Wow! I thought we were ambitious driving down the Eastern Seaboard and then over to Texas." I looked past him to his rig, a Class-A mammoth beast with all the bells and whistles. "You sure made a leap from the Phoenix. That's a Challenger, right?" Howie must be doing all right for himself, living the dream in his retirement.

He beamed a wide grin, nodding his gray-haired head. "You betcha! We sold everything, and it's basically our home now. When the kids left the nest, we wanted it to stay that way. Can't come back if they can't find us!" He chuckled to let me know he was kidding.

His eyes zeroed in on the "Magical Mystery" logo I'd painted on the side between the two windows. "That's from the Beatles album, right? Nice touch. Maybe I should paint "Charlie" on mine. That's what we call her. Charlie Challenger. Although if you ask my wife, Laura, Charlie is short for Charlene. Can I give you a hand with your hookups? I've done them so often for the Phoenix, I could do them in my sleep."

"If you want to give me pointers, I'd be good with that, Howie. I really want to get the hang of this. It's only my second time setting up camp." I led the way to the driver's side of the vehicle and opened the compartments where the electrical line was stored.

Howie grabbed the line and headed toward the post where the connections were mounted. "You've got most appliances unplugged, right? I find just leaving the microwave on when I do the electrical works well. No blown fuses that way."

I gave him a thumbs-up. "That was first on my list of instructions."

He nodded. "Attagirl. Are you staying here for a while? It's a nice spot, close to the ocean. We've been here two weeks."

"It seems pretty nice, but we're planning on visiting family in Charleston, South Carolina. We were going to follow the coast as much as we can."

"Oh, that's a pretty route." He came over and grabbed the waterline. As he worked with the hookup, he glanced over. "If you're planning on stopping in North Carolina, I can't recommend Hatteras enough. It's well worth a stopover. We spent a month there last year."

While Howie quietly extolled, at great lengths, the sights and amenities of the cape, I rummaged for my thick rubber gloves to begin the—yuck—graywater line and sewer. I'd noticed that Howie hadn't jumped in to do this part. Hooking the hoses up wasn't difficult, but still, I took my time making sure that I did everything correctly.

When I finished with the sewer-line connection, I was anxious to get inside to wash my hands and see that we were up and running. Howie must have noticed my glances at the door of the rig because he wrapped up his travelogue with a smile.

"I'd better let you get inside to finish settling in. I've probably talked your ear off, anyway. At least that's what Laura always says I do. If you need anything, don't hesitate to ask." He edged away, giving me a wave of his hand before turning to join his wife.

I went back inside, noticing the flashing light of the microwave oven letting me know that the power was a go, hooked up correctly—thank you, Howie. I tested the water and then scrubbed my hands before grabbing a cold beer from the fridge. The bite of the brew was heaven in my mouth after a day of driving. That wasn't even taking into account all the twilight-zone crap that had happened. It was surreal, even to me!

Flopping down onto the leather sofa, I picked up the remote to turn the big-screen monitor on but kept it muted because Maren was still asleep despite my banging around. This was the one luxury I insisted on when I'd purchased this home on wheels two weeks ago. It had to have satellite connection for the TV, music, and internet. There was no way I was missing Netflix or my email. I didn't care what it cost.

My gut tightened at my next thought. All my life I'd scrimped and saved, trying to make ends meet on a waitress's earnings, so that Josh and I could have a roof over our heads and the typical stuff a kid growing up, needed. Now I had enough money to live out the rest of my life without ever worrying about paying a bill again and still leave a good starting stake to my son.

Living long wasn't in the cards though.

I gave my head a shake. Stop. At least I had this trip with my sister. Reconnecting with Maren was something I had hoped to do for years.

She didn't totally turn her back on me when I got pregnant. But by the time I did, she was already a mother of twins and still running the real estate investment company with her husband. Sure, she made a point of sending birthday and Christmas presents, but...

I lived in a two-bedroom apartment in the more run-down area of Auburn, while Maren and Wayne had beautiful homes—at least after they'd fixed them up to sell and start over again with another one. While I did get invited to their annual Christmas party, there were pool parties and barbeques in the summer, along with dinner parties the rest of the year that I just wasn't invited to. One of the things about being a waitress (don't call me "server"; I hate that term) is that you're pretty much up to date on town gossip. There were a few regulars of mine that knew Maren and Wayne pretty well, so I knew about most of her parties.

I guess I sort of embarrassed her. She was the one with the MBA tearing up the world, while I was the continuously underachieving sister, getting high on weekends and partying on. I guess I was an embarrassment to Maren. Definitely to her husband, Wayne the Weasel. We had disliked each other on sight.

I did leave my party-hardy days behind when I got pregnant with Josh. His arrival made me a lot more conventional for the last nineteen years, for sure. But by the time I had him, my reputation was pretty much locked in, y'know?

Shit! Josh! I grabbed my cell phone from the front console to send a text to my son. He hadn't heard from me for three days! Just wait till I told him about the alien thing and Maren's new powers! He would be totally smoked.

"Hey!" Maren stretched her arms over her head and let out a shuddering yawn.

I looked over, doing a quick scan, checking her eyes and her balance as she climbed out of the shotgun seat. "You're finally awake. How are you feeling?" She looked relaxed, her eyes heavy lidded, while the lines bordering her mouth had vanished. She was calmer than I'd seen her in years.

Bending to get a vodka cooler from the fridge, she smiled as she twisted the cap off. "I feel a-mazing! I can't remember having a better sleep than that." Her one eye closed as she tilted her head, peering at me. "Did all that really happen? Did I dream about saving that kid and—"

"It was no dream, Maren. You really did it." I held up my cell phone. "I'm just writing a text to Josh to tell him about it and that abduction thing. He's not going to believe it!"

"Wait!" She sank into the spot next to me. "Don't do that. I don't think we should tell anyone—at least not yet.

Not until we figure all this out, Kara."

I couldn't help my eye roll. "Too late for that, I'd say. Did you notice the people onshore with their cell phones, taking videos? We don't have to tell anyone, Maren. It's all out there on video. That's why I turned the TV on. I'd be surprised if that didn't make the national news, but for sure, there's got to be local coverage. It's almost six, so it should be on soon."

"No. No. No." Her fingers threaded through her hair, fisting handfuls. "Shit! I don't have a good feeling about this getting out. This is so not good."

"Why? You're a hero, Maren! I've been thinking about this while you were sleeping. We made a mistake, taking off from that picnic area so fast. I wished we'd had the presence of mind to talk to the boy's parents, at least. I'm sure they'd have wanted to thank you."

I leaned closer to get her attention. "This is the kind of thing that would get you on Oprah or The Today Show! Jimmy Fallon, Maren! Can you imagine that? We'd be famous!"

Maren's face morphed, her mouth falling open like that famous painting The Scream. Her dark pupils were rimmed with white, totally horrified. Before she could say another word, the picture on the TV set caught my attention. I unmuted it, and yup, they were doing a story about a boy almost drowning.

I pressed the button on the remote, turning up the volume before shushing Maren with a sweep of my hand. I wanted to catch what the commentator was saying.

> *"...can only be described as nothing short of a miracle, folks. Little Danny Miller had slipped under the floating barrier and into the current of the Potomac. At that particular spot, the river is narrow, and there are a series of white-water rapids a little past the*

swimming spot.
What we're about to play for you are
two videos taken by onlookers. They
show how young Danny miraculously
emerged from the swirling waters, and
was held airborne for a moment or two.
He was then set down gently onto the
safety of a rock jutting out of the flow."

Maren jumped up, staring hard at the screen. "Shit! You can even see me at the riverbank in that clip!"

Ignoring her, I sat mesmerized as the news station played the two clips a couple of times each. Yeah, for sure the kid had been airborne hovering above the rock before he was set down as gentle as a mother putting a baby down for its nap. There was no mistaking what had happened. It was all out there in living color. And Maren had done that!

The screen went black and I turned to see her with the remote control in her hand, scowling at the TV. "They don't know that I saved that kid. We could have been anyone just standing there watching that poor boy. They can't pin this on me, and that's the way it's staying, Kara."

I took a long drink of the beer and glowered at her. "I don't get you. Not at all. It really should have been me that got these superpowers. This is so like you, Maren. Always cautious, never wanting the spotlight or taking credit. Like when you backed out of that photo shoot for the contest in that home-reno magazine. You were a shoo-in to win, but you didn't want all that publicity, featuring your home and family. Well, for once, I think you should take some credit. Especially now, with that Weasel Wayne trying to screw you out of everything in a divorce settlement."

"Forget him! This is waaay bigger than Wayne, Kara. And certainly, bigger than getting an award for decorating."

She shrank into the sofa next to me. "If you're right—and I'm not convinced you are—this teleport-thingy happened after we passed out for three days."

"When we were kidnapped by aliens," I corrected her. Why was that so hard to believe? Especially now that she had this superpower?

She slashed at the air. "I'm not buying that explanation, okay?"

"So, what the hell do you think happened?"

"Beats the hell out of me! I don't need to jump to some woo-woo, out-of-your-mind explanation at the drop of a hat! I'm just sticking with the facts!" She jabbed a finger at me. "You ought to try it sometime!"

Now this was the Maren I knew! I put my arms around her and hugged her.

"What the hell are you doing?" she said. But...she did hug me back.

"You were so spacey after saving that kid, I was scared you had brain damage or something," I said in her ear. "But now, I know you're okay. The old Maren is still in there."

She was silent for a moment. "That really, really was something else, wasn't it, Kara?" She disentangled from our hug but held my hands. "Look, I don't know what happened when we were out cold. But I do know that if word gets out about what I did, our government and every kook out there would want to know more about that. At the very least, I'd be a freak in some media sideshow, and at the worst...well, Homeland Security or the NSA would want to study the hell out of this. Hell—out of me! And my life would be ruined."

"So, we're not telling anyone about this? Not even our kids?" But I already knew the answer to that question. I could see the fear in her eyes and in every line of her face. She was totally frightened, not by the power, but by people's reactions to it. Rather than fame and fortune, this would destroy my sister.

"Not my kids or yours either. Swear to me you'll keep this between us. We don't know why this happened and if it will last. Let's give this time to process and then decide what to do. No one needs to know any of this. Not yet."

She started for the back of the rig. "I need a shower. Is everything set up so that I can do that? Notice, I'm not whining about the fact you didn't check us into a hotel like I asked."

"I appreciate you not bellyaching about showering here and not at a motel. But Maren, if you want me to stay quiet about all this, you have to promise me one thing." I couldn't help the smirk that glinted in my eyes.

When her head dipped, waiting, I added, "From now on, you look after the sewer hookup. That gift of telekinesis will mean neither of us has to physically touch those lines anymore."

She grinned. "Sounds fair. You got a deal."

Ten

Maren

Freshly showered and with a full meal in my belly—compliments of Kara—I offered, "I'll clear the table and get the dishes done." I pointed at her empty plate and smiled when it levitated up off the table to float over to the kitchen sink. Next, mine became airborne.

"You're such a show-off now, Maren," Kara sat back scowling at me. "Still not freaking fair. Not by a long shot."

"You're just jealous! Face it. If this were you, you'd be levitating everything in this rig." I grinned and sent the salt and pepper shakers to the counter. "Want a beer?" Okay, maybe I was showing off as I flipped the fridge door open and floated a cold one over to Kara.

"Show-off." Kara snatched the beer from midair, and twisted the cap off.

This was truly amazing! I couldn't explain how I'd suddenly got this power to levitate stuff, but who cared? It was fun and even functional! Smirking at Kara as she guzzled her beer, I bragged, "I'm getting good at this tele-thingy, aren't I?"

"It's TELE-KENISIS!" Kara barked it out at me.

"Whatever." But I could see from the way she picked at the beer bottle label, her face twisted in a knot, that I was maybe pushing her buttons too much. This was totally something Kara would love to be able to do. Time to ease up a bit.

"Thanks for cooking dinner, Kara. It was really good. You're sooo much better of a cook than I could ever be." Flattery usually worked with my sister. But it was also true. She was a natural at practically anything she set her mind to. The problem was attention span. She'd get bored, or if it proved too challenging, she'd give up.

She shrugged. "Work for years and years in a restaurant and you practically learn by osmosis."

One of our cell phones went off, and the "Black Velvet" melody filled the air. Kara jumped to her feet to grab her phone from the counter.

"That's Josh! He's finally answering my text." She glanced over at me. "Don't worry. I didn't mention the abduction or your new superpowers. I just asked him how school was going and how he's doing."

When she turned her attention to the phone, I got up to start running water to do the dishes. Josh was a good kid, and he'd done well to get into college in Syracuse. Later, I'd check in with my own kids and see how they were doing. Wonder what they'd say if they knew about my new powers—not that I was going to tell them. Still, it'd be fun to see their faces.

When Kara let out an angry huff, turning away from the phone, I looked over at her. "What's wrong? Is Josh okay?" But her face showed more disappointment than worry, so that had to mean Josh wasn't hurt or something.

"He hadn't heard from me for three whole days, and it's like he didn't even notice." She stared down at the floor, setting the phone on the counter. "And then when he answers, it's all about his new roommates and how ridiculously expensive his books are. He never asked about our trip or how I'm doing."

"He's nineteen years old, Kara. And he doesn't have to worry about money anymore, right?" I knew she had forwarded a few thousand from her winnings to him to help with living expenses, so he wouldn't have to take a job. And him being caught up in his own life, the first time away from home adjusting to school was understandable.

"Yeah, but…" She folded her arms across her chest. "I didn't think I'd…well, not matter anymore, y'know?"

I took a deep breath as I set a pot onto the drying rack. Been there, done that with my kids. "Yeah, I know. When the twins went off to college, I didn't hear from them for the entire first week. And when I did, they both said that they needed more money." At the time, it hurt, but in retrospect, what did I expect?

I smiled when I looked over at Kara. "I wanted to kill 'em for being so selfish, and cry because they didn't need me anymore." A glance at my sister showed her eyes filling with tears, so I dried my hands and went over to give her a hug. "I realized something then."

She sniffed. "What?"

Pulling back, I looked into her eyes. "Them not needing me, them not being clingy meant that I had prepared them for the world. I prepared them for growing up." Giving her arms a gentle squeeze, I continued. "So, congratulations on a job well done, sis. Like me, you raised a self-reliant kid! Self-centered, too, but that comes with being nineteen!"

"He probably won't phone tomorrow either."

When I turned away to drain the sink, she muttered, "Hey, I get to wallow, okay?"

I turned back to her and dried my hands. "Sure you do. You even get extra wallow and kudos because you did this entirely on your own. As much as it pains me to admit it, I did have Wayne at my side as we raised our kids; you did this all by yourself."

I held her gaze and we stared at each other in silence for a pregnant pause. I took a breath, and Kara held up her hand like a traffic cop. "Don't, Maren."

"But—"

"No. We made that agreement when I told you I was pregnant, and again when he turned thirteen. Don't."

She had that look in her eyes; the "I'm really, really serious" look, but I kept at it. Things are different now, for Pete's sake!

"Kara, things are different now. I don't understand—"

"No!"

I held up my hands in surrender. "I'm sorry, then. I don't think you're being fair—not to me, and certainly not to Josh. The boy should know who his father is."

Kara closed her eyes. I knew she was silently counting to ten. As kids, Mom and Dad drilled into us, like nobody's business, that when you're about to explode all over a family member, you have to count to ten in your head first. After you do, if you still need to, okay. But you have to take that last one step back before. Dad said, "At least you give the other person a chance to escape so you stay out of jail!" laughing as he said it.

She opened her eyes and her lips were a thin line. "No," she said. "I worked it out with Josh years ago. He's not crazy about it, but he accepts it."

"For now," I added.

Her eyes flashed at me. "For now," she repeated. "And if that's good enough for the boy, it damn well is good enough for you, Maren West!"

She was right. I didn't agree, but it was her call. I exhaled a long breath. "I'm sorry." I held out my hand. "Pax?" Dad taught us that too. At the end of a quarrel, one of us has to man up and say the magic word, pax. I had to look it up; he said he got it from a movie.

Kara held my gaze for another moment and then took my hand. We clasped and shook once. "Pax," she replied.

This was hard on her. She'd sacrificed and worked hard to raise Josh on her own. I mean completely on her own. A twinge of remorse hit me just then. Josh's father hadn't been in the picture at all, yeah.

But his only aunt could have done a better job too.

I had to give her credit for that. She could be flighty as hell, but she'd done right by her kid.

Moving over to her again, I put my arm over her shoulder. "Let's go find the ocean. What do you say?"

***

We locked the doors of the rig and went onto the roadway. The campground had been filling up all afternoon; now many of the spots that had been empty had rigs in them. We headed to the main office to find the best way to reach the ocean. Our campground was in a wooded area, but I knew from the website that the seashore was really close by. I just wasn't sure which was the best way to take.

Up ahead of us were two younger kids, about twelve or so, playing a game of catch in the roadway.

One of the kids jumped to catch the softball but missed. It came flying through the air right at me. Without even thinking, my hand rose and the ball stopped still in the air. I made another gesture and it went arcing silently back toward the kid. Oh God. I hadn't even touched the ball! I don't know how I knew how to do it, but I did it! This crazy energy shooting from my fingers was amazing. I just hoped they hadn't noticed that the ball never physically made contact.

The kid's eyes were round as that softball, and he just barely managed to catch it before it bonked him in the chest. He looked at the ball and then gaped at me. "Uh...sorry. But thanks for throwing it back...?" His face was a puzzled knot when he tossed the ball to his friend.

Shit! I had to be more careful when I was out in public. He'd noticed that the ball hadn't touched me. There hadn't even been a slap of it contacting my hand. The last thing I wanted was someone seeing this crazy power. I hurried on while Kara muttered, "No problem. Have a nice evening."

She caught up with me, smirking. "Nice catch there, sis! But I wish I'd grabbed it first. Hopefully, that kid won't give it much thought."

I shrugged. "I shouldn't have done it, but it was more just instinct. Sounds crazy, but I just did it as naturally as if I had actually caught it. That puzzles me."

"What does?"

"Just how…" I held my hands out in front of me. "How much a part of me this gift has already become."

Kara looked over her shoulder at the two boys. "Well, they're not staring at us, so I think you got away with your public display this time."

I nodded. "I'll have to be more careful, for sure. But here's the thing—people don't see stuff they don't believe." When I saw her eyebrows knit in puzzlement, I added, "They say 'seeing is believing,' right? Well, you also have to have a frame of reference to see stuff too. If that kid saw what just happened on TV, sure he'd understand that I have"—I waved my fingers—"tele-thing powers. But out in the real world? Nope. He would just think his eyes played a trick on him, because this tele-thingy—"

"Telekinesis!" she said, her teeth gritted.

It was fun needling her. "Yeah. That. Well, what I'm saying is that the kid sort of just knows that doesn't happen 'in real life.' So no, he didn't 'see' it. There are accounts of first contact with Native Americans from the earliest days of settling in the New World, that they weren't able to actually see the ships in the bay at first because they had absolutely no frame of reference for sailing ships. I think it's the same thing with that boy."

"You sure?"

"Well, it fits, doesn't it?"

She nodded. "Y'know, you're pretty smart, Maren."

I did a fake curtsy. "Why, thank you!"

She pointed to an arrow sign up ahead. "There! Doesn't

that say, The Beach? It must be a shortcut."

I just wanted to put as much distance as I could between me and those kids. Here I'd given Kara hell about telling the world about this tele-thingy power I had, and it was me who screwed up. My eyes narrowed trying to see the sign she'd mentioned. Sure enough, a white sign with a red arrow was tucked next to a large shrub with yellow flowers. A narrow strip of hard-packed dirt led deeper into the trees.

When we left the road and were out of sight, I held my hands up, gazing at them. It was still hard to believe what I could do with just a thought harnessing whatever power was now in these hands.

Kara must have noticed me gaping at them, when she commented, "Y'know something? There's gold in those hands of yours!"

I looked over at her, noticing the wide grin on her face. "What do you mean?"

"See how you flipped that softball around? You could go to a football game, bet big on the underdog, and from the stands make sure that the other guys don't score a point!" Her eyes widened. "Or you could go to Vegas and mess around with the dice on the craps table! Or the ball on the roulette wheel!" She looked at me, her eyes glinting. "We could be partners, Maren! Maybe we should make Vegas one of our destinations on this trip."

"Sure. That'd work well. The cameras at those gaming tables wouldn't notice two old broads like us, breaking the bank with our winnings. Not bad enough I have to worry about some kid noticing my weird power, but we'd have the Lottery and Gaming Commission to deal with. I don't want to end this vacation in a jail cell." Trust Kara to come up with some get-rich-quick scheme.

"Oh, come on!" She nudged me playfully. "We'd plan it out and move around to different cities. They'd never catch us. Think of Wayne's face when you show up in Auburn driving a Lamborghini. You could buy up the whole block where the real estate office is and squeeze him and Suzanne out. Think of the fun you'd have."

It was hard not to get caught up in her excitement and fantasizing revenge. "Forget that! I'd make sure all his tires were flat every time he went out to show a property." I started giggling at the next thought. "Think I could do something to his little dick so that he'd never get it up again? Deflate all his plans with his girlfriend? Would she even notice though?"

"Probably not." Kara grabbed my arm and lifted her head, taking a deep breath. "Do you smell that? I smell the ocean."

I paused and took a deep breath. Although I couldn't smell anything past the smell of pine and the loamy forest, the hiss of waves rolling to shore and children's laughter was faint in the air around me. "I think we're almost there. It's been a long time since I've been to the ocean."

"I've only been once. That summer when Josh was nine and we went down to the Jersey shore? Even though there's tons of lakes near Auburn, it doesn't compare to the ocean." She let out a long sigh. "That was ten years ago. God, where does the time go?"

Before I could comment, the phone in my back pocket vibrated and it chirped with a text message. When I scooped it out and looked at it, I could see it was from Derek Scott. My mind nose-dived to catastrophe mode. What the hell was wrong? What had Wayne's lawyer come back with, answering my lawyer?

"Who is it?"

Ignoring Kara's question, I brushed the screen to read what he'd written.

"Wayne was served with divorce papers earlier today. I've just received an email from Anthony Dunleavy, his legal representative that he is contesting the grounds of adultery. He will agree to no-fault on the grounds that you have had

irreconcilable differences over the past six months. His representative is trying to make hay about you burning his client's clothes, questioning your judgment, if not sanity. This is all bluster, of course. The adultery charge really got his nettle up. I'd advise that we stay the course but I had to update you on your husband's response."

"Maren? Is everything okay?"

For a moment I found it hard to focus on Kara's face. Even though I knew Wayne was going to fight back, the fact he'd hired Anthony Dunleavy was bad. Hell, I would have retained him but he was retired! He'd come out of retirement for this? What was Wayne paying him?

My mouth was suddenly dry and I croaked an answer to Kara. "He's got Anthony Dunleavy as his lawyer. He wants a no-fault divorce even though I've got him dead to rights on adultery. Derek thinks it's bluster but...if it were any other lawyer than Dunleavy, I'd agree."

"Oh shit. Dunleavy sued the town five years ago over a proposed landfill site. I heard about how he got them to change, as well as millions for his clients. But he retired, I thought. A friend of mine worked the banquet for his send-off bash at the Palisades."

For a few moments I considered replying to Derek and telling him to agree to a no-fault. Knowing Dunleavy, he'd put me on the stand and grill me about the clothes-burning, making make me look like a total lunatic! The guy was ruthless.

My eyes narrowed, remembering Wayne brazenly waltzing into the restaurant and the scene between us. He'd acted like I was the bad guy, but I was in the right here. He'd screwed around on me once before and I'd let him off for the sake of the kids.

Kara inched closer, looking into my eyes. "What are you

gonna do, Maren? You have to stand up for yourself, or Wayne's gonna get everything. Are you sure you shouldn't get Alex Johnson instead of this Derek?"

"I think Derek knows his stuff. As for Wayne...I wasn't the one screwing around. My days of being his doormat are over." I took a deep breath and tapped Kara's shoulder. "But I'll deal with that later tonight. Right now, we've got a beach to see."

Eleven

Kara

We emerged from the path and stood stock-still for a few moments gazing across a roadway to the beach and ocean beyond it. A line of tall palm trees stood like swaying sentinels along the side of the road, and just beyond them was the beach, the sand glinting in the late afternoon sun.

Only a few handfuls of people walked along the wide swath of the shoreline. But it was the azure blue of the ocean streaked with frothy surf that was truly gorgeous. I took a deep breath, infusing myself with the hint of seaweed in the salty aroma.

This. This was what I had hoped to see when I'd planned this vacation.

Maren smiled as she gazed at the panorama. "It makes you feel pretty small, doesn't it? The water just goes on and on forever."

I nodded. "When I stand here, it's hard to believe everything that's happened to us since we started this trip. Yet it's as real as that ocean."

"Yeah. It makes the problems with Weasel Wayne pale in significance," she replied.

Hell, it even made my own mortality more acceptable. At least I'd been able to see this, relishing every moment with my only sister.

Both our parents were long gone. They had us later in life. Dad passed away in his late seventies ten years ago, and two years later, Mom joined him in heaven.

Aside from Josh, Maren was my only living relative. And it's different being with her. I love Josh to the end of the world, but I felt it would have been wrong to have gone on this trip with him. I knew Maren all my life—she's only two years younger—and despite our previous estrangement, we reconnected without any animosity. Okay, maybe a few speed bumps after being abducted, but...I had missed being with my kid sister for many years.

I grabbed her hand and squeezed it tightly.

"What?" she asked. "Worried about me crossing the road? You used to do this all the time when we were little." But she smiled when she squeezed back.

"Well...uhhh...I'm just glad you're here."

"I know."

"Oh yeah?" I looked at her sideways.

"Yup." She squinted her eyes a bit. "Your aura's bright as anything. I guess that means you're happy."

"That's got to be weird." Weird but wonderful. Why couldn't it have happened to me? "Do you see auras all the time?"

"No, I don't. I have to sort of think about it and focus a little before they appear." She gave a little shudder. "Thank goodness for that! If I saw them all the time, I'd probably go crazy with all the colors."

"Do you know what the colors mean?"

"No, not really." She gave me an elbow in the side. "But

I'll bet you can tell me everything I need to know, right?"

I snickered. "Yeah, I probably have twenty bookmarks on my computer just for auras!" I remembered following what one online guru wrote, practicing on trees and plants, but aside from getting a headache, no wavery color ever showed. Still, I believed some people could see them and it fascinated me.

We hustled across the road, still holding hands, and went down to the shoreline. At about ten feet from the damp sand, we toed out of our sneakers and tucked our phones in them. Wearing shorts and T-shirts, we went out past our knees into the frothy surf. The afternoon was warm and balmy; the breeze from the ocean caressed my skin.

"Hey! I wonder if I can make the water move like I can with objects?" Maren's eyes sparked as she grabbed my arm, tugging me deeper out into the water. "This is going to be fun to try—as long as I don't create a tsunami."

The ocean's hissing surf called to us. It was like we were kids again, letting out shrieks of joy at the coolness of the ocean on our legs, wading deeper until the bottoms of our shorts were drenched.

Suddenly a spray of water droplets cascaded over my head, soaking my hair and face. At Maren's hoot of laughter, I spun to face her, just in time to get another face full of salty water. Her hand was waist high, but with a flick of her wrist, she'd caused a crest of water to splash over me!

"Stop that! No fair!" I bent lower and scooped water, sending it in an arc at her, drenching her head. It wasn't by telekinesis, but did the job.

Maren squeezed the water from her eyes, and looked at me, her face shining in joy. "I did it! I did that tele-thingy with water! It felt more smooshy, but it worked!" She looked from where we stood back to the shore. "I wonder how big a wave I can make."

No tidal waves, okay?" I said. I really wasn't worried, but still. But then, just how big a wave could she make, I wondered? It couldn't be all that much; I mean, we were only twenty or thirty feet from the shore.

Her hand went out, hovering over the rolling surf. Spotting a lone woman up the beach staring at us, I stepped toward Maren, grabbing her hand. "Don't do that. Look! There's a woman watching us."

The woman's eyes appeared black, they were so dark and piercing, practically glaring at us. The ends of the silver headscarf covering most of her hair fluttered in the breeze over her shoulder like a short cape. Her skin was an almond hue, almost a shade of gold, and her nose was straight with a slight downward hook above full ruby lips. She could have been of Middle-eastern descent but I didn't think so. Still, there was a something exotic about her.

She was gazing at us openly, fully facing us with her hands on her waist, making no attempt to hide her interest in us.

When Maren tried to pull her hand away, I continued, "Hey! You're the one who doesn't want to attract attention. That woman over there is watching us like a prison guard. The next thing you know she's going to pull out her cell phone and film us." I looked past her to the dark-haired woman standing at the edge of the water about fifty feet away.

Maren's head turned and she lifted her other hand to give a friendly wave to the woman. The woman didn't acknowledge the gesture in any way, not with a smile or change of expression. Instead, she took a step closer, shielding her eyes with her hand from the water's glare.

The longer we stared at each other, the more my gut tightened. There was a threatening malignancy emanating from her in the perfect stillness of her body. "Maybe we should go back now, Maren."

Maren's gaze never left the strange woman. "There's something about her that—"

"I know. I've met some creepy characters in my time, but she's something else."

"It's not just that. It's the color of the energy around her.

It's dark red, almost a burgundy. I don't know what the different colors mean, but I definitely don't like hers. Who the hell is she and what does she want with us? Why does she keep staring at us?"

As Maren and I waded through the water, heading toward the shore, I kept glancing at the woman. "Maybe she's the local weirdo, off her meds or something."

"There's something off about her, all right." Maren swore under her breath. "Shit! We were having such a good time together, playing in the surf. Why'd that looky-loo show up to ruin it."

.When we reached the hard-packed sand, Maren took a step toward the woman, sneering at her. "You got a problem, lady? Take a picture, why don't ya? It'll last longer."

The woman was about fifteen feet away from us. She didn't react at all, just continued staring at us.

"Maren, let's just go, okay?" The last thing we needed was getting into an argument and creating a scene. That bitch was weird, and we should just get away from her.

But rather than calm my sister down, my suggestion added fuel to the fire in Maren's eyes. "No! I'm done with people trying to intimidate me." She darted to our sneakers and grabbed her cell phone. "We're not leaving this beach without at least a selfie! Come here, Kara."

Oh God, Maren was on a roll. It was starting to feel like that scene in the Italian restaurant when Wayne barged in. But this time, she was way more assertive. Normally, it would be me feeding it back to someone who teed me off, not Maren. I was the blustery one. Maren's style of confrontation was more like a shark—she'd come at you from where you weren't looking and whammo! But here on the beach? My sister was about three steps away from catfight city, for sure. And we weren't even drunk!

Yep, this was a different side to Maren, and I liked it. She was more like me right now and that felt wonderful.

"C'mon, Kara! Selfie time!" She spun around, so our

backs were to the woman behind us now.

My chest swelled with pride at Maren's attitude as I stepped closer to her and smiled at the camera she held out. The reflection in the lens showed just the tops of our heads as she angled it to capture that woman's face in the picture.

"See how she likes being stared at and getting her photo taken," Maren muttered.

What the—? The screen only showed Maren and me. She twisted the phone to the left and then to the right. My eyes followed the lens but only the beach and an older couple in the distance showed.

"What the hell?" Maren spun around. "Where'd she go?"

Where the woman had stood was now empty. And there was no sign of her hurrying away up the beach in any direction. What the hell?

Maren trotted over to where the woman had been. "There's not even any footprints in the wet sand, Kara. She was right there!"

Twelve

Maren

My mouth fell open as I stood, gawking around the beach. Aside from a few kids tossing a Frisbee farther up and another old guy walking a dog, there was nobody else nearby. And not a single sign of the strange woman. How was that possible?

I looked over at Kara. "She was here, right? Or am I losing it, Kara? I mean we both saw her. You saw her, glaring at us."

She shielded her eyes with her hand, peering around the sand. "What the hell? Who is she, Houdini? How could she just vanish like that? As soon as we went to take the picture, she just disappeared!"

This was all too weird. Waaay too much to process in one day.

After a few moments, I stared at Kara. "Are you thinking what I'm thinking? This morning, waking up after missing three days, things just keep getting wonkier and wonkier. First there's this teleport thingy, and then some random woman just vanishes into thin air."

I folded my arms over my chest, and a shudder skittered through me. "This isn't fun anymore, Kara. It's too weird. I mean, what's next? I'm not sure I want to know." It was like starring in The Black Mirror, and I never even watched that show, except the few times Kara had it on. But this was my life, not some creepy thriller.

Kara stepped closer, putting her hand on my shoulder. "Aside from giving us a scare, nothing really awful happened, Maren. No one got hurt. And that bitch is gone now. Who cares how it happened? Good riddance, I say."

"Yeah, sure, I guess." I let her usher me alongside her, heading back to where our shoes were. Of course, Kara took this all in stride, but for me, it was hitting me like a wall. None of this made any sense! The tele-thingy was fun, but how could all this be happening? Hell, I shouldn't be able to move things with just a thought, and forget about people disappearing into thin air.

"Look at the positive side. You saved a young boy today, Maren. If not for you, he wouldn't be alive. There is that to consider."

I nodded numbly. "Yeah. I know I saved that kid." Slipping my feet into my sneakers, I mentally reviewed all that had happened. That woman had pissed me off, but if I hadn't been showing off just now, trying to use this tele-thingy to splash Kara, we wouldn't have caught her attention. And for her to literally vanish when I'd confronted her... I gave my head a shake. If it wasn't for the fact that this day had already been off the charts in the strange-things column, I'd be frightened right now. People just don't vanish like that.

But then...people don't splash water by waving their hands at it.

Kara continued to plead her case. "I think you're right about keeping your new abilities under the radar, Mare. We really need to downplay it and keep everything just between us. I'd like to know who that was though."

"Maybe just a curious onlooker who doesn't speak English?" I said in a weak voice.

Kara shot me a look. "No, and you don't believe that either. The vibe we got from her was…" She groped for a word.

"Malevolent," I said. "Her aura was malevolent." I don't know how I knew that, but I sure as shooting did know it.

"You serious?"

I nodded. "Let's get out of here."

As we walked across the beach, heading back to the campground, I thought about that odd woman. She wasn't dressed like most people walking along the beach, not with the silver headscarf and the tailored tunic over tights. If anything, she looked like she was going to a cocktail party, not a beach outing.

Turning to Kara, "She was weird, but her disappearing was really spooky. Do you suppose, I can maybe see ghosts now?" But immediately, I dismissed that. "No, I saw her aura, so she had to be human."

Kara nudged me with her shoulder. "I saw her too, y'know. No, she was there. Maybe she's an alien. After what's happened over the past week, anything's possible."

Gawd! Aliens again! But one thing she was right about, were the strange things that had happened since we'd started this trip. I forced a smile before we crossed the road to go back to the trailer park. "Believe it or not, the way this day's gone, I'm not going to rule anything out anymore, Kara. She could be a ghost or an alien. But one thing is sure, she wasn't normal, not vanishing like that. If we see her again, I think I'm going to try levitating her." I rubbed my hands together. "See what she does then!"

As we entered the shortcut leading back to the RV, I started chuckling. Maybe I was losing my mind. "I can't believe what is happening to my life. Just a month ago, I was crazy busy with remodeling that old house we bought, and now look at me. Traipsing across the country in a camper with my kooky sister, abducted by whatever, and getting these magic hands! And this is all while I'm going through a shitty divorce!"

Behind me, Kara snarked, "You call me kooky? Miss Magic Hands who wants to levitate aliens to teach 'em a lesson? I'm the kooky one?"

I batted my eyes at her. "We've just been living together for a few days, and you're rubbing off on me, I guess."

"Ha!" Kara grinned. "I guess it's not hard to tell nowadays that we're sisters. But seriously, they made a mistake giving you the magic hands. That bitch back there would be clinging to a buoy in the harbor, if I'd gotten that gift."

"Yeah, yeah. Easy to be tough now that we're safely away from her." I pulled up and put my hand up in the air. "Wait a second. This is a little stranger than just that woman."

"Oh? How so?"

"I'm a nice lady," I said, pointing my index finger at my heart. "You're a nice lady," I added, pointing to Kara.

"So what does that have to do with that bitch?"

"Exactly!" I looked away for a moment, thinking it over. "All she was doing was watching us while I levitated water and we wound up splashing each other."

"Yeah, and then that bitch vanished."

"That's it! That bitch!" I snapped my fingers. "We never met her before, right?" When Kara agreed, I continued, "But both of us, both of us hated her on sight! Why? She didn't do or say anything to us, other than watch us, right?"

Kara nodded again. Her eyes were thoughtful.

"But even so, Kara, she's a bitch."

"Yeah. No doubt about that."

"Yeah! I feel the same way! But there's no good reason, is there?"

"Not that I know of."

"Exactly." I turned and looked over my shoulder at

where we'd come from. "We're not like that. But yet in this case, we are." I shook my head slowly. "There's something about that woman."

"About that bitch."

"Yeah. Let's get back to the rig, then, okay?"

As we stepped onto the road leading through the campground, I sighed. "Magic hands and vanishing women aside, I'm glad that we're doing this trip. It's been too long since it was just us." Aside from her pranks when we were younger, we'd been close. That was before our paths took us in different directions.

"Yeah, I know. And me winning the lottery enabled this. This trip has always been on my bucket list, especially doing it with you."

I paused for a moment and turned around to face her. Despite her life choices, turning her back on higher education and an easier life as a nurse, she was a good person. She might dress like a boho renegade with the fringed shawls and campy T-shirts, but under that free-spirit façade, she was smart and honest, working long hours in a menial job, and always with a smile on her face.

"If anyone deserved to win the lottery, it was you, Kara. You've worked hard all your life and raised a good kid. I appreciate being here, even though it's had its eerie moments. With my life getting upended by Jerk-Face, I needed to get away for a while."

We both needed this trip, Mare." She leaned in to tuck a lock of my hair behind my ear, and her eyes were bleary with tears when she looked into my eyes. "Even though we were both caught up in living our own lives, I always knew you were there if I needed you. You know that, right?"

I nodded. "Ditto. You've always had my back, too, even though we went in different directions when we left home. But we're together again, and as strange as this trip is, I'm enjoying being with you."

She grinned and turned back to our journey. The two of us fell into step together walking to the roadway leading to our site.

As we neared Howie's campsite, all was quiet like they were tucked in for the night. The sun was now down, and campfires flickered like fireflies along the roads of the campsite.

"Looks like we've got a new neighbor."

I followed Kara's gaze to the pale, bubble-shaped camper hooked up to a Dodge truck. It was parked in the site between Howie's rig and Kara's camper. My forehead bunched as I stared at the odd little contraption. As we passed by it, I leaned in to whisper, "That thing is basically the size of an oversized closet! It's like Howie's rig laid an egg."

Kara murmured, "I looked at one of those years ago, when I first thought of taking a road trip. Even though that thing's tiny, it's got a sink, stove, bed, and bathroom. It's amazing how they design the Boler campers. And that one's a classic."

As we walked by it, I couldn't help but stare at the odd little camper. Again, there was no sign of life, aside from the yellow glow behind the curtain covering a small porthole window. Turning to Kara, I whispered again, "I'm glad you didn't buy that model. I can't imagine going cross-country in something that small, although it is kind of cute. We'd really be at each other's throats in that."

"No kidding. I wonder if it's a young couple in there, getting down and dirty? I hope they don't keep us up all night." She shrugged and winced. "I think I'm getting old, y'know that? Grousing about young people?" She laughed lightly.

But instead of any moans and groans, the harsh rumble of a male voice drifted from the small camper. It was immediately interrupted by a coldly feminine series of sharp words, until the two voices combined became louder.

My hand flew up to cover the chuckle as I peered at Kara. "You were worried about screams of ecstasy. Looks like it's the reverse. Doesn't sound like they're getting their freak-on to me! Great. I hope they settle their issues and it doesn't get worse."

Suddenly a blast of light shone from the window at Kara and me, spotlighting us as the busybodies we were! A man's face—his eyes locked with mine—peered out.

"Shit!" Kara tugged me along, hurrying to the door of our rig. Beside us, the conversation had quieted, with only the odd snippet of the woman's voice snapping. She fumbled with the keys trying to unlock the door. There was no way either of us wanted to get involved in their drama, even though I'd listen in case it escalated into violence. What were Howie and his wife thinking of the noisy neighbors?

Finally, the lock snicked and the door opened. We were barely inside when Kara hurried to the side window to draw the blinds, but not before she took a final peek over at the small camper. When I snuggled in next to her, I saw that a man had stepped outside, the light from his rig highlighting his head and shoulders. His face was in shadow but I could see the soft, curly halo of his hair and wide shoulders in a plaid shirt.

Feeling his gaze fix on us, Kara flicked the blinds shut, cutting all contact, while I stepped to the door to lock it. I let out a long breath now that we were safe in our shelter.

"Crap! He saw us eavesdropping on their argument. He stared right at me, Maren. I hope they're gone when we get up in the morning. If not, it's going to be awkward."

I stepped over to the fridge to grab us a couple of drinks. "I guess a campfire is out of the question, not that I have the energy for it."

I took the vodka cooler from her and took a long sip. Just one more quirky thing about RV travel. You never knew who you'd end up with as a neighbor, I guess. "Yeah. I wonder how often stuff like this happens? I mean, getting stuck parked next to idiots arguing."

But Kara wasn't listening. She'd gone back to the window, peeking out between the slats of the blind. Her gaze flew to me and she hissed, "He's still out there watching us! That's weird. I'd rather he went back to arguing with his girlfriend than checking us out. What the hell is he doing?"

The absurdity of the situation—Kara getting all paranoid about some idiot looking at our rig—after all we'd been through since we'd come on this vacation—hit me. I smirked, holding up my hand and wiggling my fingers. "Do you want me to go out there and ask him? If he tries anything, I'll bet I can toss him through the air like a Frisbee. Maybe I'd be doing his girlfriend and everyone a favor."

"No! Don't go out there. Let's just sit down and have our drink and ignore them. We've had enough close encounters of the strange kind today." Kara slid into the bench seat at the table.

I took a seat across from her and pulled out my phone. Reality sank in my gut like a stone. I still had to send a reply to Derek about terms of the divorce. And then there was an email to Amy and Jordan. I had to touch base with them, especially after being out of touch for the past few days. As crazy as this trip was turning out to be, I still had responsibilities to look after. Before I had a chance to open Derek's email, Kara was once more on her feet, glued to her spot at the window, peeking out.

"He's still out there, staring at our camper, Mare!" She snapped the slats shut and spun around to face me. "He's starting to creep me the hell out!"

"Just ignore him. We're safe in here." I started to draft a reply to Derek, and then my hand faltered. This was insane. "What is with this place? First the woman on the beach staring us down, and now some clown next to us does the same thing? I had no idea two middle-aged women could be so fascinating. Either that, or else the people around these parts need to get a life."

It was only then that I saw the weariness on Kara's face. She'd done all the driving that day while I had slept. With everything that had happened, it was catching up with her and making her just a tad jumpy. "Why don't you go to bed, Kara. I'm going to stay up for a while to catch up on my emails. I'll keep an eye out in case that guy over there does something." Which I was pretty sure he wouldn't. He was just a nosy parker, like the woman on the beach.

She nodded but grabbed her phone and set it on the table. "There's an email confirmation of my payment for this spot. If he tries anything, the campsite office number is in it for you to call."

I sat back and stared at her. She looked really worked up about some guy in a camper next door acting a little strange. "I don't know why you're so worried about this, Kara. Normally, it would be me getting worked up."

"It is strange. That guy's odd, Maren."

I barked a laugh. "He's just some low-rent guy in a camper, Kara. Considering that we lost three whole days, let alone what I can do with these babies"—I waved my fingers at her—"some guy having an argument with his girlfriend feels practically normal."

She shrugged, but her face was still lined with worry. "I don't know why, Mare. There's something about him…or maybe I'm just paranoid after what's happened today. But if we're going to carry, on, I guess I'd better lighten up, huh?"

"Ya think?" I got up, and placing my hands on her shoulders, I turned her to face the back of the rig. "Go to bed. You had a long day. I can look after things for a while. I'll be in after I finish my emails. 'K?"

"Okay."

I left her in the bedroom and turned to go back to my correspondence. But before I sat down, I peeked out the window and saw the Boler Guy standing next to the door to his rig. He was still staring over at us.

Thirteen

Kara

The smell of bacon and coffee twitched my nostrils, luring me from a deep and restful sleep. I creaked an eye open, noticing the sun casting slivers of light through the blinds on the window. Maren's bed at the other side of the small space was empty. I threw my covers aside and got up, grabbing my housecoat.

When I wandered into the main area of the rig, Maren looked over from where she stood at the stove, cooking breakfast. Dressed in jeans and a green hoodie, with tendrils of hair escaping a messy bun, she was the epitome of a morning person, unlike me, stifling a yawn.

"I knew if I started cooking, you'd get up. How'd you sleep?" She left the frying pan and poured a mug of coffee, leaning closer to hand it to me. "Here. You look like you need this."

"Thanks." It was going to take more than one mug of

coffee to kick my brain into gear. I sank down at the table, and rubbed the sleep from my eyes.

"I've been up for an hour. I showered, did a power walk around the campground, and chatted with Howie and his wife for a while. Boler Guy and his girlfriend are still here but all's quiet on that front this morning, thank goodness. Although it would have been nice to see them gone when I got up." Maren dished out the eggs and bacon as she talked, finishing by setting the two plates on the table, along with cutlery.

The caffeine worked its magic, and I could actually focus now. "He better not try staring at us again today or I'm going to say something to him. Did Howie mention anything about the argument Boler Guy and his lady were having?" I downed the rest of the mug and got up for a refill.

"They didn't hear a thing! But Howie said they were watching a movie, so that's probably why. They asked us if we wanted to join them for dinner but I wasn't sure what our itinerary was. Are we staying for another night or pushing on?"

When I took a seat across from her, I smiled. "What would you like to do? I'm okay with staying another night, but I thought you might be anxious to get to Charleston and hold that new granddaughter."

"I am!" Her grin was ear to ear. "And to see Amy, of course, and Harry. But to be honest, I feel like we were cheated from seeing the ocean yesterday. I'd like to hang around for a day, maybe even go swimming and see some sights."

Just as I was about to ask her about the "tele-thingy," she looked over at the stove, and her hand lifted higher. In a flash, the salt and pepper shakers sitting there, lifted up and floated over to the table by her fingers.

She did a shoulder shimmy, beaming over at me. "I've been practicing. I'm still smoked that I can do this! There was a tree limb that had fallen onto the road when I was out walking. I took care of that too."

It was still amazing to watch even though I had seen her do stuff yesterday. And I hadn't seen Maren look this thrilled about anything. In her entire life. She had always been the low-key sister. It was great to watch. I snorted a chuckle at her. "Something tells me that if that weird woman shows up at the beach, she's going to be going for a swim, whether she wants to or not."

"You got that right! It doesn't mean I'm going to flaunt this levitation thing, but if that woman gives me a hard time, I'm gonna let her have it."

"Whoa, Maren! Tough cookie, huh?"

She paused and stared at the ceiling. "Yeah. Maybe it's the change or something, but...yeah. I'd let her have it for sure if she pushes me." She went back to cooking and then paused in the middle of adding pepper to her eggs, and looked over at me. "That's another thing I got done while you were sleeping! I spoke to Derek about Jerk-Face and his lawyer wanting to change to no-fault. There was another text from Derek. Can you believe he offered to drop the cost of replacing the clothes I burned—like those polyester suits and cruddy clothes were worth ten thousand dollars!—in exchange for the SUV and the funds in the four-oh-one k."

"What?" I slapped the table so hard it spilled a little coffee on the Formica top. "It's easily worth three times the value of his stupid rags."

"I know! And he offered me twenty thousand for my half of the real estate firm, a firm which I helped build, which is easily worth half a million, according to Derek. The only thing he was halfway reasonable about was the current shit hole we were fixing up. Again, something that I spent hours slaving on, which he will give me exactly half the value of." Her eyes sparked in anger, and the vein in her forehead popped out a little.

Maren's eyes narrowed, but there was a sly smile on her lips. "Derek thinks I should stand firm at seventy percent of everything. It's a good starting point in negotiations. He thinks Wayne is anxious to get this wrapped up and that his big goal is getting complete ownership of the business. The rest is chump change compared to that."

"Why? It's a small town, and the business is as big and successful as it's ever going to be. Aside from the prison nearby and some historical stuff, it's just a Podunk town. Why is he so interested in the business?" There had to be more to this. I only hoped her lawyer was smart enough to figure out Wayne's angle. And knowing that Weasel Wayne, there had to be an angle.

"People moving out of big cities to small towns? Everyone is working from home if they can. That's got to be it. Wayne sees big potential. Too bad he doesn't have me at his side instead of Suzanne. I never wanted him to hire that money-grubbing bitch. I hope they run the business into the ground after I get my share." Maren went back to eating, stabbing a piece of bacon with her fork.

Maren stood up and took her half-finished plate to the sink. "Enough divorce drama for one day, I think. I'll clean up while you shower and get dressed. After that, let's hit the beach again and explore the town."

I rose from the table and headed to the bathroom to get ready for the day. "Is it warm enough for shorts and a T-shirt? You mentioned going for a swim."

"It'll be warm enough in an hour or so!" Maren was busy directing the salt and pepper as well as cutlery to float over to the sink, using just a pointed finger. She then snapped her fingers and the water started pouring from the tap over the sink. "Awesome!"

As incredible as it was, I felt a stab of envy. Why her and not me? But the total glee in her grin cheered my heart. But then, why not her? Her life had been a bed of roses and was pulled out from under her after twenty-five years with the guy. Hell, go for it!

"Show-off!" I tipped my head, peering at her closely. "So how do you feel when you do that? Yesterday it kind of wiped you out at the river, but not so much when we were at the beach. Is it my imagination or are you getting something more out of this? I mean besides being totally smoked by it?"

Her cheeks held a bloom of pink and her skin looked clearer, fresh-looking even. It looked like she'd shed a few years and the line between her eyebrows was almost nonexistent. She looked great despite my concerns the day before.

Staring at me with a wide-eyed look, she gushed, "It's the craziest thing, Kara. I feel energized when I do this. At first, I must have still been in a state of shock, zoned out after that thing with the little boy in the rapids. But now? I could run a marathon and still have energy left over. Whatever happened to me, has supercharged me."

I stepped over to her and gripped her wrist. "I could use some of that. Got any to spare?" But all I felt was her warm skin, no jolt of energy like she exuded. I felt fine at present, but for how much longer was anyone's guess. But I wouldn't think about that now.

Her other hand rose and I felt myself being swept upward! It was like being in a current of water pushed up into weightlessness! I gasped when my gaze shot downward and saw my bare feet hovering a few inches above the linoleum floor. "Maren! Oh my God! I'm floating!"

Her hand fell and my feet gently connected with the floor again. "Holy shit! That was insane! Do it again! Float me over to the bathroom! C'mon Mare!"

She extricated herself from my grip, and with two hands free, she let them raise higher. Along with me! Again, that unseen force cushioned my body, gently buoying me up while my jaw dropped open in wonder. There was just a faint tingle in my muscles but absolutely no pressure points anywhere on my body!

When my head nudged the roof of the RV, I had to use my fingers to push myself down. I felt like an astronaut hovering in zero gravity! My body swung slowly around till I was facing the rear of the rig where the bedroom was. The hem of my bathrobe flared outward as I glided toward the bathroom door. My hand touched the handle, and my body once more settled lower, until the tips of my toes scraped the floor.

"How was that? This is so freaking amazing! I feel like I could burst, I'm so excited!"

I could only stare at her, with my mouth gaping wide. Amazing didn't begin to describe it! It was better than I'd imagined any ride at Disney would be. And it was my sister who had done this! As easy as waving her hand and I'd been airborne.

The next thing I saw was her hands drop along with her gaze. She lifted her hands up slowly, watching her feet. Her face tightened and she bit her lower lip, concentrating hard.

"Rats! I thought I could make myself lift up into the air, but it's not working." She went for one last try, splaying her fingers and urging whatever force she hooked into to raise her up. But nada.

"Hey! Take it easy, Maren! You levitated me, don't forget. Maybe you need to recharge or something. I'd say you were doing pretty damned good for your second day with telekinesis. This is going to be hard to keep to ourselves." Maybe it was a good thing she got this gift and not me. I'd be on Jimmy Fallon and Joe Rogan in a heartbeat, if it were up to me.

"You're right. Y'know, I'd love to show my kids and even Wayne! Who would ever believe this if they didn't see it with their own two eyes? But that's also not the thing to do, is it? This is special, but I'm not willing to let the world know." And just like that, the bubble of her excitement popped and she frowned. "This is just between us and that has to be enough. We went through something odd together and this is the result. No notoriety or fame for me, thanks."

"I'm afraid so. But that doesn't mean we can't have fun with this when it's just us, Mare. At least for now."

***

When we emerged from the door of the rig, I searched the campsite next to us for any signs of Boler Guy and his partner. It was almost eleven and still the door was closed as well as the curtains. The ground around the egg-shaped camper also showed no signs of life, not even a tablecloth on the picnic table or clothesline strung up for their dishtowels.

As I locked up our camper, I glanced over at Maren. "Let's hurry and get out of here. The less we see of that pair, the better. I wish they'd left."

There was a creak and small thud before Maren murmured, "Too late for that."

Turning around, my gaze locked with Boler Guy's. His eyes were deeply set under arched eyebrows, the color of dark autumn honey. His nose had a little uptilt at the end, giving him a boyish, innocent look. Now that I saw him in the light of day, I was struck by how classically good looking he was with the chiseled cheekbones. Seeing us, his smile faded, covering teeth made whiter against the almond hue of his skin—skin that was all too well displayed, covering a muscular bare chest above the cut-off denim shorts.

Okay, he was good looking. But considering he was probably in his early forties, he was way too old to be making a ruckus arguing with his wife and disturbing everyone.

Catching my gaze, he looked like he wanted to say something, his eyes taking on a look of concern: his eyebrows a little squinched and his gaze intent.

He took a breath, and to be honest, I wanted to hear him speak. But then he gave his head a small shake and darted back into his camper, the door slapping against the frame like a sharp denial.

What the hell was that all about?

"Hmph." My chin rose higher when I saw him retreat back into his camper, shutting the door behind him.

Maren signaled with a nod for us to get going. "Quick, before he comes back outside." When I joined her, she mused, "We should stop and tell Howie and Laura if we're going to have dinner with them. We never came to a decision about that. Do you want to?"

The question yanked me back to the moment, rather than dwelling on Boler Guy and his partner. "Sure, I'm okay with that. They seem like a nice couple even if he does talk nonstop. How 'bout you?"

"Sure. That'd be better than us spending the evening alone, especially if that Boler is still there. I'd rather share a campfire with them than have Boler Guy and his wife hanging around ours."

Her eyebrows bunched when she glanced over at me. "That was kind of weird the way he popped back into his rig like a turtle pulling its head back into the shell. Come to think of it, that's sort of what his camper looks like—a turtle's shell. Hope he stays there and minds his own business."

I shrugged. "As long as there's no repeat of last night, I don't care what he does." Still, those eyes and the expression on his face played in my mind. He didn't look like the belligerent type, especially shying away when I looked straight at him. It was a totally different feel to what had happened the night before, him staring at me—but then it was daylight, way less disconcerting. It struck me that there was an element of...worry in his expression? But worry for who? Maybe he was concerned that we'd call the camp's office to report him for noise.

He probably was just going to apologize for all the noise last night.

Whatever. We headed over to Howie and Laura's massive rig.

When we rounded the front fender of the mammoth motor home, they were sitting at the picnic table, playing cards. Laura looked up, and a smile broke the smooth ebony skin of her face.

"Well, if it isn't the sisters up and around on this fine morning. Where are you two off to? Are you joining us for dinner, ladies?"

Howie twisted around to give us a two-fingered salute. "Morning, ladies. I make a mean burger, and Laura's potato salad is to die for. How about it? Why don't you join us?" The smile he flashed was inviting and not uncommon, judging by the deep creases framing it.

They were so friendly; it was hard not to smile back at them. "Only if you'll let us bring dessert. We're going to hit the beach and then noodle around the town. I'm sure we'll find something delicious to bring."

"Nothing chocolate! But if it's caramel anything, we've got a deal." Howie winked. "Seriously, just bring yourselves. We'll be happy for the company."

Maren shook her head. "No, we insist. And we'll pick up wine or would you prefer beer? Name your poison, Howie. Laura?"

"We're teetotalers, but you bring whatever you want to drink." Laura stood up and rested her hand on Howie's shoulder. "We won't keep you from your sightseeing, ladies. This is going to be a lovely evening. It's a full moon too! But I warn you, we're not night owls, so dinner at six, as we usually retire at eight-thirty."

I couldn't help the chuckle that burbled up. Laura was a no-nonsense straight shooter. It would be an early night after all. It would give me time to catch up on Facebook and my emails.

"Six it is, then! We'll see you later!" I waved my hand before Maren and I continued on past other campsites. Only the odd person sat reading or puttering around, tidying up litter around their blackened campfire. People must be at the beach or in town.

As we headed for the path we'd found the day before, my pace slowed while I sent a text to the main office to let them know we were staying another night. I didn't think it would be a problem, considering the campground had many vacant spots. Maren darted ahead of me, walking quickly into the break between the stately pines.

"Wait!" I took a deep breath and hurried to catch up with her. As I went by the large trunks, lifting the branch of a spruce behind it to find Maren, I listened for her footsteps. The path took a sharp bend to the right, becoming even narrower, with maple saplings forming a net with their spindly shoots, scratching at my bare legs. I came to a stop, peering ahead through the foliage to see where she was.

Her sharp cry propelled me forward.

Fourteen

M aren!" Ignoring the brambles ripping my skin, I
kept going until I saw her. About ten feet away,
she stood staring into the ferns and brush beside
the path.

I gripped her upper arm when I got to her. "What're you
doing? You scared me when you—"

"Don't you see them?" Her eyes practically popped out
onto her cheekbones before she turned back to peer at the
undergrowth. Taking a step off the path, she swept the
green growth to the side. "Where'd you go? Hey! Come
back!"

"Is it an animal?" I followed her, peering for…what? "If
it's some kind of wild animal, you should leave it alone,
Maren. Or is it someone's cat or dog?" But if it was a lost
pet, wouldn't someone be out calling for it, trying to find it?

Maren spun around to face me. "It was an elf! I can't
believe it, but an actual elf—two of them, even! Oh my
God! It was so awesome! Their ears were pointed at the tips,

110

like Mr. Spock's. One was a boy and the other a girl."

I stepped back from her, openly gawking. Elves? First, she's able to see auras, and now elves? Or is it...oh shit...was she losing it? After a moment, my gaze flashed to the side where she had been looking and then pinged back to her. She grabbed my arms, squeezing them while she bounced on her toes.

"I know how this sounds, but they were there, Kara! The girl had these big and round eyes that were the color of emeralds! But it was her ears! That's how I knew she was an elf! And the boy was—"

"An elf?" I swallowed hard, staring at my sister. Talking at warp speed, she was so excited she practically quivered. I couldn't believe my ears.

I took in the wooded area. Nope. Nothing. Maybe they really weren't there. Maybe she was hallucinating.

"They were right here! From the look on their faces, they were as shocked to see me as I was to see them. Where'd they go?" She turned her attention to the bush a couple feet away. "Come back. I just want to say hi. I won't hurt you."

"Wait a minute, Mare. Maybe they were people dressed up for some play or maybe kids playing a prank? There was no such thing as elves; everyone knew that.

Shooting me a frustrated look, she continued. "No! They weren't actors. Why would there be actors hanging around outside an RV park?"

I shook my head. Oh my God. Her insistence was making me uncomfortable. Would I be able to calm her down and get her back to the camper? She needed to lie down while I looked for the closest doctor to examine her. Whatever was happening inside her brain right now was downright scary. It's one thing to think you're seeing auras—lots of people claim to. But elves? What's next? Orcs? Hobbits?

She jerked and her hand flew to her neck. "There!" Leaping forward, she cried out, "On that rock next to the maple tree!" Grinning like a hyena, she beckoned me to join her.

I peered where she pointed, but there was only a big old granite rock sitting there.

"Hey, there. I'm Maren and this is my sister, Kara." She held her hands with palms facing them, the nonthreatening way you'd approach a strange dog to let them sniff you.

I felt like I'd stepped through the looking glass, watching Maren approach the big rock. Except that this was all in Maren's head.

Unless…it wasn't. No. No, that couldn't be. There was nothing there but that big gray rock and the tree next to it. No elves or fairies or even a garden gnome. I wished there was a garden gnome, even the tacky, plastic ones!

Her voice was soft with wonder. "This is amazing. Do you talk? Do you speak English? I can't believe this is happening. Holy shit."

She pulled back and her head tipped to the side, quietly watching the rock. After a moment, she exclaimed, "Why yes! I can most definitely see you. Yeah, I know! This is totally mysterious!"

Shooting me a look, before turning to gaze at the rock once more, she continued, "No. I don't think my sister can see you. It's just me who can."

Again, there was silence before she spoke once more. "I don't know why. Something really strange happened to us and now I can move objects with my mind. I can also see you! It didn't happen like that for her. It was only me."

Great! My sister was in full-blown psychosis, having some kind of conversation with her new imaginary friends. Maybe it would be wise to play along so that she didn't totally freak out.

"What are they saying, Maren?"

Never taking her gaze from the rock, her voice was just above a whisper. "They said that this is really rare for a human to see them. They've only heard tell of it a few other times in a land far away. They thought it was a myth until I showed up."

Rare? As in never! Unless you were in Ireland, drunkenly weaving on your way home from a pub, I'd bet. When I started to ask another question, she shushed me with a wave of her hand.

"Wait. They're speaking again, Kara."

Silence descended once more as Maren cocked her head, stepping closer to the rock. This time was longer than the other as she stayed listening to whatever voices only she could hear.

Finally, she shook her head. "No. Don't worry. I won't tell anyone about this. I mean, aside from my sister, but she's okay. You can trust her."

"You going to introduce me?" I asked.

Maren shot me a look of surprise. "Oh! Good point." She turned back to the rock. "My name is Maren, and this is my sister, Kara. How do you do?" Her eyes widened and tracked from the rock to the ground in front of us. "They said they're going to formally introduce themselves."

Maren stepped back from the rock. "They're coming off the rock; give them some room, okay? She watched the empty space, and a smile lit her face. She clapped her hands. "So, you're Pia," she said, pointing in one direction, "and you're Dool. Is that right?" She gave a brisk nod. "Let me do this as formally as you did."

She murmured to me, "They did this really cool-looking bow, Kara; I'm gonna return the favor." She stretched her right leg way out in front of her, and then began to bend her other leg, lowering her butt toward the ground while bending forward at the waist with her arms straight out from her sides. "Ooof!" she cried as she tipped over.

She looked to where her imaginary friends were. "I guess I did look silly, but it's not that funny. I just don't have your sense of balance, I guess." Her eyes narrowed. "Oh, I see. You flutter your wings to hold you up when you do the formal bow, huh?" Her eyes glinted and she teased, "Well, that's cheating!"

"Wait. They have wings?" I said.

She nodded. "I guess I didn't notice them before, but yeah, they have wings. Like a dragonfly's, all shimmery."

"They have pointy ears?"

"Yes."

"Their eyes...are they big and almond shaped? Like a deer's?"

"Yes! Can you see them now?"

"No I can't. But I know what they are. They're not elves, Mar—"

She cut me off. "Can you guys fly?" Her gaze went straight up into the air. "I guess you can! Look, Kara! They're up at the treetops! They're just hovering..." her gaze tracked back down to the spot in front of us. "No..." she said, "I can't fly. But"—she waved her hands—"get a look at this!" She turned and gestured at me.

And yeah, just like that I was five feet up in the air. "Maren! You could have at least given me a warning! Put me down!" I gently returned to the earth. Ooooh! So not fair!

Maren was ignoring me, her eyes focused on her "friends." She held up her hand. "What does that mean? I don't understand that word." She nodded again. "Sorry, I only speak English. Was that Irish or something? No? Is there an English word for it?" She paused and gasped. "Really? For real? Are you sure? I've always been told there's no such thing!"

"What are they saying!" Damn it. Now I'm being sucked into her delusion!

She glanced over at me. "I'll tell you later, okay?" and went back to her "friends." She laughed again. "Surprising to you? Ha! I'm stunned! At least you knew humans existed! I've never seen guys like you in my entire life!"

As I watched her chatting away to some imaginary beings, I thought of the fact that she was now able to levitate objects. This was Maren, never one to give any credence to anything supernatural. Hell, there was still a part of her that wasn't buying that those aliens were responsible for us losing that time. Yet, here she was having a

114

conversation with fairies of all things!

Rats! Why couldn't I see them if Maren could? I huffed. I caught myself and sighed. Either my sister wasn't losing her mind, or else I just got on her crazy train. She's really talking to invisible beings.

"I understand. Of course, you need to return to your people and tell them this. Are they nearby? I'd be happy to go with you—"

Her silence was then followed by a nod. "I get it. You have rules and protocols. Her face went serious again and she slowly nodded. "Of course. I'd be honored." She gestured at me. "We'd be honored." Moon Dance? That's a big ceremony? Okaaay. Is there something we should bring or wear?"

She let out a short laugh after a few beats of what to me was silence. "Of course we can! Something like honey? Really, really sweet? Or strawberry jam or sugar…whatever sweet treat we have is yours! Hell, we have to pick up a dessert for dinner tonight, so I'll buy you a pecan pie. There's nothing sweeter than that."

My jaw dropped lower and lower as I stood there. Whatever these things were that Maren was talking to, it looked like they had a serious sweet tooth. I'd have to ask her how their teeth looked. They must have serious dental issues.

Again, there was silence as she stood there beaming at the big rock for a few beats. Her hand rose and she fluttered her fingers. "It was very nice to meet you, Pia and Dool! We'll be back here to meet your elders… 'neath the midnight moon—got it. Her gaze shifted to the side and she smiled. "You take care too." Then her gaze went up in the air, through the treetops. "They're gone now. We're coming back here tonight."

Maren whirled around to me. "There's freaking elves living here! Can you believe that? I wish you could have seen them, Kara! This is your jam more than mine, but even I'm shocked. Elves!"

"Mare? Should I be worried? I mean, you feel okay, right?" I examined her closely. Her eyes were wide, but her pupils weren't overly dilated. Even though she was talking a mile a minute, her words were still clear, and even if it sounded crazy, there was order and consistency in what she was saying.

"I'm fine!" Her fingers fisted a handful of hair as she looked off to the side. "I feel more alive than I've ever felt before, Kara. My senses feel sharper. I can smell the seaweed in the ocean, even from here. When I look at the leaves on that tree or this bush, I see waves of energy surrounding them. I swear I can sense streams of water flowing under our feet, making its way to the shore. So yeah, I'm better than okay! I'm tuned in, like I'm on a different frequency or something."

"This is all happening so fast. With every hour that passes, you're changing, Mare. You've gone from levitating to now seeing creatures—beings that we always thought were mythical."

"Like us! That's what Pia and Dool said about us! That humans who can see them are really, really rare. But some do! And now I'm one of them. It makes me want to explore, go running through the forest to see what else is out there." She shook her head and took a deep breath.

"Tell me again what they looked like. You said they have wings and pointy ears—"

"Their skin was an almond color and kind of glowed. Aside from their eyes being larger than ours, they looked like us, but with small noses and. Their necks are longer than a person's. And the wings were like a dragonfly's wings, translucent with two big sections."

"And when they left, they flew away, right?"

"Pia shot straight up and was gone in a flash, but Dool took his time, skimming the bushes, and keeping an eye on us. The wings move so fast that it's like a vibration more than flapping like a bird's wings." Maren looked away in the opposite direction, wistfully. "They left so they could talk with the old ones, the ones who know about people like us. I think those two elves were a bit spooked by all of this."

"Spooked by us?" My eyebrows arched to my forehead. "Well, they aren't the only ones. This is all surreal, like in Alice in Wonderland. If a white rabbit came rushing by, it wouldn't surprise me. Not. At. All."

"I know, right? And they invited us to come back tonight at midnight! For their ceremony. How cool is that?" She squeezed her eyes shut and let out a squeal of delight.

I tried to picture the creatures she'd described before musing, "If they had wings like a dragonfly, I don't think they were elves. Did they actually say they were elves?"

She screwed up her face. "No! Why would they? It's pretty obvious that—"

"No. Elves don't have wings, Maren. Fairies, or as they are sometimes called, the Fae folk, have wings and fly." If she ever did any reading, she'd know this! Duh.

"Elves, fairies! What difference does it make? They had wings and they flew. I saw them, not you, so I'd have a better idea of what they were, and I say they were elves." She turned back to scan the trees and brush around us.

"It matters, Maren! We share characteristics of apes but that doesn't mean we're orangutans, swinging from trees! If they flew, they were fairies!"

She huffed, "Oh, so that makes you an expert, does it? You read some stuff online and watch movies, and now you're some kind of PhD or something? You think you know everything about them. Well, the so-called 'research' was make-believe, but I saw the real thing, for your information." Turning, she took a step deeper into the woods, peering around and dismissing me.

It made my blood boil, just like the times when we were younger when she'd made fun of my watching Peter Pan so many times. I'd loved Tinkerbell, and when Peter asked everyone watching to clap their hands to save her, I'd clapped so hard my hands stung. Okay, it was a really old movie and kind of hokey, but it was still great.

"They were Fae, Maren. And from the looks of it, they're gone now, right? We should get going too." I kept checking her out, noticing the bright spots of color on her cheeks and how excited she was. "We want to hit the beach and then a few stores, don't we?"

Maren spun around, gawking at me like I had two heads. "Are you kidding me? Go to the beach after I just encountered elves? I'm staying here! Who knows if there aren't more of them around? Now that I've seen two elves, I want to see what else is here."

My jaw tightened when she turned away again to resume her search. It stung that she kept saying she'd seen them, while I was a total outsider. Why her and not me? "They left. You said it yourself. Besides, you don't know what else you may encounter. I think you should come to the beach. You made plans to see them tonight. Besides, we need to buy desserts for that and for Howie and Laura."

She threw her hands up in the air, and practically barked at me, "You go, if that's what you want to do! I'm staying and checking out these woods. You might as well go, since you can't see them anyway!"

I stiffened, clenching my teeth so hard they clicked. "Fine! You stay here if you want, but I'm going down to the beach—Virginia Beach, one of the nicest beaches in the world. Have fun, Maren." Turning back to the path, I stormed down it, heading for the ocean.

Why'd she have to be so difficult? Bragging that she had all this power now and could even see fairies. And they were fairies, which she would know if she wasn't so ignorant.

Shit! I'd planned this trip, bought the RV, and she was the one getting all the perks! It wasn't fair. Worse yet, these powers were wasted on the likes of Maren. It should have been me!

The highway was busier than I would have expected for a Saturday, and I had to wait a few minutes for a break so I could cross. And, of course, being Saturday, the beach was packed with families and kids. I'd be lucky to find a spot near the water to set my bag without getting sand kicked in my face from kids running by.

I had to walk down the beach a bit, getting closer to the long dock and the sailboats moored there, but finally I found a section that was less rowdy. Plopping the bag down and spreading out the towel, I sank down on its surface.

Maren! I'd forgotten how snitty she could be. It reminded me of the times when our parents had to intervene, with Dad always taking Maren's side. Of course, she was his favorite and never let me forget it. Always doing the right thing, acing every exam she took, while I was lucky to scrape by with a C. "Little Miss Practical One," Dad called her once. Why couldn't I be more conscientious like her? How many times did I hear that growing up?

Elves! As if. And what was it they called their gathering for later that night? Moon Dance! Van Morrison would be happy to know he'd inspired that name with his song. My forehead knotted. Maybe he'd been inspired, by fairies.

How did it happen that she was the one gifted with all these powers? Would it have hurt to give me just one? Just one! I'd rather be able to see Fae folk but I'd settle for telekinesis. It wasn't fair, especially considering my health and all. Just a glimpse of one of these creatures? But no. Maren got everything! Good looks, good genes, and she was Dad's favorite. Not that I'd wish her harm or anything, but still…

As I sat peering out at the ocean, I thought of her back there. Could it be possible that she'd find any more? A coldness sank in my chest at my next thought. Oh God. She'd seen mythical creatures. What if Bigfoot and vampires and demons were also real…and back there with Maren?

Damn it! I jumped to my feet and shoved the towel back into my beach bag. I'd only gone a few feet when I noticed the Boler Guy and a woman walking across the sand, coming toward me.

My mouth fell open. It wasn't just any woman—it was that same woman from yesterday, and she even had the same headscarf covering her hair! That was Boler Guy's wife or girlfriend? The one he'd been fighting with the night before? They both stopped dead in their tracks staring back at me like I'd caught them doing something wrong. What the heck was with those two? I couldn't care less about them arguing and acting nosy. Not with Maren alone in those woods!

Ignoring the odd pair, I took off at a run, heading across the sand. Maren didn't know anything about vampires or Bigfoot or a yeti. They might be feasting on her blood that very moment! Damn! I should never have left her alone there. If anything happened to her, I'd never live with myself.

Fifteen

I arrived at the spot, totally out of breath and with a serious stitch in my side. Even though I was in decent shape from slinging hash in a restaurant for most of my life, I was no marathon runner.

"Maren!" Finally, I managed to get a yell out.

She popped out from behind a large oak, staring back at me with wide eyes. "Be quiet! You'll scare anything away and I'll never catch them."

"I'm pulling rank, Maren. You have to come with me. Now!"

Her mouth snapped shut as she glared at me. "Pulling rank? That only worked when we were kids! I'm a grown woman, and you're not the boss of me, Kara."

"You don't know what's in these woods! You saw fairies, but what if there's nasty creatures, with long, bitey fangs as well? Enough is enough. Let's go get the stuff for tonight." Seeing her be so huffy, I couldn't help the next words that leapt from my tongue. "And I am, too, the boss of you! It's my rig and I'm the captain. You're only the co-pilot. And you're still my baby sister."

Her lips pulled to the side. "Okay. I haven't seen anything else here. But you could be right, I suppose." As she walked through the growth of ferns and bushes toward me, she rolled her eyes. "You're more of an expert in this kind of crazy shit. Elves or fairies or God knows what. Even though you're not the boss, with everything that's happened, we should stick together."

It was the closest thing to an apology that I'd ever get from my sister. "At least we agree on that. We need to stay together. Too many weird things have happened since we started this trip." When she joined me on the path, grudgingly, I added, "Sorry. I'm pretty envious of your new powers, y'know. It should have been me who got them."

"Yeah. That would make more sense. So, why me?" She let out a fast sigh. "Although I'm not complaining. This is freaking awesome, Kara."

Sixteen

Maren

It was way later than we'd planned when we got back to the campground, laden down with packages. We'd picked up four different kinds of desserts, souvenirs for our kids, as well as a few items from the local Wicca Crystal store. All afternoon, the excitement of seeing the elves later tonight bubbled in my chest—so much so, that I'd even bought a present to give to them.

I held the new necklace out from my throat, peering at it. "You really think this stone is something the elves will like? I mean, I've never heard of lapis lazuli, but it is pretty."

It was the shade of the ocean on a summer day with ribbons of white, like frothy surf threading through it. Even though the silver chain was delicate, the stone was chunky. It was too bohemian chic for my taste. Really more like something Kara would wear. I'd got a couple of these necklaces, intending to give one to the head elf.

"You heard what the shop owner said, Mare. Lapis Lazuli is known as being beneficial for calmness and communication. Plus, it's associated with Taurus, your astrological sign, and then there's that third-eye thing."

Okay, all of that was Greek to me. I'd never even been in one of these woo-woo New Age shops before, with all their crystals and other assorted bullshit. Tarot cards? Smudging supplies? All kinds of "out there" stuff. But the woman at the counter came off like she knew what she was talking about. And yeah, Kara sucked up every word. I frowned, looking over at her. "I didn't want to ask her and sound like a newb, but what the heck is a third eye? Or chakra? She said something about that too.

I pictured the plump shopkeeper, her long dark hair secured by a paisley headband and the layers of silky skirts swishing across the floor as she walked. She was everything I would have expected running a place like that.

Kara actually groaned as she rolled her eyes at me. "Chakras are energy points in the body. The third eye is one of them."

I jerked back when she tapped the center of my forehead, continuing. "That's where it is, your third eye. It's responsible for perception beyond ordinary sight."

My mouth fell open and I grinned. Perception beyond ordinary sight. "Like me! What I have!"

That would explain seeing the elves and auras. I rubbed at the spot she'd touched, but of course only skin touched my fingertips, no bump or anything odd, just a few wrinkles there.

"Exactly like you. So, I'd say the Lapis Lazuli stone is a perfect gift to give to those elders tonight."

"I hope so. I'm so stoked about seeing them again!" Looking over at my sister, my stomach sank lower with guilt. Here I was going on again about seeing them, when poor Kara would give her right arm to be able to do that. Plus, I didn't want to get her back up again, arguing with her.

I decided to set the elves aside, changing the subject a bit. I knew Kara was probably right—they were actually fairies, or "Fae" as she called them, but I did so enjoy getting under her skin. "Well, the one thing she said, that it would remind me of the waves and surf on the ocean, was right. I wish we'd gone back to the beach for a bit, but with Boler Guy there and that woman..." Why did they have to be around to ruin things? First, her on the beach, staring, and then the two of them showing up earlier, when Kara went down there.

"We can go to the beach tomorrow before we pull up stakes. But, you know, there'll be other beaches we'll visit without Boler Guy and his lady gawking and creeping us out."

As we walked down the road, I noticed Howie's big rig just up ahead. We'd spent a long time that afternoon, having lunch and browsing shops. I pulled out my phone to check the time, and swore. "Shit! It's almost eight o'clock! Laura said dinner was at six. We lost track of time shopping, so we're really late. We gotta hustle, Kara."

Kara pulled a face. "She'll understand. She's a woman, so she knows how easy it is to lose track of time shopping. Besides, they're retired with all the time in the world."

The smells of barbecuing meat drifted into my nostrils, reminding me that it had been hours since we'd stopped for a seafood lunch at that patio. As we neared Howie's RV, the aroma got stronger, making my mouth water.

Kara paused and took the box containing the caramel-glazed cake from the bag of pastries, before handing the sack over to me.

Muttering, "Hang on while I drop this off to Laura. She'll want to refrigerate this right away. I'll be right back." She stepped away, heading to their campsite.

With her no longer blocking my view, I could see Howie and Laura in the area next to their camper.

My eyes opened wide and I gasped. Oh my God! What the hell had happened to them? Their hair! It was no longer neatly trimmed but had grown into a shaggy mess, extending down their necks to the top of their shirts! And their arms and legs bristled with matted fur! They looked more like animals than people! How was that possible?

At Kara's voice, apologizing about the time, Howie spun around from the BBQ. His eyes glowed red above a snarling yap, showing pointed incisors like a dog's...or wolf's.

I froze in place, my mouth suddenly dry, watching Kara approach Laura, extending the cake. "We kind of lost track of—"

"You're late!" Laura barked. Her hairy arms crossed her chest as she tapped her toe on the hard-packed ground. "I said six o'clock and that's what I meant! We eat early and we go to bed early."

Finally, I managed to get the words out, "Kara? You need to come back here." All the while my heart pounded like jackhammer.

Kara shot me a puzzled look before turning back to them.

At the grill—filled with enough meat patties to feed a platoon of soldiers—Howie paused and shot a snarling grimace over at Kara. His hand rose as he twisted his wrist and very pointedly checked his watch.

Oh crap! Kara was right between the two creatures, holding the cake out as a peace offering. She looked confused, like a deer in the headlights as Howie bellowed, "These burgers are burned! I turned the flame down, but I'm sure they're dried up like shoe leather." He shook his head from side to side, letting out an exasperated snort. "I thought we made our timelines perfectly clear. We asked you to respect them, and what do you do? Show up late!"

The way they glowered at Kara sent a spike of fear through me. They rounded on her, edging closer and closer. Quickly, I pointed my fingers at the cake in Kara's hand, feeling a surge of energy shoot forth and lift it in the air. I aimed it at the center of the table, next to a vase of flowers, but the cake landed with a thud, rattling the cutlery and plates.

Kara stared at me in horror. "Maren!" Right after that, she turned on the irate pair. "This was supposed to be a casual dinner. Yeah, we're late, but it sure as hell doesn't warrant getting this bent out of shape. What's wrong with you guys?"

I darted over to her and grabbed her arm, yanking her away from the old couple. "C'mon! We're leaving! Now!"

As I pulled her along, she kept scolding Howie and Laura. "For Pete's sake! We brought you caramel cake like you asked! You're acting like we committed the crime of the century!"

Finally, I got her to the roadway, frog-marching her past the stupid Boler and to our own rig. All the while she protested. "Has everyone gone crazy? Even you, Mare? Why'd you levitate that cake right in front of those two nut jobs?" She twisted out of my grasp, glaring at me.

As I grabbed the door handle and yanked the door open, then grabbed her arm again to steer her inside, I hissed, "They're werewolves, Kara! I probably saved your life."

Seventeen

Kara

Werewolves?" I spun around to face her, watching her lock the door. Werewolves. Oh my God! Maren had seen that, just like she'd been able to see the fairies. We were supposed to have dinner with a pair of werewolves? Or were we the dinner? Along with that shitload of meat patties.

I darted over to the window. But outside, there was only the Boler parked beside us, no Howie or Laura coming down the roadway to get us. Thank God!

Maren dropped her supplies onto the table with a thud. "I saw it as soon as we were at their site, Kara! I could hardly believe my eyes! Howie's hair was longer, poking below his ball cap...mingling with the tufts of fur on his face and neck. When Laura yelled at us, I saw big pointy teeth. Even the shape of her face had changed so that her nose and mouth were extended like a wolf's. That's why I had to get us out of there!"

Her description didn't jive with what I'd seen, but I believed her. How could I not, after all that had happened? I pictured Howie standing at the grill flipping burgers and then the...Oh my God! A growl! I heard him grumble—and it was deep!—but I'd dismissed it as some weird thing Howie did when he was pissed. But now that I thought about it, it was a growl, not a grumble.

I clutched Maren's arm. "I heard him growl! I can't see them like you do, but I heard that! Maybe whatever happened to you is starting in me." This was amazing! My feet did a happy dance and I actually squee'd.

Maren's voice was hesitant. "Yeah...there was definitely a growl. I was more focused on how they looked but yeah, I heard it too. And you actually heard it?"

You'd think I'd won the lottery...again! I grinned, continuing my jig. "Yeah! I heard it. I heard it, Mare! I can't wait to visit with the fairies tonight. When did they say to meet them? I won't see them but I'll be able to hear them!"

"Are you crazy? We can't go outside! There's a full moon tonight with two geriatric werewolves on the prowl. They eat people, don't they?" Maren shook her head, backing away from me until she flopped down onto a chair. "No way am I going out there, not even to see those elves." She looked at me pointedly. "We should get the hell out of here."

"What? Just when things are getting good? Just when I can start to hear them?"

"Kara!" Maren shot out of her seat and jabbed a finger toward the window. "There's WEREWOLVES OUT THERE! And it's a full moon! Are you out of your freaking mind?" She shook her head at me. "We need to disconnect the rig and blow this place!" Her eyes boggled. "I wish we had a gun."

"You'd need silver bullets."

"What?"

I shrugged. "Only silver bullets can kill a werewolf. Not

regular ones."

"I take it this is from all your time with your woo-woo stuff, right?"

Her jaw just swung open as she shook her head at me. I held up a hand. "But we got way, way better protection than any gun."

"Wha…"

I stepped over to her and grabbed her hands. "We got these sis. I'm not afraid of any creature, human or mythical, if you're at my side. All you'd have to do is flick your wrist and you'd ruin their day. Especially if you thought I was in danger, right?"

"Well, I guess so." Her eyes went big. "B-but werewolves!"

I shook my head. "Nope. I'm not scared." I waved my hand at the window too. "And I'll bet your new friends know all about them. And they're still throwing that party."

Maren burst out laughing. "Good grief! You're still a party animal! Werewolves? No problem! Let's party on, dude!"

"C'mon, Maren…they said they were going to bed, didn't they?"

"That could be a lie."

"Look, my gut is saying that we'll be perfectly safe, okay? And you do have those magic hands, better than any gun or whatever, as far as I'm concerned." I watched her struggle to make up her mind, and let my voice fade.

"Well, I really do want to meet more of those elves," she said, glancing up at me.

"They're FAIRIES, dammit!" Why in the world couldn't she get that through her thick skull? With a huff of exasperation, I took a seat across from her and leaned forward. "We have to, Maren. This is the chance of a lifetime. We need to go out there and visit with these fairies."

Damn! I'd just gotten this ability to hear these mythical beings, and that crazy pair in the giant RV screwed it up!

Freaking werewolves. My jaw clenched tight before I sat back, blinking a few times.

Werewolves. They actually existed. As strange as it had been learning about the Fae living alongside us, now there were werewolves too? And rather than being in a total state of shock at that fact, I was more pissed that they were messing with me seeing the Fae. I really was in Bizarro World.

Maren got up to get a glass of water before peeking out the blinds. "No sign of them, but they could be lying in wait. That's why they were so pushy about us having dinner with them. We were going to be the main course."

Her words barely registered as I tried to puzzle this out. There had to be a way to visit those Fae tonight. "Look, Howie and Laura were angry we were late, because they have a strict schedule going to bed at eight. That means they won't be out prowling around! They'll be in bed." Bingo! Problem solved. I rose to rummage in the fridge for something to eat, since our dinner plans got waylaid.

Maren snorted, "You believe that? How do you know they won't be out howling at the moon and hunting—as in people? I'm not willing to take a chance that we're not their next meal, Kara." Her voice softened. "Those poor elves. I hope Howie and Laura don't attack Pia and Dool."

I grabbed a frozen lasagna from the fridge and turned to her. "Do you honestly think that the fairies don't know about Howie and Laura? If anyone would know there's werewolves in the area, I'd say it would be the fairies. Yet they're still having their Moon Dance tonight. They aren't worried. So, neither should we be."

"But maybe werewolves can't attack fairies," she said in a small voice.

I wracked my brain trying to remember movies and books I'd read about werewolves while I unwrapped the frozen food and popped it into the microwave. They ate meat, although it was mostly chickens and sheep. But then, maybe when they were ravenous, would they kill and eat people...or fairies?

Maren let out a chuckle. Which became a giggle and then turned into howls of laughter. I couldn't help smiling when I took a seat at the table. "What's so funny? You go from being scared shitless about werewolves attacking you, to laughing your head off."

Tears rolled down her cheeks. "This! Listen to us! We're actually discussing the social dynamics and eating habits of fairies and werewolves." She slapped the table as another fit of hilarity claimed her. "Just the other day, my biggest worry was fighting Weasel Wayne in a divorce and then getting back on my feet. Where will I live? What will I do to earn a living? Meno-freaking-pause hot flashes, and would I ever date again." She shook her head. "Now? Now it's werewolves and elves!"

"Fairies!"

"I know, I know!" She waved at me. "But it's too funny watching you get pissed off about it!" She started to giggle again.

Her giggles were infectious. The situation was beyond crazy. I giggled, trying to get the words out. "Now you're worried a werewolf will eat you before you get a chance to do the Moon Dance with fairies and give them a gift."

She scooped the necklace from inside her shirt, smiling wistfully as she stared at it. "Damn. It would have been so cool—"

"Maren!" My gaze became riveted on the silver chain and the filigree scrollwork clasping the crystal. "Silver! Werewolves are repelled by silver! That's why they use silver bullets! Iron is better, but they don't like silver either. You have a second necklace you were going to give to them! I'll wear it!" I grinned at her. "We'll be able to go to the Moon Dance."

She paused in the midst of swiping the tears of laughter from her eyes. "What? Silver? Are you sure about that?"

Rolling my eyes, I sighed. "You're asking me a question about something supernatural? Have you met me, Maren?

Of course I'm sure! And one other thing…if Howie and Laura ate all those charred, old hamburgers, they're not going to be all that hungry. That's assuming they even have the energy to sneak out and go howling at the moon. I think we're good to go."

Maren looked at me silently for a few beats. Finally, she nodded. "Okay. But I'm also bringing a knife. Who knows if there are even stranger creatures out there? I'm going to be ready if something tries to eat me."

"I already told you that we have protection."

She didn't reply. I face-palmed and stared at her. She watched me and finally asked, "What?"

I flopped into the loveseat. "Stand up."

"Why?"

"Just do it." She complied and stood up in front of me. "Okay. Now lift me and the couch up in the air."

Her eyes lit up. "Oh! Yeah!" She pointed at me, and with a slow bend of her wrist, me and the couch floated up a foot into the air.

"You okay?"

"Fine!" she said.

"Great. Now pop me and the couch to the end of the room and—"

Before the words got out of my mouth, me and the sofa whipped across the room. She whipped me back and forth two or three times before gently putting me back down in the sofa's spot. I'll admit it, I hung on for dear life for a second or two, but it was fun!

I blinked up at my sister. "Silver? Iron? I don't need no stinkin' silver! I got me a Maren!"

She stood there blowing on her fingernails like a gunslinger.

"Hey," I said. "You scared anymore?"

"Nope."

***

After we had dinner, we each retired to different areas of

the rig to catch up on emails and send text messages to our kids. There was so much I wanted to tell Josh but the timing wasn't right.

The more weird and wonderful things that Maren could now do, the greater the threat to us. It wasn't just from people who were obsessed with anything paranormal; it was the government as well. Who wouldn't want to know about mythical beings existing alongside us in a parallel dimension? How could that dimension be breached and the beings studied or exploited? Even weaponized. To say nothing of Maren becoming their newest project. No thanks.

But at some point, I'd tell Josh all about this—along with the truth about his father. It was the one thing that I'd always felt deep shame over—lying to my son. But it would all come out before it was too late. I prayed he'd forgive me.

There was a tap on the doorframe and Maren filled the opening. "Ready? It's eleven-thirty. Time to go."

Shaking thoughts of my health from my head, I smiled at her. In her long, knitted burgundy sweater coat, with the hood framing her dark locks, she looked like she'd fit right in with the Fae folk. The necklace was on full display above the scoop neck of her cream-colored top.

"You look great." I slipped my jean jacket over my blue hoodie and followed her to the kitchen area. Seeing the silver lapis lazuli necklace on the table, I looped it over my head and picked up the box containing the pecan pie.

Maren held up a flashlight but then slipped it in her pocket. "I won't use this unless we really need it. No need to broadcast our location to the world, specifically Howie and Laura. Something tells me the fairies will see us, even without the light."

Now that we were on our way, actually going to meet up with the elders in the fairy world around us, my stomach did a flip-flop. Being able to hear Howie's actual growl made me think that maybe I'd be able to hear the Fae folk when they spoke. Woo-hoo!

When we stepped out into the cool night air, I noticed

light inside Boler Guy's camper, but there was no noise or arguing. Great. Just when I needed them distracted, they were quiet as church mice. When Maren turned the key to lock the door, the click sounded loud. I shot a look at the Boler but the curtain covering the window remained unchanged, no peeping Tom or Bob or whatever.

We stayed close together, tiptoeing away from our truck to the narrow roadway threading through the RV park. Holding my breath as we eased by Howie's ginormous rig, I searched for any light or sign of movement inside. All was quiet, which could be a bad sign. My hand drifted up to the silver chain around my neck, as I said a silent prayer that they were inside, enjoying a sound sleep.

Above, the full orange moon lit the way, coating the roadway with a faint silver sheen. We passed a few other RVs before we came to the break in the trees, where the path was. Maren took the lead, walking quickly and blending into the shadows like a wraith.

When I entered the path, pinpricks of light sparked through the trees in the distance. It was late in the season for fireflies, but considering we were south of home, maybe that was normal. Or maybe it was something else? Could it be possible that I'd be able to see these fairies? Maren's power was growing in leaps and bounds, so why not mine?

I bumped into Maren and then jerked back. "Sorry. I guess we're here, right?" She turned, and even in the low light of the moon, I could see her gaping grin under eyes as round as that celestial sphere above.

"Can you see them?" When I shook my head, she cupped her ear with her hand. "Listen! It's really faint, but it's there, Kara."

I held my breath, listening hard for any sound. The only thing coming through was the rustle of leaves. Darn! My gaze met hers and I shook my head. "Nothing."

"C'mon." She plucked my sleeve, pulling me after her as she stepped off the pathway into the inky blackness of the trees. "I can see them, Kara!" With that, she was off, leaving me standing there.

"Maren!" I stumbled into something when I plunged after her, barely stopping myself from falling, but banging my wrist pretty good. As I tried to rub the sting out, balancing the pecan pie, I heard it—snippets of a song that I'd boogied to, back in the day. Even then it was old, a relic from Woodstock and the hippie era. Yeah, it was Van Morrison's "Moondance," but being played on flutes and other instruments.

Huh. Moon Dance was what they called their celebration, so what better music could you ask for, right? I wondered if Morrison had been able to see them, or had the fairies just hijacked his song when they heard it?

No matter. I had to find Maren and get closer to whatever was happening. I made my way through the darkness and headed in the direction where the sound was coming from, the music all the while becoming more distinct and now interspersed with laughter.

I jerked when someone grabbed my arm, spinning me around and yanking me into a clearing to my left. Maren's eyes and cheekbones were highlighted by the moon overhead. My heart fell back into my chest, seeing my sister and not Howie or Laura Werewolf.

"It's happening, Kara! There's got to be at least fifty fairies here." She looked around. "No, there's more arriving through the trees! I wish you could see them all decked out with flower garlands and shimmering robes, dancing in a circle and—"

A breathless, feminine voice interrupted. "Linette, these are the humans we told you about. This is Maren and her sister, Kara." Her voice dropped to a whisper, "Linette is our leader. Behind her is Tien, her scion, and Sebille, the chief counselor."

Oh. My. Gawd! That had been a fairy speaking!

At that moment I heard the sound of bells. It started with an almost whispery series of tinkles, cascading like raindrops. It then grew in volume with fuller sounds until it was all I could hear; a fantastical melody danced in my ears. Peering hard into the moonlit clearing, I saw only my sister, sweeping lower into an awkward curtsy and bowing her head. Even though I couldn't see these creatures, I followed Maren's lead, dropping my chin to my chest, hardly breathing from the excitement.

When the bells ceased, Maren gushed, "It is an honor to meet you, Linette. I could never imagine your people are actually real." She wiped her eyes. "I'm…so grateful to be here."

A smoky voice, feminine and mature answered Maren. "It is a wonder and indeed rare for us as well to be seen by your kind, Maren." That had to be Linette, their leader. She paused for a beat and added, "It's just you who can see us, Maren? Your sister…"

I could almost feel her peering at me, before Maren finished the sentence. "That's correct. But even though Kara isn't able to see you, she can now at least hear you. Oh wow! I wish she could see you."

"What's she look like?" I asked.

"Oh Kara, it's amazing! Linette glitters and shimmers like she's under a spotlight in a Broadway play! But it's coming from within her! Small points of light pop on her, then fade and another appears." Maren held her arms out to where the rest of the fairies must have been gathered. "All these lights and glimmers are all around us right now, drifting through the air in pulsing wisps and pinpoints. Oh, Kara it's beautiful." Her face brightened like a five-year-old's. Now the lights are spinning around both of us like ribbons!" She held her arms out, gazing in wonder at them. It's like we're being adorned in these gentle lights."

I giggled. "Like a couple of middle-aged Christmas trees?"

Maren chuckled. "Like a blessing, Kara. Like a blessing." She looked over to where that Linette must have been. "Am I right? Are you blessing us right now?"

"We welcome you, Human. You come in peace and

good will and are welcome here."

Maren's eyes widened. "Oh Linette, your aura's so beautiful! She waved her hand in the air. The colors shimmer and move all around like a living painting...so beautiful."

"You see auras too?" This was a masculine voice, husky and hurried. "I don't understand—"

"Tien, I am the one leading this parley. This is not the time for you to speak," the older fairy woman chided the male and turned back to us.

Her tone was gentler when she continued. "This is as extraordinary for us as for you, dear child. It has been years and years, centuries long gone, since our cloister has spoken with a human." Her voice took on a somewhat anxious tone. "There has been a screen, a veil between your kind and ours for millennia." She paused and said, "Even so, never did I dream that I would experience this, to speak to an actual human."

Her words were followed by excited murmurs. I could feel the excitement sparking in the air, mirroring my own. This was not only a thing for us but for them as well! There were so many things I wanted to know about Linette and the fairies. Before I could think more about that, the air around us began to swell again with the sound of those bells. The melody rose and then faded, leaving the glade silent.

"Oh, Kara..." Maren said. "Someone new has just showed up."

"Who?"

Before she could repeat, a third voice spoke. "In ancient times, when mankind was young, magic was as natural as the seasons changing or the moon in the sky."

My forehead knotted trying to tell if it was male or female. There was a powerful timbre of authority in it but not commanding. This voice was proffering wisdom and sagacity. The entire area grew quiet as it spoke. Hell, I even hung on every word.

The voice continued, "The Fae, along with other beings, lived in harmony with humans. In many ways, it was symbiotic, each species benefiting from the gifts and talents of the other."

"What happened? Why did that end?" Maren asked the question that was pinging in my mind as well.

The silence hung for a moment. Then with a forlorn sigh, the wise one spoke. "I am but a counselor and historian to our cloister, Lady Linette. It is your decision as our leader what to disclose to this young human lass."

Lass? Geesh. Both Maren and I left our "lass" days behind decades ago! I bit my tongue though.

Linette's smoky voice filled the air. "Thank you, Sebille. Your wisdom has guided us for uncounted ages." When she spoke again, she was closer to me and my sister. "In ages past, humans and the Fae folk, along with all the other mystical beings, did live in harmony. Even though there were some challenges to our relationship, it did work. All our species lived our own lives, but like members of a large extended family, our differences were not enough to break our shared bond of beings upon this world..." Her voice faded.

"What happened?" Maren asked. "How come you guys became but a legend to humans, then?"

Linette answered in a matter-of-fact tone. "It was you humans. Your kind lost your way. Leaders rose from your ranks who weren't satisfied with being chieftains of humans, but wanted to be chieftains of all. Wars and battles of conquest began at first. Taking and pillaging." Her voice grew sharp. "By the time I came into being, these wars were wrapped in the armor of religious fervor. Before even the ancient Greeks and Romans, your kind learned that you could perform the most cruel actions, if bidden to do so by your gods." She spat out the last words.

"All of the mystical folk withdrew from you, leaving only legends in our wake." She snorted. "It did not take long for you to find other prey—you fell upon one another. And that has been your history ever since. War without end, amen."

She continued. "We mythicals wove the veil to separate ourselves from your kind when you were still but a collection of tribal groups of nomadic hunters or settlements of small villages. When you learned to plant and harvest, when your tribes built hamlets, then towns, then cities, we were long apart from you." She let out a small laugh. "We do walk among you to this very day, but your kind is blinded to us by our veil."

"You must be talking about pagan times that ended when the church expanded. That was in Europe, a long time ago, right?" I thought of novels I'd read, trying to make sense of all this.

"Far, far earlier than that, child. As I said, we separated from humans long before you could write; your so-called religions of those times weren't even written down. The expansion you talk about only began in the last two millennia; we created the veil ages earlier. For eons we watched in wondrous horror as you made such blood-soaked war upon one another."

"But that's changing?" Maren broke in. "You said the veil is damaged in spots and other people can now see you. Like me. How many of us are there?"

"I don't know. But I do know the number is growing. I sense a revival, people turning from empty ambition to what is real and meaningful. Magical power is in all of us, but for your kind, it's been relegated to the recesses of your brains instead of celebrated."

"Celebrated?"

"Of course! What do you think this Moon Dance is?" Linette's joy in the celebration bubbled in her last few words, and the music started again as if on cue.

"A marvelous night for a moon dance," I sang, wishing I could see these Fae dancing, longing to join them. With my head swaying side to side, I hummed the next line, imagining them.

"Your aura, Kara! It's gone from orange to a shimmering

yellow! And it's expanding! Oh my God. I wish you could see it." Maren turned her head to the side. "Why can't she see you, too, Linette? Her aura is getting brighter, like mine."

"That is not for me to say, Maren."

Again, the male voice—Tien?—spoke, "The real question is, where do we, as members of this cloister, go from here? These two women know about us. I, for one, refuse to accept that!"

"Tien!" Linette's voice took on an edge. "You speak out of turn!"

"Forgive me for breaking protocol, but this is a dangerous road you're taking us down with these humans! It's hard enough living alongside, watching their kind create havoc everywhere they go and with everything they touch, without this added threat. When they tell the rest of their kind about us, you know what will happen! We'll be destroyed. We can't allow that to happen, Linette."

"Do no harm, Tien. That is how we've lived for centuries, and we're not about to change now."

"And we lived for ages without their kind among us! Have you forgotten, Linette? Do you not remember the Days of Reaping? The slaughter of our kind suffered at the hands of humans?"

At his words, an arrow of fear shot through me. He was threatening us. When Maren's hand closed over mine, squeezing it, I knew she also saw the danger we'd walked into.

"The old ways aren't relevant anymore, Linette. Those were simpler times. The world is too complex, and the danger to us and our offspring is greater now. You've seen the violence their kind is capable of. We must protect ourselves again. The only option is to remove these women from their kind and repair the veil." Tien's voice had an edge to it, challenging the older fairy leader.

Holding Maren's hand, I took a step back, tugging her with me. The way that guy was talking, we might have to try to make a run for it. But these creatures could fly. What chance would we have if this got ugly? Shit!

Maren jerked her hand from mine and scooped the silver chain from her neck. "Please. We won't tell anyone. Take this necklace as a token of my sincere promise. We don't want anything to threaten or hurt you. Just for the record, we don't trust our leaders too much either."

The lapis lazuli stone dangled, swaying back and forth from the hand she extended. "Kara and I promised each other we'd keep all of this to ourselves. No one will know about you or about any of the events we've experienced the last days. Not even our children know about any of this."

I watched the necklace leave her fingers and levitate to a spot a couple of feet away, just hanging there in the air. And then it was gone!

The strange sexless voice spoke again, "I agree with Linette, Tien. And I fully recall the Days of Reaping—I was there. But time moves on, and these women are innocent of those days. We shall trust Maren and Kara. Their hearts are pure."

"Bah! Their hearts are human! Their kind changes with the wind!"

"There are other forces that threaten our people—forces more powerful than these two women."

Even though I breathed a sigh of relief that Tien was outvoted, their points made me glance over my shoulder, into the inky blackness outside of the glade. "Other forces, like werewolves? You guys know that there's two werewolves around, right? They're parked just two campsites away, and it's a full moon, so—"

The tinkling bells sounded again, followed by laughter. A lot of laughter, like an audience at a comedy theater had filled the forest. Just how many of them were here? What the hell? I felt my cheeks heat up, even though I had absolutely no reason to be embarrassed! I was trying to warn them about werewolves, for Pete's sake!

"Wait. You act like werewolves aren't threatening? Are

you nuts? Sheesh!" Maren had my back, shrugging her shoulders and giving me a sideways glance.

Linette spoke again after clearing her throat and getting everyone to shut the hell up with all their giggles. "I accept this necklace in the spirit of friendship and trust. As for Howie and Laura, their bark is worse than their bite." She tittered a giggle. "The full moon rekindles the romance in their bedroom, but that's about it. They pose no threat to you or us."

A picture of Howie and Laura flashed in my mind—the two of them sniping and growling about us being late. We'd thrown a monkey wrench into their amorous plans, delaying them. I couldn't help smiling. The poor old things just wanted to get their freak on. No wonder they'd laid out such a strict schedule in their dinner plans.

Maren chuckled. "Eeew. But it's good to know, I guess." She paused for a beat before asking, "So, how many other beings exist in your world? It's like some kind of parallel dimension? There are werewolves, okay? Anything else? I mean, anyone else?"

"Yes, there are others. Sprites, for example."

"What's a sprite? Are there any we should be afraid of?"

"Linette!" Tien shouted before Maren had even finished. "These humans should not even know about us! Yet, you've told them about werewolves and sprites as well. Do not divulge any more information to them. In the name of the Guild, I demand that you remain silent."

A deadly hush followed, and I held my breath waiting for the leader, Linette, to answer. Seconds felt like minutes before she spoke, ominously soft in tone. "You demand? I caution you to remember your place, Tien. You are still scion, my heir, not in a position of power."

"Yet! But it is becoming clear that perhaps I should be. Especially with so much at stake. You have forgotten our history, and what these creatures have done. I can't stand idly by while you—"

"It is you who has forgotten, Tien! Forgotten your

manners as well as your place. This matter is not open for discussion, particularly on this night with our guests. Return to court and stay there until I summon you." The steely tone of Linette's voice along with her words, drew more than a few gasps around me.

Maren leaned closer to me and whispered, "Well, this is getting awkward. Looks like some kind of power struggle going on with these guys. I don't like the look in Tien's eyes, glaring at us."

A blast of wind, littered with leaves, hit me square in the face before a high-pitched whir disturbed the quiet. I knew even before Maren whispered, "He's gone! He zapped out of here as fast as a hummingbird! A group of them left with him."

"My apologies to everyone and especially to our guests. Tien spoke out of turn, but I take responsibility for that. Nevertheless, let us resume Moon Dance." When Linette finished speaking, the ringing of bells was followed by stringed instruments and voices singing.

It was as if the disruption with Tien hadn't happened. But it had. Despite the awe of being in the company of fairies, dancing and celebrating the moon, it was now tinged with unease. Tien had made ominous threats to Maren and me, and I didn't like that one bit. And there had been a group of fairies who had agreed and left with him.

I stiffened when the air became warmer, filled with a scent of roses. I couldn't see Linette but I was aware that she had stepped closer to Maren and me. Her voice was gentle when she spoke.

"There are more things in heaven and earth, Horatio, than are dreamt of in your philosophy. The Bard's words, Shakespeare, were never truer than now. We coexist with many mystical creatures in my world, but elements of magic still thrive in your plane too."

"What do you mean?" I asked.

"Why, witches of course! Yes, they practice the old ways, delving into magic. Some would even say that you two have stumbled into that state of being, yourself!"

As she spoke, I noticed Maren's jaw falling lower and lower. For me, it was music to my ears! For years, I'd followed anything supernatural, and now it looked like I was totally on the right trail.

Maren's eyes bulged like golf balls. "Witches? You're saying that because I've got this power now, that I'm a witch?"

The silvery, androgynous voice intoned, "You have been gifted; that is certain. By whom, I do not know. It doesn't matter the source. It's how you will go forth with those gifts that matters. Our dictum to do no harm has served us well. I would advise you to adopt it."

"I smell sweetness!"

I swear I felt a gossamer touch on my arm—the one holding the box with the pecan pie.

Even before I raised it, Maren gushed, "The pie! We also brought pie for you. Pia said you love anything sweet!"

The box left my hand, floating a few feet away from me before it was opened and the pie divided up amid excited squeals. I saw it disappear in bite-sized pieces as squeals and sighs of pleasure filled the air. They sure made short work of the dessert.

I noticed Maren focusing on something to her right, leaning in to whisper, "You weren't kidding about the fairies having a sweet tooth, Pia. I wish I'd brought a dozen more."

"We have something for you as well." Linette said before she clapped her hands twice, ending the music. Immediately, two tiny dark rings appeared, one floating to Maren and the other to me.

As I took the one meant for me into my hand, I felt the fine braiding of strands of fiber, thin and supple as thread, woven to form a small ring. A nudge on my palm was immediately followed by this ring slipping over my forefinger.

The androgynous voice spoke again: "These are rings of protective energy. They are woven from the root of the hawthorn tree. In addition to protection, they will immediately identify you as friends of the Fae cloister in this region should you encounter other beings from our realm. That in and of itself will provide safety to you."

I gazed at the ring on my finger, admiring the artistic intricacy but also feeling a slight tingle where it clung and molded to my skin. It felt alive with power seeping into my pores and spreading up my hand and arm—tingly like when something tickles your nose making you want to sneeze.

Maren started to speak but I interrupted before she could say thanks. I'd read somewhere that saying thanks to a fairy was rude. As weird as that might be, I wasn't going to risk offending them. It was bad enough that our presence had incited Tien's threat.

"We accept your gifts, Linette. You honor us." I elbowed Maren when she started again, and she shot me a scowl but stayed silent.

"We honor each other on this Moon Dance night. A rekindling of the once lost friendship between Fae and humans. When you wear these rings, know that we are always a heartbeat away, should you need us."

Again, the sexless voice spoke, "It is time to retire from our festivities this eve. Sleep well, Maren and Kara. Safe travels to you."

No! It couldn't be over this quickly. I had a million questions. Surely, if anyone knew what had happened to us, why Maren had these powers, it would be the Fae. I had to know!

"Linette? My sister hasn't told you, but for three days, we were essentially gone! When we woke up in the RV, we had no memories of those days. I think we were abducted by aliens—"

"Kara! Linette doesn't want to hear about your alien theory. Something happened, sure, but aliens?" She scowled at me before flashing a warm smile and turning slightly away. "Before you go, I want to hear about the others who can see fairies. How will we know them?"

Several pinpoints of light glowed in the clearing and the music faded. I glanced at Maren, with her mouth hanging open, blinking. I already knew they'd left, and the disappointment on her face proved it.

"Damn. That didn't last nearly long enough. It was so cool while it lasted…aside from that loudmouth Tien." Her mouth set in a straight line as she crossed her arms over her chest.

I stood there for a few moments, fingering the ring while trying to relive the magical time with the Fae. Maren was right. It had ended waaay too soon, like living a wonderful dream. But only the cool night air, filled with the sounds of crickets and the odd firefly remained.

It was over.

Looping my arm through hers, I pulled her along, stepping through the brush and out of the clearing. "I guess when they announce they're leaving, they mean it. Meeting them was amazing, although it got kind of scary with that Tien guy. I'm glad Linette made him leave."

"Yeah." She sighed before squeezing my arm. "I wonder how Howie and Laura are making out?"

"Making out?" We looked at each other and started laughing. A midnight meeting with the Fae followed by two senior werewolves getting it on. Yup. We had gone through the looking glass, all right.

Eighteen

Kara

I rolled my fingers over the ring that Linette had given me as we walked back to our RV. It still felt tingly, like it was alive with energy. "How does your ring feel, Maren? Can you believe she gave us these rings, like we're now part of the club?"

"I think the term they used was Guild."

"No, they said 'cloister.'"

Maren shook her head sadly at me. "Kara, Kara...listening is really not your strong suit sometimes. The Fae live together in a 'cloister.' That cloister is joined with other 'Mythical Beings' in a Guild."

"If you keep doing all those finger quotes, you're gonna hurt yourself," I chortled. "You probably have an organizational chart all made up in your head, don't ya?"

She blinked and nodded. "Duh! Damn right."

I rolled my eyes at her. "Now answer the question,

would ya?" I held my hand up again. "This ring…it feels like it's almost alive on my finger. Does it feel the same way to you?"

She held her hand out and stared at the ring for a moment. "It's got its own aura, Kara. It pulses a yellowish glow that's separate from my own aura." She looked over at me. "Your ring's got the same aura. But it's not 'alive' like a creature would be."

"Well, that's good to know; I wouldn't want some Fae worm disguised as a ring wrapped around my finger."

"Ick." Maren shuddered. "That's an icky image in my head." She shook her head. "No, this isn't anything like that. I do sense a kind of vitality, though, like a hug or something." She looked over to me. "I feel a sense of comfort emanating from it." She snapped her fingers. "That's it! The sense of comfort is just like when we'd visit our nana when we were little kids! Remember that big quilt she'd spread on us when we'd be watching TV? That big ol' quilt of hers? It would be a little chilly, but snuggling under that quilt was heavenly, right?"

Wow. Nana's quilt. I hadn't thought of those memories in some time. We were just little kids—she passed away when I was seven—but we'd visit her, Mom's mother, every Thanksgiving or else on Christmas Day.

I closed my eyes for a second, and with my other hand, I stroked that ring and—like a movie—I could see me and Maren snuggled under the quilt on Nana's big old "chesterfield" as she called it, watching Christmas movies while the grown-ups' voices droned from the kitchen. Warm, well fed, snug as a bug…it was a comforting memory.

I nodded and opened my eyes to Maren. "Yeah, I remember that; I haven't thought of it in years."

"Me neither. But I think this ring makes it easier to recall stuff like that." She held her hand out before her, admiring the woven jewelry. "This is all so unbelievable, but this ring…it proves we actually joined them in that ceremony.

We met real-life elves tonight."

"Fairies, Maren. Get the terminology right, okay."

She looked over at me and smiled wistfully. "I wish you could have seen them. Linette was so regal, yet friendly and warm at the same time. And beautiful...her eyes had an upward lift at the outer corners, and her cheekbones were like Audrey Hepburn's. Actually, every feature on her face was perfection; even her complexion was smooth and unlined."

I tried to picture her, and thanks to Maren's comparison to Audrey Hepburn, that star's face filled my mind. "Linette is their leader, right? I wonder how long they live. Do they go through menopause and crap like we do?" And then my mind bounced to that androgynous voice.

I tapped Maren's arm. "What about Sebille? I really couldn't get a reading when she, or was it he, spoke?"

"That's a good question." She shook her head before continuing. "I saw Sebille, and honestly, I couldn't tell you if it was a he or she. The silvery outfit included billowy, loose pants but the top had voluminous layers." She shrugged. "I couldn't tell if there were boobs or not. The close-cropped haircut was kind of masculine but the face... It could have been male or female. Whatever. It doesn't matter. Sebille was on Linette's side and that's what counts."

I looked up at the night sky, twinkling with stars. I'd never forget this night. It was a mystical and wonderful experience. I could live in this moment forever, reveling in the wonder of meeting actual fairies. Despite the dispute at the end with Tien, Linette and her cloister had been amazing. My life would never be the same.

Maren broke the silence. "That Tien! I hope Linette gave him shit for making a scene. He was the only negative thing about tonight. Even Howie and Laura weren't as frightening as him."

"Yeah, I didn't like him."

"You don't think we're going to have any problems with him, do you?"

"Hell no. Linette slapped him into line."

Howie's rig was completely dark and quiet when we passed by it. The moon was lower in the sky and if I had to guess, I'd say it was close to three in the morning. Time had flown. I looked over at Maren. "How are we ever going to be able to go to sleep? I'm still stoked about meeting them."

She started to walk faster. "I don't know about that, but I know I have to pee." She hurried by the Boler to get to our camper. "C'mon, Kara."

"You go ahead. I'm going to sit outside for five minutes to try to decompress. My head is a whirlwind."

I jerked when the door slammed behind Maren going inside our camper. Shit. Hopefully that didn't wake the Boler Guy and his girlfriend. I peered at the Boler, checking to see that he hadn't wakened to gawk out his window. I wouldn't put it past the nosy parker.

As I stood there checking the other camper, I heard the sound of footsteps clopping on the road. I ducked into the shadow next to my truck, and took a peek to see where they were coming from. The moon cast light on a lanky figure who was weaving, before letting out a loud belch and coming to a halt next to Howie's rig.

I could smell the reek of booze from here. The guy was plastered.

When he started whistling a low haunting tune while continuing on, I tiptoed my way to the door of our camper. Whoever was out at that hour of the night—drunk—wasn't someone I'd care to meet.

"Hey! Hold up a minute, lady."

Tight fingers dug into my shoulder as I reached for the door's handle. Before I knew it, I was spun around to face dark eyes like coals in a pale, angular face. He looked around my age, but I wasn't positive in the nighttime lighting. Definitely in his forties anyway. The smell of liquor wafted in the air when he belched again, loosening his grasp on me when his hand flew to cover his mouth.

"'Scuze me. Sorry. You wouldn't have any smokes,

would you?" He patted the pocket of his black shirt and started hiccupping, "I ran out an hour ago and the store in this campground is closed."

Great. My luck that I hadn't gone in with Maren and avoided this lout. What the hell was he doing out wandering around in the middle of the night? It didn't help that he was at least a foot taller than me and drunk as a skunk.

I reached behind me, my hand fumbling for the handle as I spoke, "Sorry. I quit years ago. You have a good night, now." I started to turn, but he leaned closer and his fingers splayed on the door of the camper, holding it shut.

"Tha's okay. I've been meaning to quit anyway. Hold on though. You got any vodka or anything to drink? Why not have a nightcap with me? I don't bite." As soon as the words were out of his mouth, he bent over laughing. "Tha's a good one!" He hee-hawed again. "Oh man, I crack myself up."

Even though he was lost in his own joke, his hand never left the door. Between his putrid breath and the fact that he had me trapped outside my camper, stuck with listening to his ramblings, I could feel a spark of anger start inside me. I'd had plenty experience dealing with drunks when the bars closed and they staggered into Denny's.

"Hey! Back off! There's no way I'm giving you any more alcohol. That's the last thing you need, trust me. Get your hand off my door. Now! I'm going inside." I watched the grin melt from his lips as he straightened, looking at me with a questioning look.

"You're not very friendly, are you? Sheesh! All I wanted was someone to talk to." He blinked at me a few times and once more leaned in. "What are you doing out at this time of night? Who are you?"

As he spoke, I noticed a snake tattoo curling up his neck to a brush of light hair, military style. Hackles on the back of my neck spiked high as I tried to project casual calmness in my voice. "If you don't leave me alone, I'll scream. I'll have you arrested for—"

"Kara?" Maren's voice was accompanied by the sound of the doorknob turning and her hand banging on it. "Why won't this open? Kara? Who's out there?"

Before I got a chance to answer, a light in the Boler next door slivered through the side of the window. The drunk's head fell back in surprise and he took a step back, grinning. "Well, this is starting to look like a party! You sure you don't have anything to drink...Kara? Just one for the road before I go back to my van." He rubbed his hands together and grinned. "C'mon! It'll be fun."

The door behind me burst open as he spoke, hitting me in the behind and knocking me squarely up against the drunk. Eew! Pushing my hands against his sweaty, damp chest, I stepped back just as Maren emerged from the camper, gaping at the intoxicated fool.

"Get away from my sister! Go on!" Maren reached for me, practically pushing me toward the door behind her. Her hand rose. "Get out of here! Go back where you came from, you foul beast!"

My heart pounded against my ribs, but even so, I whispered, "Foul beast?" Still trying to process Maren's odd choice of words, my mouth fell open when the drunk flew up, jetting through the air like he'd been hit by a tractor trailer. He landed with a loud oof and a series of belches on the other side of the road.

"Don't come back here ever again! Next time I see you, you'll really get a hurting! Beast!"

The door to the Boler opened and the guy stepped out. "What's going on? Are you two okay?" He slipped his arm into the shirt he was carrying and looked over at the drunk. "Who the hell is that? Was he bothering you?"

Maren turned on Boler Guy. "Not anymore! I don't know who he is...some drunken idiot, I guess." She pointed at Boler Guy. "You'd be better off just staying away from him, okay? Good night!"

Maren turned to me. "Get the hell inside, Kara!" she hissed. What the hell? As if this night wasn't crazy enough,

Maren tossing that drunk away, displaying her power for him to see? It was the icing on the cake! It was a good thing that it happened before Boler Guy came out.

But what about the drunk? No. Forget him! He'd think he dreamed it up in his drunken stupor.

Maren locked the door behind her. When she turned around, her face was as white as the moon outside. "That guy was a vampire, Kara!" Her hand flew to her chest and she gasped, "He had long fangs, and his eyes glowed red like fire! There was no aura around him. That's what vampires are, right? The undead?"

"A vampire?" It came out as a high-pitched squeak. Oh my God! Could this night get any weirder?

I shook my head. This couldn't be, not another mythical creature. "No. He was just a drunk, Maren. The smell of booze reeking off of him almost turned my stomach!" But as I stood there, I couldn't deny that Maren could see things I couldn't. If she said he was a vampire, then he was.

My jaw dropped slowly open. A vampire? First the horny werewolves, then a bunch of fairies having a Moon Dance and now…a vampire?

Wait a goddamned minute! A drunk vampire?

"Oh, he was a vampire all right! And don't correct me and say that he was a zombie. I was wrong about the elves, but I'm definitely not wrong about what that thing out there is. You're lucky I came out when I did! He might have sunk his teeth into your neck!"

Maren lifted her hands and gazed at them. "I'm getting stronger. Did you see how far I hurled him? That had to be twenty feet!"

I fell onto the bench at the table. "What the hell is going on with us, Mare? I know I was kidding about stepping through the looking glass earlier, but this is just—" Watching her as she grabbed two drinks from the fridge was like looking at a stranger. How come Maren didn't seem all that freaked out about any of this? She was the rational, no-nonsense one, and here she was rocketing vampires across the road like she was batting a fly away. What was happening to her…and me?

Grinning triumphantly, she handed me my beer. "I sure served that guy some serious whup-ass, didn't I? He had no idea who he was tangling with when I showed up." She clinked her vodka cooler against mine, "Here's to us, Kara! We may be getting older, but by hell, we're sure getting better."

I swallowed half the beer in one long haul. I definitely needed that! Being with the Fae had been thrilling. It was a night I'd never forget, but this? Vampires and werewolves prowling among us? What would have happened if Maren hadn't shown up when she did? Would I have been attacked? Became one of the undead? Or just killed? And what about all that stuff in the movies about vampires being sexy and irresistible? That guy was a stinking drunk.

Maren took a seat across from me. "Should we stay a few more nights here, Kara? I'd love to see those fairies again. We hardly got to ask them anything before they ended it." Maren picked at the bottle's label, staring down at it. "I wish we could see them again."

"Yeah, that'd be cool." I mumbled. But my mind was screaming something entirely different.

As if! I was wondering if I should just disconnect right freakin' now and get out of this so-called campground. I don't know what the hell it was with this place, but fairies? Werewolves? AND NOW VAMPIRES?

Still feeling dazed, I got up to check the window, tweaking the blinds apart so I could see. There was no sign of him out in our space or on the road, so that was good. Movement across the way caught my attention, and my gaze flitted to the Boler parked in the next site.

I jerked back seeing the Boler Guy in the doorway of his camper, staring over at us. It was decent of him to check on us earlier, but why did he always seem to be watching us? And considering that his girlfriend was the same woman who had freaked us out at the beach, before just disappearing into thin air, I had to wonder about Boler Guy too. What the hell were those two? Frankenstein and his bride or something?

No. If that were the case, Maren would have seen it. But who were those two?

Turning and propping my butt against the counter, I peered at my sister, who was still picking nonchalantly at the label on the bottle. "Maren? I know you'd like to stay and see the Fae again, but I'm not sure that's such a good idea. This campground is giving me the willies. I was fine with the Fae and even the geriatric werewolves, but vampires? And those two in the Boler are odd ducks. I don't know what their game is."

She looked over at me. "Yeah. Something's off about them. They keep watching us and their aura is such a strange color."

"What do you mean?"

"Well"—she pointed at me—"at the moment, your aura's orange with spikes of red shooting through. I think it's because you're upset right now." She pointed next door with her chin. "But those two? First of all, their auras are exactly the same, and I don't think that's how it's supposed to be; everyone's aura is their own. But those two? The lady at the beach and him, they both have the same aura." She pointed at me again. "Yours pulses, kinda. I mean it gets a little bigger, and then relaxes...like your chest when you breathe. But theirs just stays the same." She chewed her lower lip. "And the color! I couldn't even tell you what it is!"

"Well, is it kind of red? Or yellow? Blue? Those are the major ones, right?"

"I guess so. But they aren't any of those. I can't describe it. But the real difference is their auras don't pulse. They just hover around them like a bell jar." She looked away. I don't know what to make of it, but my gut says that there's something out of whack with those two. She looked over at me. "Funny, we haven't seen her at the campsite with Boler Guy. We heard her the first night but we've never seen her here."

"Another one of her disappearing acts?" Even though I tried to be flip, the feeling of unease in my gut grew. I had to admit that the vampire was the topper. Other than being annoyed with him—asshole drunks do that to me—I hadn't recognized the threat he posed. But Maren had.

"Yeah. We should leave. I really want to see my new granddaughter and...Linette made it seem like this is just the beginning." Maren held up her hand, wiggling her finger that the ring was on. "We might see more fairies and sprites and God only knows what else besides geriatric werewolves, or, ugh...vampires in our travels."

Her hand covered mine and squeezed. "I can see that you're worried. It's not only in your eyes, but your aura is fading and is getting kind of muddied. We'll pack up and leave later today. But I'm going to need another couple of these coolers if I'm ever going to fall asleep."

We sat there for another hour, having more drinks as Maren continued gushing about the fairies. I nodded and smiled, but I couldn't shake the feeling of foreboding that smothered my earlier excitement. Even twisting the fairy ring on my forefinger did little to ease the dread.

And that dread felt familiar, believe me. When I was in the waiting room at the doctor's office, I felt that dread. It was so black that the news he gave me was almost a relief. As if a death sentence could be that way. But it sort of was...at least I wasn't wondering anymore. And that's what I hate—the not knowing.

I made a mental note to send my son a text before I went to sleep. I'd never experienced premonitions before this, so why now? Is that what this was? Was this my gift? Maren could levitate and see mythical beings. Although I could hear those beings, maybe this sense of dread was actually premonitions. Was that my gift? That I could sense impending doom?

Great. Just freaking great.

Nineteen

Kara

Surprisingly, Maren and I both managed to sleep in until almost eleven that morning. I think I would have stayed snuggled in my bed if it weren't for the clamor of some camper with a bad muffler driving by. The noise woke me right the hell up. I looked across at Maren in the twin bed next to mine.

Swiping sleep out of her eyes, she grumbled, "I guess it's time to haul ass, right?"

I threw the covers back and slipped my feet into my slippers. "Yup. I could have used another hour of sleep though. It felt like I just dropped off and now we're getting up."

Maren grabbed her housecoat and slid her arms into it, tightening it over her plaid nightgown. "Yeah. That was quite a night. I'm surprised we got any sleep."

When I wandered out into the kitchen area to start the coffee maker, bright sunlight beamed over the counter. Lifting the blinds to check outside, I rolled my eyes seeing Boler Guy next door, sitting in a lotus position meditating on his picnic table. I guess it had been too much to hope for that he'd have pulled up stakes and left.

Although his creepy preoccupation with us bothered me, he was easy on the eyes. Who was I kidding? He had a perfect body, sitting there in cutoffs and a tank top. His eyes were closed and his head tilted up toward the morning sun—probably working on that perfect tan of his—showing his perfectly sculptured face for all the world to see.

I let out a sigh. Here I was spying on a wannabee stalker.

I needed to get laid.

Speaking of wild sex, I saw Howie hanging towels on a clothesline at his campsite, while his wife swept the rattan mat that served as their patio. "Howie and Laura are still here," I called over to Maren. "Surprised they have so much energy."

"So, any idea where we'll end up today? I think pushing through to Charleston will be too much, especially considering our late night." Maren eased in beside me to pour two mugs of coffee for us.

"My thoughts exactly. Let me get my computer and we'll check out some routes to figure it out." When I returned from the bedroom where my laptop was, Maren was pouring cereal into two bowls and getting our breakfast laid out.

I took a seat next to her and set the laptop across the table. For the next ten minutes we discussed routes to ocean properties in North Carolina. "So, Havelock it is. That's not quite four hours and should be a snap. We'll get there and have plenty of light to get settled in for the night."

Maren sat back and smiled. "I'll make you a deal. If you get us out of the congested areas and onto the highway, I'll take it from there. It's about time I got comfortable driving this thing so we can share the burden. It's not fair that you do all the driving, although you'll still have to take over when it comes to parking it."

You could have knocked me over with a feather. Maren had been reluctant to take this trip initially, but when she agreed, she made it clear it was strictly as a passenger. Now she was offering to share the driving? Whatever changes she'd been going through over the last couple of days was changing her nervousness about wheeling this rig around.

"It's a deal! It's not really that hard to drive this. It's just a bit bigger and longer than a full-size pickup. I think you're going to like it, Mare." I snapped the laptop shut and grinned at her. "I bet once you get the hang of it, you'll want us to step up to a Class A, like Howie's monstrosity."

"Don't count on getting me to drive that mansion on wheels!" She extended her hands, lifting the bowls and empty mugs into the air. One hand directed the bowls to the sink and the other deposited the mugs down in front of the coffee maker. "But hey! If I can do this levitating thing, then I should be able to handle driving this rig down the highway, right?"

"After seeing you toss that vampire aside, driving this will be a cakewalk!"

Smirking, she replied, "He's probably nursing more than a hangover today. Too bad he showed up, putting a damper on our evening. It was so cool being with the fairies. I'm still amazed that they exist!"

As I watched her dreamlike gaze sitting there lost in the memory, I came to a decision. It was broad daylight and with her strengthening powers, why not?

"Look, I'm happy that you're going to share the driving, Mare. Why don't you go see if those fairies are around so you can see them one last time and say goodbye. I'll look after pulling up stakes here." The way her eyes lit up when I suggested one last visit, confirmed I'd made the right call.

"Absolutely!" She popped to her feet and as she rushed to the bedroom to get changed, she called over her shoulder, "I promise I'll be back in an hour. This is awesome! Thanks, Kara. I'll do all the hookups when we get to Havelock, even the sewer one."

As I poured another mug of coffee, I nodded. "I'll hold you to that! Be back at one, okay? No dawdling and losing track of time." It would be nice to go with her and hear them but I'd pretty well had it with this campsite. Especially after that creepy vampire last night. Time to move on.

Carrying my mug of coffee, I stepped outside to enjoy the sunshine. It was already seventy degrees with a clear blue sky overhead. Boler Guy had finished his meditating session and had disappeared inside his camper. Just as I was about to settle at the picnic table, I noticed Howie wave before getting out of his lawn chair to head over.

"Good morning!" He flashed a wide smile that extended to the crinkles at the corners of his eyes. But it was the way he carried himself, like he was cock of the walk—practically prancing across the vacant campsite—that made me chuckle. Amazing what getting laid could do to a guy.

If I didn't know better, he looked like any normal retired guy in his late-sixties enjoying the day. But this was a werewolf, and one who'd put new meaning to howling at the moon. I smiled at him. "You look well rested, Howie. Did you have a good night after Maren and I left?"

For a moment he seemed to start, the smile dropping as he peered at me. But just as quickly, he recovered, "We did! I'm sorry we got so out of sorts with you gals. It's just that we have a routine, y'know? It sucks getting old. Time was, we could stay up till dawn...er...chatting and watchin' movies. Now..."

The door behind me opened and Maren called out as she stepped outside. "Hey, Howie! I hope you and Laura enjoyed that dessert last night. Sorry we screwed up your schedule." Her eyes met mine, and I had to look away or I'd burst out laughing.

"Not a problem." Howie watched Maren walk to the road instead of joining us at the table. "Where you off to? You look like the cat that swallowed the canary, Maren."

"So do you! I'm just going for a hike! Actually, we met some lovely folk on the path yesterday, Howie. I'm gonna try to catch up with them to say goodbye." With that, Maren broke out into a jog, cutting off further conversation with the old werewolf.

I held up my hand, wiggling the finger that the fairy ring was on. In the bright light of day, it was even more impressive, seeing the filigree crafted out of the tree's fiber. When my eyes met Howie's, his mouth had fallen open and the smile was gone.

"So, Laura was right about you ladies. She said you weren't what you pretend to be. Where'd you get that ring?"

My knowing smile was the only answer I volunteered.

"Okay. I guess you met them." He looked up at the sky and added in a low voice, "So, I suppose you know everything…about Laura and me." His already dark complexion became even darker and he looked down at the ground for a moment. "That's where your sister is going. To see if any of the Fae are around." His gaze stabbed mine with intensity. "Look! This is no game, Kara. You can't—"

"You're telling me! We had a visit from a vampire when we got home last night. But if you're worried that we're going to tell anyone about any of this, Howie, don't be. Who would believe us anyway? Fae, werewolves, and vampires?" I leaned in closer, "You have nothing to be concerned about on that score."

When I saw the lines on his face ease, I added, "It's us, too, Howie. We can never explain all the things that have happened or what we've become."

Seeing the confusion on his face, I decided the trust thing went both ways. "Linette said that the veil between her world and ours is fraying in spots, but I'm not sure that accounts for everything that we've been through over the last week."

"You met Linette…and Sebille?" He hit his forehead with the heel of his hand. "Hell's bells! Of course! The Moon Dance. You were at the Moon Dance with them."

"Yeah! Don't you think that's really strange? We were just ordinary women going on a road trip across the country, but now? Now, we're not. Maren can levitate objects. She sees the Fae and other beings we always thought weren't real. I can hear them, and I think I'm maybe developing some premonition ability, but—"

"But why you?" Howie's chin tucked into his chest as he watched me. "Linette thinks there's some kind of rip in the veil. I get that. So, you two just walked through it or something?"

I just shrugged. "I don't know." Even though I had an idea, of course. That blinding light and the missing days? That must have been this veil thing. But again, that niggling feeling told me I should keep quiet about that, and I trusted my gut.

Howie huffed. "So, if you two can just cross over it, then who else can step through? Is it just in this location, or are there more places where humans can actually see us?"

I shook my head, letting out a long sigh. He was seeing this only from his own perspective, of course. "A rip in the veil doesn't explain everything that's happened—not everything that's happened to us, especially not Maren's abilities."

Something else didn't make sense to me. "And this thing of you being a werewolf…" I rolled my eyes. Werewolf. Something I'd never dreamed I'd actually say to someone, let alone sitting here chatting with one! "Maren sees Fae and that vampire, so of course, she knew what you were when we stopped for dinner. But why am I able to see you at all, if you're supposed to be all mythical?"

His bushy eyebrows rose, and his voice dripped with sarcasm. "Maybe it's because I'm human? I'm not always a werewolf, y'know."

He glanced at the Boler before leaning in closer, and lowering his voice. "Look, our kind are floaters. We drift between the two worlds depending on the phase of the moon. So, of course, everyone can see us. It's just when the moon is full, that the change comes on. Something, of course, your sister saw right away. And you don't have to worry that we're going to attack you." His eyes narrowed. "You're safe for another month."

The bite of his words struck a nerve and I fed it back to him. "From what I heard last night, attacking isn't really on your agenda. Not unless you and Laura are into some real serious sado kink. Not that I want any sordid details."

"Lord love a duck! Stop it! I was teasing about attacking you." He looked down, digging into the soft earth with the toe of his sneaker. "I didn't ask to become a werewolf, Kara. It happened so long ago." His eyes met mine. "I was only eighteen years old, thinking about Amy Everly as I walked home from the dance at the high school. I got jumped…"

He paused, rolling his eyes. "Not that way! True, it was a woman, but she physically attacked me. I managed to fight her off, but she left me bleeding with a gash in my arm. The next full moon, I knew though. When hair started sprouting on my face and body, my bones stretched painfully as my mind became obsessed with hunting, killing, and…oh God, was I horny." His voice dropped. "That woman was—a she-wolf. The bitch turned me."

For a moment I could only look at him with pity. It was clear he wasn't happy to end up living his life like this. "But you don't hunt and kill people, right? Please tell me you don't."

He shook his head. "No. It'd be too dangerous. There was a time when our kind did, but that's over. Now, with such advanced police technology, it'd be too risky. The most we do now is hunting and killing wild animals like fox or deer. And that's just the younger generation, certainly not anyone my age."

"Are your kids like you? Werewolves?" Even though I considered myself educated in all this supernatural stuff, this was a real education—getting it from the wolf's mouth, so to speak.

His shoulders slumped lower. "We don't have children,

Kara. That's just a story I tell people when I meet them. We appear more normal, joking about boomerang kids. Early on we made the decision to never have children. No way would I put any child of mine through this."

He took his ball cap off, tapping it against his thigh before continuing in a flat voice. "And our schedule of being in this world, is tricky without adding kids to the mix. Laura and I follow a strict dietary regime. When the moon is in the waxing gibbous phase until after it reaches full, we consume meat at every meal. A lot of meat. That's why I chose to become a butcher. If people knew how much meat we ate, they'd be appalled, and then…well, they'd wonder. And that's the last thing we want."

"Good to know, if I ever ask you to dinner at my house. Immediately I regretted the flip remark when he let out a long sigh. "Sorry. I'm sure it must have been difficult. But there must be some positives about being…well, being a werewolf."

His smile was wan. "Think of the best qualities of a dog. Great olfactory sense, jaw grip like a shark, and loyalty. And we're strong. It must be all that meat."

I glanced over at Laura. "So how did you two get together?"

He burst out laughing. "On the prowl, little girl!" He leaned over and jabbed at me with a finger. "On. The. Prowwwlllllll." His eyebrows bobbed and he grinned like a maniac. "It was a full-moon night, and we caught each other's scent. All that night, instead of hunting and feeding, we tracked each other down!" He rubbed his hands together. "Full moon! Lemme tell ya, it was 'lust at first sight'! He cackled another laugh. "Been together ever since!"

I chuckled before another thought popped into my head. Now I had a handle on werewolves, but what about that vampire? "What can you tell me about vampires, Howie? Specifically, that drunken one who was going to attack me before Maren tossed him aside. Do you know who I'm talking about?"

He sat back and scratched his head, smirking. "If he was drunk, my bet would be Mike. Thin, looks like he's in his fifties, wearing a Stones T-shirt, probably whistling 'Angie'?"

"Yeah! That was the tune! I couldn't place it before but... So, Mike? You know the guy?" Crap! What was with this campground? Were there were more of these creatures around, living right under our noses?

I continued, "He asked me if I had any cigarettes or booze and kind of cornered me. He was annoying as hell, but when Maren saw him, she flipped out. Or rather, flipped him across the road would be more accurate."

Howie chuckled. "I would have loved to have seen that. Mike handles being a vampire kind of like we handle being werewolves. Except rather than eating copious amounts of meat, he drinks. Although I've got my doubts that he always behaves himself at work."

At the vacant look on my face, he added, "He works as an undertaker. You know, draining bodies to inject them with embalming fluid. I'm not sure all that blood makes its way down the drain."

"Eew! Gross!"

Ignoring my look of disgust, he continued. "He lives in Pittsburgh and vacations here every fall. We meet up with the Fae folk if they're around."

"Linette mentioned a Guild."

"Yeah, that's it. Anyway, we all meet up here now every year. Mike drives a van. Well, on the outside it looks like a van, but if you look inside, he's got himself a sweet little studio apartment on wheels, let me tell you. A nice sitting area, with a stove, a fold-down bed, all the necessities." He nodded. "I like my space, but Mike's rig's nice enough."

Howie took my hand. "Look, you're human, but you should understand. Full moons are hard on my kind as well as on vampires. It's when the urges become stronger. He's figured out how to handle it so he can exist with humans, so more power to him. It's the younger generation that I'd worry about being around, Kara. They're still trying to figure things out."

He placed his hand on my shoulder, and his eyes glistened when he looked at me. "What about you, Kara? I smell sickness on you. I noticed it right away when I helped you with the hookups, yesterday. How bad is it?"

Twenty

Maren

My feet fairly flew down the path on my way to the glade. Please let some of the fairies be there so I can see them once again. If you had told me a week ago that I'd be racing off to meet up with fairies, I would have wondered what kind of cheap drugs you were on. Yet here I was, the skeptical, level-headed younger sister doing just that! What's more, it was thrilling. Yes, the world had become much, much more exciting for sure. And a little scary too: vampires? werewolves? What other wonders are there in this world that I'd been dismissive of?

If there're fairies, maybe there are elves for real? Maybe? Yes, I'll admit it. I crushed on Legolas twenty years ago in the Hobbit movies; sue me! I laughed slightly at the thought. Wait!

Could hobbits be real too?

Get a grip, Maren! Next thing you know you're going to

be trekking up to Canada in search of Santa Claus's workshop at the North Pole!

I slowed to a walk, pondering this. Vampires, werewolves, and fairies pretty much blew skepticism to smithereens. But where does it end? Am I so nuts wondering about Santa Claus now? Really? I shrugged. At the very least, old St. Nick has been moved from the 'It's just a legend to tell kids' category over to the 'I really don't know, could be'… category.

Santa was now in the company of UFO's, stuff from the Bible, the adventures of those ghost hunters Ed and Lorraine Warren's Annabelle, and other stuff I couldn't remember at this time. The top of this box in my head had a label on it. A label that said 'Could Be? Maybe?'

"I'm gonna need a bigger box!" I laughed out loud.

The world had become a place of wonder and I felt like a child again. And that made me grateful. I looked up at the sky. "Thank you," I whispered.

The day was clear with not a cloud in the sky, the air warm on my skin as I continued down the path in the trees. It was probably too much to hope for that Linette would be there, but perhaps Pia and Dool, the fairies I'd met the day before, might be around. What had they been doing in the forest? How did they spend their days? Aside from the fact I knew they liked sweets and celebrated the full moon, I knew basically nothing about how they existed. Did they ever work or go to school? There was so much I wanted to know.

As I walked deeper into the trees, the smell of pine and lush undergrowth filled my nose. I gazed around, looking for movement in the branches sweeping high above. The only thing I noticed were a few birds and a squirrel leaping from the branch of a tall maple to another tree next to it. I came to the big granite rock and stepped off the path, my arms separating the low brush and ferns apart as I headed for the glade.

The sound of bells tinkling in a cascade of melody

caught my ear. Oh my God! That had to be them. It was the same sound from the night before, ringing each time that Linette finished speaking. With barely a thought to the bristles tugging at my shirt and arms, I bounded deeper into the forest. I stopped when I saw movement. A streak of electric blue darted up into the air and stopped. I could make out the figure of a young male, hovering above a patch of vibrant green grass. When his head turned, I recognized the face. It was Dool!

"Hello?" Waving my arm frantically, I forged ahead. "Dool? It's me, Maren. Wait up." I grinned when I saw him flit closer, landing at the edge of the clearing, staring at me. "I just came to say goodbye. My sister and I are leaving soon, but—"

Oof. The words were knocked out of me when I was shoved from behind, landing face first. A blinding pain spiked between my shoulder blades. Before I could even register that, my hands were yanked back. "Ow!" Something had my wrists in a vise like grip so tight it hurt! What the hell? My heart thudded fast against my ribcage. What the hell was happening?

"Wrap her up!" a voice commanded behind me. I knew that voice, and a chill swept through me. The owner of that voice wanted me dead last night and had been sent away for his opinions, and now he was back.

"Let me go, Tien!" I shouted. Which became a cry of fear as I felt thick tendrils begin to encircle me. An image of a giant python attack from some YouTube video sparked in my mind. I struggled to look and see what was happening, but my head along with the rest of my body, were completely immobilized as this ropey thing slithered up my legs, wrapping itself around them and coming up toward my head! "Make it stop!" I screamed.

This thing pulled tighter on me; now it slithered to my arms, whipping around them and lashing them together. Someone grabbed my hands and wrapped them in some sort of leather strips.

"Let me go, Tien!" I shouted. "Dool! Make him let me go!"

"I shall not, Maren," he replied. "Tien is right about your kind."

"Where's your sister?" Tien said. "We want her as well."

This was not good. I tried flexing my fingers, imagining that electrical charge shooting out and breaking whatever the hell was keeping me pinned and tied down, but whatever they wrapped my hands in kept me from moving them at all.

Tien spoke again. "Stop struggling. This will be less painful if you relax. There's no way you can break free of those vines."

"Vines? It's not a python?" Well, that was some kind of plus, wasn't it? I mean, snakes scared the shit out of me.

"It isn't my intention to harm you. But you must be silenced."

I scoffed. "That's not how you sounded last night, buster!" I tried rocking from side to side, but he was right. I couldn't move in the slightest. "Look, Tien, I told you! I'll never tell anyone about you! You have to believe that."

He barked a laugh. "A human asking us to believe them!" I heard others chuckle. It was more than just Tien and Dool here. "These creatures lie to one another as easily as they breathe, and this one expects our faith? Our faith in their word?" They all had a pretty good laugh at that.

He squatted down next to me. "We do not believe the word of your kind, Maren. As I told you, I shall not harm you, nor allow you to be harmed. But you shall spend the rest of your days in banishment from your kind."

"Then you may as well kill me now, Tien!" I spat. "Without my family, I'd rather be dead!"

His hand stroked the side of my face. "Such a childish thing to say, Human. Your loved ones will grieve at your absence, yes. And your only way to cope with that grief is your own death?" He breathed a sigh. "And you wonder why my kind fear you and your kind? Such a violent people you are." He shook his head. "No, when I assume the role of leader of my cloister, you'll be banished."

"Some kind of prison, huh? Fairies have prisons too, huh? You guys aren't so different from us if you need prisons."

"It's nothing like the hellish places your kind have created, foolish child. In fact it's a place of plenty and comfort. Unlike your kind, we do not revel in nor value cruelty." His voice took on an edge. "You are so cruel to each other in the names of your gods and your so-called justice!" he spat out. Taking a breath, he continued in an almost soothing voice. "You simply cannot leave, but instead will live the rest of your days there." He patted my cheek. "And you shall have your sister with you throughout it all."

"You make it sound like you're sending me to some kind of a resort."

"No. It's banishment. It's not cruel, but it is a harsh thing to do, nevertheless."

From behind me, I heard Dool speak. "What about her sister? Should we wait here until she shows up?"

My gut tightened hearing Dool's young voice. He was definitely on Tien's side in this, going against Linette's wishes. He was the one who lured me into this situation! Someone on my other side, gripped my arm, steadying me.

"We'll take this one to our sanctuary and return. I don't want any of Linette's allies to find her or us. Not yet. The other one will show up soon enough. When she does, we'll be here again."

"Will that Kara human heed you as easily as this one did, Dool?"

"I'm not sure. Maren can see our kind, but we're still unseen by her sister."

"Just as well. That may work in our favor."

"She also lacks the other powers Maren has. She's unable to levitate objects the way this one is able to do. I know that."

"Very well. When we have both of them captured, I'll

have a discussion with Linette then. It's time for her to hand over the leadership of the cloister to me." I felt the toe of his foot tap me. "Putting our safety in the hands of the likes of this one is perilous. Prepare her for our flight."

A black hood was thrust over my head, blocking everything. Great. I was trussed up like a damn turkey, my hands completely immobilized, and now I was blind. And this bag stank to high heaven with a sweet, sickly odor. I could barely keep from gagging as I drew breath.

My legs became heavier and heavier as I stood there listening. Even my arms felt warm and kind of numb. I panted softly, feeling woozy. I tried to blink eyelids that felt like they weighed a ton. The sack on my head. There was something in the fabric. Some drug. My eyes closed, and everything went black.

Twenty One

Kara

How bad is it, Kara? How sick are you?" Howie's eyes held my own.

All the air left my lungs and I stared back at him. Oh my God. He could smell my illness? Then I recalled reading an article about animals used to detect certain diseases. Of course Howie would smell it. Werewolves gotta werewolf, right?

I swallowed hard before I spoke, "It's bad."

"How bad?"

I said it out loud. For the first time. "Stage four pancreatic cancer." My voice cracked, but I held it together. Somehow, not saying it out loud, not saying it to anyone made it not real. Not really real or something. And now?

Now it was really real. Howie still held my eyes, but I could feel my chin do that thing.

You know that thing. That damn chin quiver? The last,

weak rampart of self-control? That if just one more thing happens, you're going to have a complete meltdown? I was right there on the edge, just by saying those damn words. All the terror I had felt and shoved down below my knees since the doctor gave me the news; all the sorrow at what I would miss in Josh's life, the…the dread of the pain that was to come. All of that was battering my heart and soul, and the only, only thing keeping me from flying apart into a million little pieces was my goddamned chin.

Which, by now, was vibrating like a hummingbird's wings.

Howie watched me, his face still as I began to breathe deeply through my nose. I sounded like a thoroughbred right after the Kentucky Derby. I sat there, inhaling so deeply I could feel the underwire in my bra cut into my ribs, exhaling like a goddamned blue whale. In and out, huff and blow, I sat there for a solid minute, if not two, while Howie just watched me.

I was so grateful to him. I'm sure that if he so much as touched me I would have crumbled into a pile of ashes.

I kept huffing until I realized my chin wasn't doing the mandible cha-cha-cha under my nose. I was able to press my lips together and hold them for a moment. I opened my mouth just a little to see if it was able to work without me falling apart and it seemed okay. I took a last deep breath.

"It's pretty much incurable at this stage. I got about five months, six if I'm lucky."

"Is there any hope?"

I sighed. "The doctors suggested radiation and chemo." My voice hitched in my throat when I continued, "But even with that, there's no guarantee of getting better. The only guarantee is that I'd be sicker than a dog—" My gaze flashed to him. "Sorry. I didn't mean to offend you but—"

He laughed. "I'm a wolf! None taken." He squeezed my shoulder. "Go on."

"So, I decided to take this trip with my sister, going cross country. It's always been my dream but I could never afford it." I huffed a sigh. "Funny thing is, the day I got the death sentence was also the day I won the Powerball lottery. I scoffed. "Hundreds of thousands of dollars! More than I'll ever spend. So here I am. I got my dream, right? And aside from one single tear tracing a line down my right cheek that I brushed away, I held it together.

Way to go Kara. Yay.

He came up to me, pulled me in and gave me a hug, rubbing my back, "I'm really sorry, Kara. I take it that Maren doesn't know this. Am I right?"

Now the waterworks started, brought on by the kindness of a stranger—a werewolf stranger at that, but they were manageable now somehow. I had a good boo-hoo before replying. "Please don't tell her. I want this trip to be the best one ever. A real memory to treasure. Besides which, she's got enough problems dealing with her divorce from an asshole husband."

"Ah, geez. That's rough for both of you." He continued holding me for a few moments, and then he eased away. "If anyone should ever meet the Fae, it should be you. You deserve some magic in your life, Kara."

I wiped the tears from my cheeks and mumbled, "That magic is certainly happening, Howie." I watched his eyes grow bigger as I spoke, but I didn't stop. His kindness opened more floodgates than my tears. Here was a sort of kindred spirit? "This all happened after we lost three days earlier this week. Three days that we have no memory of." I grasped his hand. "It sounds crazy, but I think we were abducted by aliens!"

He eased down onto the bench at the picnic table again. "From what I've read, you wouldn't be the first person to claim to be abducted. It changes them. But this is the first I've heard of anyone getting paranormal powers. But, hey! I'm just an old werewolf. What would I know?"

"Have you...ever met any?"

"What? Are you crazy? No!"

We both stared at each other. Finally, I started to laugh.

"Sure. Fairies, auras, werewolves, and vampires are all perfectly normal. But aliens? Ohhhh noooo! That's crazy!"

He let out a full-bellied laugh and pointed at me. "You got it!"

"Thanks for talking to me, Howie. You've been kind to me today. Aside from my doctors, you're the only one I've told about the cancer." The knot of that diagnosis buried deep in my chest, loosened a bit. It felt good, like slipping into a hot tub and feeling your muscles melt, just being able to talk to someone about it.

Howie touched the fairy ring on my finger. "I don't think I'm the first person to know this about you, Kara. That ring is super special. It's from the hawthorn tree, the highest element of protection there is. That tree is revered by the Fae. He tapped the ring again. The Fae don't give these out very often, you know. In fact, I think you're the first non-Fae I know who has one."

"Really? Why did she, then? I mean, I can understand her wanting to suck up to Maren or whatever—she's got all kinds of powers. But me?"

"You'll have to ask her that yourself. Linette sees something in you, that's for sure. Something that I suspect goes past the cancer." He tapped the ring on my finger again. "Even so, wearing this sure as shootin' isn't going to hurt.   That's   for   a   fact."

"You think it can heal me?"

"I don't know a damn thing about Fae medicine. But I know that having a hawthorn ring's a big deal."

My mouth fell, and I felt a ray of hope lighten my chest. But before I could say another word, Howie placed my hand in my lap, murmuring, "I don't know if it will work, Kara. But a Fae ring is powerful."

He squeezed my hand. "Keep the faith, girl, and I'll do the same."

Twenty Two

Kara

For the next half hour, Howie helped me unhook the lines and prep my rig for departure. When we finished, Laura joined us, carrying a tray of sandwiches and colas.

"Supper got derailed, but at least we can have lunch before you gals head out." She looked sheepish as she set the food on the wooden picnic table. "Sorry we were so sharp with you last night, Kara."

Howie finished drying his hands and then wandered over to his wife. "They know everything, Laura. You were right that there was something different about them. They met Linette last night. Maren is over in the clearing the Fae love so much in these parts." He chuckled. "She's gone to say goodbye to them."

Laura also laughed lightly. "So they gave them each a hawthorn ring?" she asked as she looked over at my hand.

When Howie nodded, she chuckled.

"What's the joke?" I asked.

Laura sat back in her chair, folding her hands under her bosom. "It's a rare thing for the Fae folk to give a non-Fae a hawthorn ring. It means that they're bound to you for all your days." She shook her head slowly. "The Fae folk don't do goodbyes. They do a 'till we meet again' sort of thing. Aaaand"—she pointed at my ring—"with that ring you'll be guaranteed that you will see the Fae again. Especially you two women." She looked over at Howie. "Don't you agree, dear?"

He nodded. "Yup. Any Fae folk in any cloister will want to see and probably meet these gals."

I peered at them both. "Why?"

Howie answered, "Because, darlin', the Fae have never given the hawthorn to a human. Not in thousands and thousands of years. They've kept humans at arm's length for ages and ages. Y'see, there was some kind of war or something that a lot of the Fae died in. They separated themselves from the human race ever since."

"The Great Reaping," I said. "Tien had mentioned it last night when we were at the Moon Dance."

Laura's eyes got misty. "Yes, that's what they call it. It was before my time, but the stories I've heard..." She gave her head a small shake. "I doubt very much Tien was happy to meet you."

I snorted. "That's putting it mildly. He was pissed off as hell."

"Yeah, that makes sense. He's the last of his line because of it. Lost his entire family in it."

"Oh!" I sat back in my chair. I don't give a damn how many years ago that "Great Reaping" was. I could understand Tien's antipathy toward Maren and I now. Despite the fact it was ages and ages before my time...grief is a life sentence.

I fingered the ring on my hand. "Maybe I should give it back?"

Howie shook his head. "Tien's but one of the cloister, despite his position as Linette's scion. I think she's decided after meeting the two of you that a healing has to take place. Linette is very wise, Kara. And with the council of Sebille at her side, she did not gift you those rings lightly." He leaned in. "So don't think of regifting them, okay?" he added with a cackle. "That would be rude!"

As. If!

"Yeah, so there's really no 'goodbye' when it comes to the Fae," Howie said. He turned to Laura and laughed. "Guess who else these two met, hon."

"Who?"

He chuckled, shaking his head. "They also met Mike and I bet he wishes they hadn't. Maren gave him what for, when she saw what he is."

"He was drunk again, wasn't he?" Laura rolled her eyes before setting the napkins and drinks out. "That old fool. He's probably sleeping it off."

I looked over their shoulders hoping to see Maren walking back, but there was no sign of her. I pulled my cell phone out to check the time. It was ten minutes past one o'clock. "She said she'd be back at one."

I tapped the icon to call her cell phone. "I'll let her know you brought lunch over! That was sweet of you, Laura."

"No problem. I'd like to try to make it up to you after what happened at dinner." The older woman took a seat at the picnic table as I stood there with the phone to my ear.

Almost immediately I heard musical notes—the Beatle song "Magical Mystery Tour," my ringtone, the one I'd loaded on her phone, signaling it was me calling. It came from inside the rig. Damn it! She'd been so excited about visiting the Fae that she forgot to take her phone with her.

I clicked the phone off and shrugged, looking over at the elderly couple. Howie paused in the midst of what he was saying to Laura and shot me a questioning look.

"She forgot her phone, I guess. I'll give her fifteen more minutes and then I'll go find her. We might as well go ahead and eat. She'll probably be back any minute. Maren is usually pretty punctual." I directed my words at Laura but found her gaze fixed on the road running through the campground.

I glanced around and saw Boler Guy walking toward his camper carrying a plastic bag with the camp's logo on it. He gave us a nod. "Nice day! Ran out of milk." He held up the bag and then stepped over to his camper, pausing to unlock the door to go inside. Was the woman I'd seen him with in there too? Funny, since that first night and then seeing them together on the beach, I hadn't seen her at all.

Turning back to Howie and Laura, I murmured, "Boler Guy doesn't look any worse for wear after the late night. The antics with Mike woke him up as well. I can't say I'll miss being parked next to him. He's kind of a looky-loo, gawking at us all the time. There are some odd people who do this RVing thing." I helped myself to a chicken sandwich from the plate of assorted meat.

"Oh, you'll find all kinds of interesting people in your travels, Kara." Laura reached across the table and her finger brushed the Fae ring. Her chocolate-colored eyes crinkled at the corners in a warm smile. "And you already have. Never take that ring off. Especially now. The Fae are gifted healers." The intensity of her gaze let me know that she knew about my health.

"I'll always wear it, don't worry. I'm still kind of in a daze after meeting them. It was amazing." I leaned closer to her and Howie. "Linette said that there are more beings in her realm. She mentioned sprites and witches. I know about you guys, of course, and Mike, but when Tien asked her to honor some kind of Guild, she clammed up. So, how many other kinds are there? Is there a Bigfoot? Mermaids?"

Laura paused in the midst of reaching for a drink. "Sprites and witches...hmmm, been a long time since I've crossed paths with those people."

I noticed that Laura didn't answer my question, tactfully dodging it. "I can understand Tien a little better with what you guys just told me; he really, really didn't like our meeting the Fae. He actually suggested kidnapping us to ensure that we could never reveal anything about them. Thank goodness Sebille weighed in, agreeing with Linette."

As soon as the words were out of my mouth, that feeling of dread from earlier washed through me again. I glanced at my phone again. It was one thirty! I should never have let Maren go to that glade to meet the fairies, not alone! Talk about stupid things to do! She had made short work of Mike but what about Tien? Who knew what powers he had, besides being able to fly?

I set the can of Coke down and stood up. "I should go find her. Maren promised to be back at one and she's thirty minutes late! I don't like this. How do I know that Tien didn't come back to make good on his threat?"

Howie gulped his sandwich down and got to his feet. "I'm coming with you. I may be old as dirt, but my sniffer's still pretty good. Just in case she wandered off and lost track of time. It wouldn't be the first time that a person lost their sense of time around the Fae. They're kind of famous for stuff like that."

When I stood, I noticed Boler Guy look over from where he sat in a camp chair, pretending to read a novel. Was he trying to eavesdrop? What was with him? He was the nosiest guy I'd ever met!

Howie patted my shoulder as we left the campsite. "I thought my neighbors back in Wesley were busybodies. They ain't got nothing on that guy. Either that or he's taken a shine to you, Kara. Maybe that's it."

"I don't think so." Casting a scowl at Boler Guy, I had no patience for him and his gawking. Tempting as it was to flip him the bird, I turned back to Howie. "He's a busybody. But y'know…if he knew what we were up to, going to interrupt my sister's meeting with the fairies, he'd really be ogling us!" The smile fell from my lips. "I'm going to give her proper shit for worrying me like this."

As I led the way from the roadway to step onto the path,

Tien's words kept pinging around in my head, and I broke into a sprint, heading for the big old maple tree where we'd seen the Fae yesterday. There was no sign of Maren, only the tree and dappled sunlight highlighting the tangled underbrush and the big rock.

Brushing aside the thin branches of saplings, I plunged deeper into the forest. "Maren! Where are you?" With my heart hammering fast, I peered about, hoping to catch sight of her. Behind and to my left, Howie also called to her. That feeling of unease curled like a viper in my gut.

"Linette? Sebille? Maren! Anyone! Where the hell are you, Maren?" My breath came in fast pants. Remembering the ring and what Linette had said, I rolled it around on my finger. "No more than a heartbeat away." Well, if that was the case, they would have broken the sound barrier getting here, judging by how fast my heart was racing!

Howie bent lower, sniffing around the clearing. "She was definitely here. I picked up her scent on the path and coming through the trees, but it's strongest in this circle."

Much as I wanted to believe that she was close, judging by his nose, I had to face facts. "That could be from last night! This is where we were for their Moon Dance. You probably smell my presence here as well."

His mouth pulled to the side. "I'm not sure about that; this scent is really fresh. But as I said earlier, she could be with them and simply lost track of time. Or, maybe they weren't here, so she gave up and went to the beach for one last look at the ocean. We can't panic, Kara. That's not helping anyone."

"Where would the Fae be, Howie? They were here last night. Linette promised to help us if we called to her. Well, I'm calling now and there's no Linette or Maren." My voice cracked a little at my last words, and I could feel tears stinging the backs of my eyes.

Howie patted my shoulder when he stepped over to me. "We'll find her. Give me your phone so I can add my number to it. I'll check the beach, and if she's there, I'll call you."

I handed him my phone and wandered around the rim of the glade, staring hard through the trees and underbrush. I could see only the odd butterfly or bird moving through the branches and canopy. Where was she?

Despite what Howie said about losing track of time with the Fae, I couldn't see Maren doing that. She was a woman who considered herself late if she showed up to an appointment five minutes early.

"Here you go, Kara."

I strode over to take my phone from Howie. "Call me even if you don't see her when you get to the beach. I'll keep looking in these woods. I never should have let her go off on her own. This is my fault."

"Take it easy on yourself. Maren will turn up even if it's tomorrow or next week. I'd take you to the home of the Fae if I knew where it was. We may be members of the same Guild, but the Fae keep to themselves mostly—well, them and the sprites." With that, he hurried back through the trees, heading to the path.

Brambles from the low bushes tore at my legs when I left the clearing, going deeper into the wooded area. I went so far that the trees thinned out, and I could see glimpses of the ocean and the highway. There was no sign of her! I headed in the other direction, toward the campground. "Maren! Where the hell are you?"

Images of that Tien fairy snatching my sister up and taking her somewhere I'd never find flitted through my head as I scrambled fast through the trees. But if he was so worried that we'd tell someone about seeing the Fae, wouldn't he need to snatch me as well. Just let him try! I'd clip his wings and make him wish he was never born.

When the phone beeped, I almost broke a finger fishing it out of my pocket. "Did you find her?"

"Sorry, Kara. She's not down here. Not even a whiff of her scent. I'm on my way back. Nothing on your end, I take it?" Howie didn't even try to hide the disappointment in his voice. "I hate to say it, but it looks like you're going to be staying another night until she comes back."

"If she comes back. And why didn't Linette or the Fae show up when I called them? They made it sound like they would show up if we needed them. Won't you give it a try, Howie? You're part of some Guild with them. Don't they have to come if you call a meeting?" I had no idea how that worked, but for sure my pleas had gone unanswered. Surely Howie could get them here.

I'd walked so far into the woods that I had circled back to the campground. I could see our truck and RV as well as Boler Guy's egg-shaped rig. Hey! That guy was always watching! Maybe he'd seen something when he'd been out buying stuff at the camp's store. It was a long shot, but at this point I was willing to try anything. Even talking to that jerk.

I stepped out of the trees and underbrush and marched across the patch of grass to his campsite. The Boler obstructed my view of his table and awning, but when I rounded it, I gasped seeing him standing there peering into the wooded area. What the hell?

Twenty Three

Kara

W ho are you? Why are you always staring at us?" It popped out of my mouth before I knew it. Giving myself a shake, I walked closer to him. "Never mind." There were way more important things to ask him than why he was such a busybody.

He turned slowly, his thumbs hooked into the back pockets of baggy, clam digger pants. In the green T-shirt and sloppy flip-flops, one thing was clear about Boler Guy. He was no slave to fashion. He had the oddest eye color— like two chips of gold. Not light brown, not yellow either. He had golden eyes. And he watched me silently as I approached him.

"Look, I'm looking for my sister. She left our campsite about two hours ago. When you were out at the store, did you see her? I thought she might be on the path leading to the beach but there's no sign of her."

As the words tumbled out of my mouth, I couldn't help but wonder where the woman was he'd been arguing with the first night? I hadn't seen her at all since I saw the two of them on the beach. And now Maren was missing. Instead of blaming Tien or even that drunken vampire, maybe Boler Guy had something to do with it? Is that why he was always watching us? What is he, some kind of government agent or something?

"She's missing? I haven't seen her since last night when you and that drunken idiot woke me up." His voice was really deep; I could almost feel it. He tilted his head at me. "I always have a hard time getting back to sleep." The look he shot me was like it was my fault Mike had been staggering around looking for smokes or a drinking partner.

"Sucks to be you, but my sister is missing!" I took a deep breath forcing myself to calm down. Getting into a pissing match wasn't helping. "What about your wife or girlfriend? Is she inside? Has she been out and maybe seen Maren? Can I talk to her?"

His eyebrows bunched as he looked at me. "Girlfriend?" Then his head fell back and he smiled. "You must mean Anjou. She's certainly not a girlfriend or mate. She departed yesterday."

"Anjou? That's an unusual name. Is she Middle Eastern or something?"

"Middle Eastern?" He blinked at me a couple of times, looking confused. "Oh! You're asking if she's from another country!" he finally said. He waved his hand. "Doesn't matter." He pointed to his chest. "I am called Rax."

"Rax? Is that your name?" Sounded more like a nickname to me.

"It is what I am called, yes."

I waved my hands in the air. "Okay, whatever! I'm Kara and my sister, Maren, is missing! Have you seen her?" I looked past him to my campsite where Laura and Howie were talking as they cleared up the lunch things. Argh! Everybody was carrying on like normal even though Maren had gone missing, possibly abducted! Crap! What the hell was I going to do?

"Oh, great." Rax muttered as his gaze flitted over to me. "Don't look now but that drunk from last night is coming down the road. Maybe he knows where your sister is."

I turned and saw the gangly drunk on a bicycle now, lifting his hand in a wave. Immediately the bike lurched to the left, and he almost ended up running into a tree before correcting course.

He grinned, showing a full set of teeth framed by deep lines at the corners of his mouth. "Good morning, or I suppose afternoon is more accurate." When he caught sight of Howie and Laura, he added, "Guess I missed lunch. Hey, Howie. Laura."

Seeing the vampire again after he'd accosted me, just made my blood boil even more. I left Rax and strode over to the bike, bringing his travels up short. "Have you seen my sister? You know, she's about five-four, brunette? The one who tossed your drunken ass across the road last night? She's been missing for the last couple of hours. What do you know about it?"

His head reared back while his bloodshot eyes popped wide at now being the one confronted. Straddling the bike, his hands rose, showing pale, yellowish palms. "I don't know anything about that bitch. I could hardly crawl out of bed this morning after what she did to me."

Howie stepped between us. "Mike! No need for name calling. That's not necessary or appropriate. Have you seen her sister or not?"

"I just got up! No, I haven't seen her. Although when I do—"

"You'll what?" I glared at Mike. "For two cents I'd report you to the main office and get you thrown out of this campground. You practically attacked me last night, you...you—"

"And woke me up!" Rax called over.

"Enough!" Laura practically bellowed. "It' time to

parley." She shot a smile at Rax. "Not you, son, nor Kara either." She pointed at me. "You keep an eye out for Maren." She gave a pointed look at Mike. "You'll join us in our rig. Now."

Parley. That's the term Linette had used the night before when she chastised Tien. Was it possible that these supernatural beings were going to call for a meeting with the Fae to find out what had happened to Maren?

Laura cast a gentle smile over at me. "You need to stay at your site, Kara. Just in case Maren returns. We'll see you in an hour or so."

As Mike passed by me, he mouthed "Bitch," making sure he was out of Howie and Laura's line of sight. I flipped the bird at him before heading back to my rig.

There was nothing I could do now but stay and wait for Maren to return or Laura to get some answers out of Linette. I rolled the ring the Fae leader had given me. Fat lot of good that ring was doing. It was as empty as her promise to be at our side in a heartbeat.

What made everything worse was that this was my fault. If I only hadn't let Maren go alone to see the Fae earlier. If I hadn't talked her into coming on this trip, she'd be safe.

At the touch on my arm, I spun around. Great. Boler Guy. My hackles rose. "What!" I snapped at him.

His eyes went as wide as they could, and he took a step back. I'd been uncomfortable with this guy from the day I first set eyes on him, but seeing him be startled like that felt like payback. He stood there openmouthed, staring at me.

"What the hell do you want?" I spat out.

"I...I would care to assist you."

"Assist me?"

"Yes." He pointed at Laura and Howie's rig. "Your elder instructed you to remain here. I can go and search for your loved one."

My elder? What the hell was with this guy? "You don't get out much, do you?" I asked without thinking.

He looked baffled now. "Are we not out right now?" he

189

said, looking around us. "We're not aboard..." He gestured at his Boler and my Phoenix.

Okay, the guy's on some autism spectrum or something. Maybe brain damage? He was as odd as his oddball nickname. Rax. Probably got hit in the head with a cue ball as a child or something.

I turned to my rig, stepping up, and swinging the door open. "How about you mind your own business, huh?" Since this clown showed up, he'd been totally preoccupied with Maren and me.

"Please, Kara. Abide here. I'll search for your sister. All will be well."

I spun around at him. "What did you say?" I came off the step, letting the rig's door slam like an exclamation mark. "What the hell did you just say?"

"I said 'Please, Kara. Abide here. I'll search for your sister. All will be well.'"

All will be well. I don't know why, but that phrase struck a chord in me. It was like when I'd be walking down the street, and something kind of hit me—a snippet of music, or maybe a scent from a perfume shop. It could just yank me completely out of whatever mindset I was in.

Normally it's scents. The slightest sniff of the right scent can transport me a million miles away to my past in a split second. One minute I'm traipsing down a promenade at that big mall in Syracuse, Destiny USA, and the next second I'm remembering my first time on a rollercoaster at Six Flags.

Well, this guy's phrase did pretty much the same thing to me:All will be well. It was such a statement of hope. Hope bloomed in my heart so quickly, it almost scared me.

He watched me with those golden eyes as I stepped up to him. "You mean that?" I said, my voice tinny.

He nodded solemnly, never taking his eyes from mine. "All will be well." He pointed at my rig. "You must abide here, per the elder's instructions. I shall go search."

I just nodded dumbly, then turned and went up and into my rig, letting the door close softly behind me.

Rax remained outside, watching me for a moment, then turned and began to jog toward the woods.

I had to sit down. What the hell just happened to me? I didn't know.

But I wasn't scared. And that unnerved me. I ought to be scared. Some weird guy says a phrase to me during a crisis and it makes me feel fine. Rax spoke with no accent at all, but it was obvious English was not his first language.

Strange things were happening. I laughed out loud. "Ya think!" Geezus! Understatement of the year!

But still…I wasn't as scared as I had been. Who the hell is this guy?

I took a deep breath. I'd abide. For a while.

"All will be well," I said.

Twenty Four

Kara

I almost jumped out of my skin when Maren's cell phone went off on the dining table. I grabbed it and looked at the screen, only to see it was just a text message from Maren's lawyer. I read its contents, that ended with a plea from the guy to set up a video call with him as soon as possible.

I rolled my eyes at her lawyer's message. Good luck with setting up that video call. Maren's divorce and Weasel Wayne could wait! I had to find my sister.

Before I set the phone down again, I saw that there were two missed calls from Maren's daughter, Amy. Crap! We could put the lawyer off for another day, but I wasn't sure about Amy. She and her husband were expecting us the day after tomorrow. Should I call her back or pretend that I— actually Maren and me—didn't notice her calls? Or try to spin it that Maren's phone was accidentally turned off or the battery drained. No way did I want to return Amy's call, not with her mother missing.

Howie's words resounded in my head; about time can go

bonkers when you were with the Fae. I'd call her tomorrow. Really, what could I tell her? That her mother had wanted to say goodbye to the fairies we'd partied with the night before? Yeah. That would be totally reassuring, and she would definitely not think I was whacko. As. If.

Damn! I slipped Maren's phone in my other pocket before stepping outside again. Waiting was never my strong suit; I gave my best shot at abiding too. I bit the hangnail on my thumb as I strode over to look down the road, hoping this was all a bad dream and she'd be ambling back. But only the hard-packed dirt road showed between rows of campers.

I wandered over to Howie's rig and stood outside the door trying to catch whatever was being said during their so-called "parley." But aside from low rumbling broken by Laura's higher-pitched murmur, I couldn't make anything out.

Feeling the vibration of my cell phone against my thigh, I reached for it as I darted back to the road. The ringtone was just starting when I grabbed it and hit the answer icon. Too late. I saw that it was Amy, now calling me! I winced and took a deep breath before holding it to my ear. Shit!

"Hello?"

"Aunt Kara! I hope I'm not catching you navigating some freeway, but when Mom never returned my calls, I got worried. Where are you guys?"

I hesitated, and in that moment the shrieking of an infant blared in the phone. "Is that Kirsten? Oh my goodness! Your mother and I can't wait to see her." Okay, I was stalling, trying to figure out what to say about Maren.

Amy cooed to the baby before she gushed, "I can't wait for that either. Normally Kirsten is an angel, but whenever I pick up the phone, she cries. With Harry back at work now, to be honest, I was hoping you and Mom would spell me for a while, you know? This motherhood schtick has a downside."

Downside? Honey, you ain't seen nothin' yet!

"Is Mom there? Can you put her on for a minute?"

"We're still at Virginia Beach, Amy. We haven't left yet. Your Mom went for a walk a little while ago and forgot her phone. She's still at the beach, I'm afraid." Not a total lie. Maren did forget her phone in the camper.

Hearing the snick of a door opening, I spun around to peer at Howie's rig. The door stayed open for a few moments before closing with a bang. What the hell were they doing? All the while I watched, Amy continued talking.

"At the Potomac? When I looked at the footage of that little boy rising in the air and landing on that rock, I saw Mom standing on the shore. I recorded it and watched it quite a few times. Even Dad saw Mom there! He called and told me! Are you going to call them? You were there."

Call them? Call who? The Tonight Show? The FBI? Not on a bet! My mouth fell open and I froze as her words sank in. She'd seen the rescue of little Timmy and had also seen Maren there. "Yeah. We were there. It was pretty amazing what happened. Unbelievable, but thank God that boy was rescued."

"So, have you contacted the news stations? They already interviewed half a dozen witnesses. I'm surprised that you didn't see it on TV, Aunt Kara! You need to call them and tell them what you saw. They're calling it a miracle." Her voice dropped. "One of the witnesses said that they saw Mom doing something with her hands. They think that Mom threw the kid some kind of rope or something. There's a video on BNN that shows Mom standing at the shore pointing and gesturing at the kid as he floated through the air."

Oh super shit.

Amy's voice dropped low. "Did Mom have something to do with all that? There's even a Twitter trend with a screenshot of that video! It's #angelofthepotomac! And wow, is it trending!"

Oh shit. Everything that Maren feared was coming true. The rescue was all over the news and now they were looking for us. Well, not us specifically since they didn't know our names.

Shit. Yet Amy and even Weasel Wayne knew it was us!

I had to come up with something.

"Oh, thaaat! Yeah, I saw that video! I've been teasing the snot out of your mom all day!" I faked a laugh.

"Wha—"

"She didn't even notice that the kid was in the water!" I laughed again. "She was being swarmed by a bunch of sand flies or something! Are you serious that people think you mother did something to save that kid? Come on!"

"Yeah, well, wha—"

"There were probably Navy Seals in the river or something and one of them shoved the kid out of harm's way from underwater!" It was good to see that my bullshitting skills were still sharp with all that was going on.

"Navy Seals?" Amy's voice got small. "No miracle? Mom didn't do something?"

"Oh, she did something, all right! I think she must have massacred about a hundred of those fleas!"

"Oh."

Total deflation accomplished. I felt like someone in a bomb squad that just kept something from blowing up. Now for the distraction. "I'll tell Maren you phoned as soon as she gets back. We'd love to look after your baby for you! Believe me, I know you could sure use the break! Guess what! Your mother even volunteered to drive the rig, if you can believe it."

"Oh…that's…great." She sighed. "Gee, Aunt Kara, I really thought there was something with Mom at the Potomac…"

"No, just plain old Maren. Sorry."

She let out another sigh. "Frankly, I'm surprised you talked her into going on this trip at all. Especially with all this crap she and Dad are going through. But y'know, maybe getting away from Dad for a while will bring both of them to their senses. Hopefully, they'll forget this nonsense and get back together."

Obviously, Maren hadn't told her about Wayne screwing around before. But divorce is hard on any child of the marriage, no matter what their age would be when the parents split up. I felt bad for her, but I also had to give her a reality check.

"Listen, Amy, your parents are negotiating the terms of the divorce. This trip isn't a respite so when it's over she'll go back to your father. That isn't happening." I tried to soften my words, but I had to get the point across. And I hadn't mentioned Wayne shacking up with his employee. Maren should have leveled with her daughter about all that. It wasn't my place to tell her.

"We'll see. I can't imagine Mom living on her own. She helps with the renovations, but it's Dad who finds the properties and negotiates the deals." Exasperation dripped from her voice. "Will you ask her to call me when she gets back from the beach? I guess you really don't need to call any TV stations."

"The story will disappear in a day or so, Amy. Sorry that there's no magic stuff for you and Twitter. I'll tell her you called. Kiss that baby for us! Can't wait to see you and her." I ended the call. Damn! She'd be expecting Maren to call back.

I couldn't think about that right now! Maren was missing, and whatever was happening at that so-called parley was taking way too much time. After glancing down the road for any sign of Maren, I marched over to the door of Howie's rig.

Despite NOT being invited, this meeting was about my sister! Who the hell did they think they were? Well, maybe not exactly "who" but more of a "what," if you're a vampire and werewolf.

Argh! Who gives a damn! They were parleying about me and my sister! I had every damn reason to be in that room, whether or not I was magical. They had some nerve! I flung open the door and stomped inside.

Twenty Five

Kara

Linette was talking: "Pia and Dool are..." She went silent, and I could feel everyone else staring at me. "Oh dear, a human's here!" an effeminate, young voice squeaked. "She shouldn't be here, right, Mom?"

When I entered, my eyes opened wider hearing Linette ask for quiet. A glance around the living and kitchen area of the rig showed Howie in the bedroom doorway with Laura pressed into his side. Mike sat at the table with his arms close to his body, making himself even thinner, but there was all this empty space next to him.

And then it hit me in a flash. The werewolves and Mike appeared crammed in because the Fae were there! They'd come to the parley.

"Linette, where is my sister?" I looked around at the vacant spots, unsure where she was parked. "Why didn't you come when I called you earlier? Isn't this ring supposed to help with that?" My jaw clenched tight as I waited for her reply.

But it wasn't Linette who answered. Sebille's smoky voice filled the room. "Our efforts were better served in finding Tien and the cadre of Fae who left with him. When we find Tien, we'll find your sister."

Linette added, "I'm worried about you, Kara. For Tien to kidnap Maren, going against my will so directly, shows how determined he is. He'll stop at nothing to ensure both you and Maren keep our existence secret. By any means necessary. In the meantime, he's convinced half of the cloister that this is necessary."

Sebille interrupted, "He's put himself in a position to break away and start his own cloister, but I suspect his real motive is to usurp the existing one. With you and Maren showing up, he's found an inciting incident to challenge Linette's authority."

None of this was reassuring. Not. In. The. Least. Maren and I had stumbled into some kind of power struggle within the Fae. Call me callous, but their internal politics weren't my concern, Maren's well-being was.

"Do you have any idea where he could be? Is he even in the area anymore? I mean he can fly, so maybe he's in California or Nebraska or—"

"My point exactly!" Mike stood up, "This doesn't have anything to do with my kind. "It's a Fae issue. But if Tien was smart, he'd ditch that bitch before she destroys him. She's not the innocent that you all make her out to be."

I jerked back seeing Mike rise in the air and land with a thud on the bench seat.

An unknown voice snarled, "Leave it to the weaselly vampire to turn tail and run. Well, not this time, Mike. The last I heard, you are still part of the Guild, so you have a responsibility to all of us."

Once more, Mike deflated, rubbing his neck and casting narrow looks at something above him. "Take it easy, you Fae brute. Honestly, that witch can take care of herself.

Take it from me."

"Enough squabbling!" Sebille ordered. "Unfortunately, we don't have any idea where Tien might be hiding. And we've looked, believe me."

Howie murmured, "That's another thing the Fae are good at—hiding."

Linette spoke, "If you're right, Sebille, that Tien wants to take over leadership of my colony, then he has to wage an attack. That's the only way that we are ever going to find him or Maren."

A solemn voice hushed the room. "For Tien to become leader, you must die, Linette. That can't happen, not for a good, long while. I'd see Tien buried in the clay before he can harm one hair on Linette's head. I hope we get this human back safely, but if it comes to Linette or her..."

"It won't come to that, Ellowen." Linette's voice broke when she continued, "I appreciate the loyalty of my brethren, the sprites. You have always had my back despite our differences."

Oh my God! Sprites? But immediately the sprite's words filled my head. Linette must die for Tien to rule. If that happened, Maren and I were as good as dead too. We'd never see our families or friends again.

Once again, the vampire couldn't keep his mouth shut. "Not to sound like a broken record, gang, but this Maren witch can take care of herself. I fully expect to get the worst of any encounter with her! She hurled me across the road like I was an empty wine bottle." Mike frowned, his gaze skimming across the room. "Have you even met her? Don't take my word for it, ask her sister! She was there!"

Mike was the only one who gave me a glimmer of hope when he said that. But I had to know more. "She's getting stronger in her levitation. But is it enough to fight off a Fae like Tien? I mean, you guys fly, and you're good at hiding, but can you fight? Could Maren blast Tien out of the air and then escape? What powers do the Fae have?"

"I think that question is one for all of us." Laura had

been staring at the floor, but now she raised her head to address each of the Guild. "Kara and Maren are new to this. They didn't know any of us existed until yesterday. There are stories and legends, but it's time she knew the truth of it. Howie has explained to her the nature and power of the werewolf, but what about the rest of you?"

The room went still, and I held my breath.

Twenty Six

Kara

S ince it is my kind who kidnapped your sister, it is
only right that I begin." Linette's voice was gentle,
caressing the otherwise silent room.

"We don't like to call our abilities 'powers,' dear Kara.
We're natural beings of this beautiful planet as much as you
or any other creature or being that exists here. Having said
that, yes, we have natural abilities, and also others that some
of us have worked to foster."

Natural, schmatural. Linette could freaking fly without a
jet pack! But I kept my mouth shut rather than argue over a
word's meaning.

"We are able to fly with a greater agility than any bird.
We can hover gently and almost as silently as a
hummingbird and then dart as quick as a sparrow. We're
very long lived—"

"How old are you?" I blurted out.

There was a pause before Linette replied, "It's not polite to ask someone their age, my child. For now, let's just say the young Pia and Dool could have watched your great-grandparents be born."

"Yeah, well, you're not immortal like me!" Mike piped up, grinning.

Linette replied with a gentle rebuke. "Nor do my kind wish to ever be, dear Michael. Your blessing's also a curse at times, is it not? Your kind live a solitary existence, no?"

Laura also chided Mike. "Let her finish, friend."

He gave a short wave toward where Linette was sitting. "Just sayin'…"

"We can communicate telepathically as easily as speaking," Linette continued. "But it is our love…no, our veneration of song that has preserved our ability to speak. Having a mind powerful enough to project thought has led some of our kind to deepen and strengthen their mental abilities. Tien, for example, is also able to move objects with but a thought as your sister can."

Sebille spoke. "We began as a people in the forests, and thus, our love of the natural world is ancient beyond years."

Linette added, "As is our mastery of the healing arts, beloved Councilor. We are grateful for the guidance you give."

Howie added, "I know you aren't able to see Linette and the Fae, but their beauty is renowned among all of the Guild, Kara. I'm not sure how that's gonna help you, but I wanted to put it out there."

"Hmmph," Laura muttered, next to him, and crossed her arms. "Thanks a lot!" she added. "You sure know how to make a girl feel special!"

Yeah, Howie will pay for that faux pas, fer shure.

A new voice, again from someone I couldn't see, spoke up. "Yes, yes, the Fae are just all manner of wonderful, aren't they?"

Who was this being? Holding my hand up, I snapped. "Hang on! Who, or should I say what are you? As Howie said, I'm not able to see beings who exist in your world. I think I have a right to know who all is here." I peered into the space where the voice had originated but, of course, only the stove showed.

Linette was the one who answered. "My apologies for not making the presence of our cousins known. It's been a difficult morning." After a beat, her voice became more formal: "I'd like to present Ellowen, Plenipotentiary Of The Sprites."

"Ellowen's title is bigger than she is," Mike scoffed. "I'm not sure how much good the sprite will be in defeating Tien and his crew. Maybe she can annoy him into surrendering that witch."

"Witch?" I'd had about enough of Mike slagging my sister when he was the one who started the scuffle last night.

I took a step across the floor, ready to get in his face and tell him off, but before I could, his face twisted, with eyes wide and mouth dropping lower.

Achoo! The bellowing sneeze coming out of him almost blew the door open. It was immediately followed by a series of more explosive sneezes. He tried to say something but it came out as a sneeze as he got to his feet, staggering to the bathroom.

"As annoying as pixie dust, Mike? Next time you insult me, it won't just be dust blown up your nose. I know where there's some poisonous toadstool dripping with spores." Ellowen followed this with a giggle when the bathroom door slammed shut. "We should carry on without him. He's gonna be in there a while."

There was a hint of laughter in Linette's voice when she spoke: "As you can see, Kara, sprites may be small as hummingbirds but they aren't without power. They're fast, and their knowledge of wood lore surpasses that of the Fae folk."

"You're darn right!" Ellowen said. "From magic mushrooms to sneezing spores, from pain relief to deadly poisons, our knowledge is also renowned!"

Howie spoke up. "She's bowing to you, Kara." He leaned forward and put out his hand, palm up. "Let my palm support you, oh, Ellowen." I watched his eyes as they tracked across the room to his hand. "There, more comfortable?"

"Always the gentleman, Howie," came the voice from his hand.

I bowed at the waist. "Pleased to meet you," I said, and decided to lay it on a little thick. "This mortal human is honored to be in all of your presences." Well, to be honest, it wasn't that much of a stretch. "I'm deeply grateful for any help you can give in rescuing my sister."

The door to the bathroom banged open. "Me too? You grateful to me too?" Mike asked, holding a wad of tissue to his nose.

I looked over at him. "You really, really give a lousy first impression, you know."

He shrugged, and Laura said, "That's true, but Mike and his kind are loyal and valiant when called up by their friends." She tilted her head toward where Ellowen was perched on Howie's palm. "You need to apologize, Mike."

He eyed Howie's outstretched hand. "Sorry, Ellowen...my bad."

"Once again, apology accepted, Vampire."

"Tell her the rest, Ellowen," Howie said in a low voice.

"Very well. Vampires and sprites have been teasing and vexing one another for ages. It's great sport between our two races."

"You sound like you're Irish," I snickered. "Hate-love's a big thing with them too!"

"Hate-love?" Ellowen asked. "I've not heard that term before!"

"The Irish and Scots are known for it," I replied. "Did you not know that?"

"No! But I love the term!" she said. "I hate-love you, Michael. With all my heart!" she added brightly.

"And I you, fair Ellowen! With all my entrails!" he

replied with a grinning nod.

Could this get any weirder?

Sebille's voice rose. Sebille ended the smiles. "Left on their own, Fae and sprites are immortal, Kara, as are the vampires. But we can be killed if our heart or head is removed. A fate that Linette will suffer if Tien is ever to take power of the cloister."

"What the hell does his power grab have to do with me and Maren?"

Linette spoke, "I think that Tien is using your presence as an excuse for him to rebel." Her voice faltered. "His reaction to your presence amongst us last night was surprising to both Sebille and I."

"Yes," said Sebille. "Quite out of character for him."

"Now, look," I said. "Maren and I never intended to start some kind of civil war among you guys."

"We know that," Sebille replied. "Nevertheless, here we are. And sadly, with Tien's actions, both your sister and you are in a perilous position, but so is Linette."

I sank down in the seat which Mike had vacated. "So, what do we do? How can we get Maren back and stop Tien?"

"You're not going to like what they're gonna suggest!" Mike stated flatly. "I don't even like it!"

A sense of dread rippled through my core as I looked over at Howie and Laura. There were no smiles or snickering now in their solemn expressions.

Linette spoke, "The sprites and Fae have scouts searching for Tien and his accomplices. Hopefully they will find him by nightfall."

The timbre of her voice shot an arrow of fear through my gut. If he was willing to kill Linette—his own kind— what would he do to Maren? "What if they don't find him?"

"If Tien is still in hiding, we must lure him out. He wants to ensure your silence as well as Maren's. I'm afraid we will have to use you as bait, Kara."

I didn't hesitate. "I'm in! I'll do anything to get Maren

back. When he shows up, you'll be able to capture him, so Maren will be free? That's the plan, right?"

Instead of their assurance, silence was the answer that made the breath freeze in my chest. A glance at Howie and Laura, seeing worry add more lines to their ancient faces, only added to the knot of dread in my gut.

"Let's cut the crap!" Mike said. "She deserves to know and you guys are wimping out!" He pointed at me. "I told you, you wouldn't like it. The fact is that it's a crapshoot whether you'll get your sister back. When push comes to shove, these fairies are going to save Linette. You and your sister might end up as collateral damage."

"Collateral damage!"

Mike shrugged and pointed toward Sebille. "Tell her the truth."

Finally, Sebille weighed in. "If it were just Tien, our chance of success would never be in question. The truth is that he's managed to convince a group of Fae that only he is capable of ensuring their safety. He mistakes Linette's kindness as a sign of her weakness."

"More than just the Fae folk," Ellowen interjected. "It causes me shame to think that several sprite have joined his cause. But there is an even more powerful force that has allied with him."

Oh my God! How many strange creatures were we up against? "What force? Do we have any chance at all?" My knees turned to jelly thinking that Maren and I could be killed. "Wha- what "powerful force" are you talking about?"

Linette let out a long sigh before continuing. "We don't know who Tien has allied with, but we know they're powerful. Tien is able to cloak himself and become invisible even to us. He gleefully demonstrated this new power to the Fae who left with him."

"How do you know this? I thought he was in hiding."

It was Sebille who answered, "Dool, the young Fae you first met, defected from Tien's group. He returned late this morning to warn us. He told us that Tien met in secret with this new ally, so DooL wasn't able to tell us who or what it is, only that Tien acquired this new ability."

"Do you still wish to do this, Kara? You may be seriously injured, or even killed." Linette's voice was right beside me. I could feel her presence and the gossamer touch on my shoulder.

Tears welled in my eyes. "I have to try, Linette. I only wish it had been me that was abducted by Tien. Not Maren, but me. She has so much to live for." As far as my being in danger? Big deal. I was running on borrowed time as it was.

I set my jaw. "Let's roll."

Twenty Seven

The night sky was completely black with clouds as if the moon itself couldn't bear to watch what was about to unfold. I was standing on the beach path, peering down the detour we had taken the night before to meet the Fae folk. Just last night the pathway was speckled with moonbeams and fireflies. Tonight, the pathway with the overhanging trees looked like a dark maw ready to swallow me up.

My knees knocked as images of malevolent Fae, wide eyed with glistening mouths, and being peppered by vicious, hateful sprites buzzing around me filled my mind's eye. They would rip me apart, limb from limb while still alive if given half a chance. I knew it. Don't ask me how, but I knew that Tien and his party were still so traumatized by "The Great Reaping," whenever the hell that happened, that they would show absolutely no mercy at all to a human who threatened their people.

The most savage of hatreds have two parents. Fear and

vengeance.

Every survival instinct in me screamed for me to turn and run.

But the deepest instincts of self-preservation are so much seafoam splashing against a wall of granite when they encounter love.

"I'm getting my damn sister!" I said out loud and strode into the darkness. Alone.

Now that I was out here, alone, it was hard to believe that the plan that the Fae and members of the Guild had devised earlier was going to work. I was on my own, walking into blackness. At the time, the strategy had made sense, giving me a sense of hope that we could pull this off and defeat Tien. But now, with shadows crouching among the trees and the insidious quiet, I was anything but confident.

Determined? Sure. Confident? Nuh-uh. Those knees were still knockin'.

Maren's life was on the line here. This wasn't anything like anything I'd tried to accomplish in the past. Dropping out of nursing school and even my half-assed attempts to get a craft business up and running was nothing to what I faced now. Even walking away from Josh's father, turning my back on a life with him, paled in significance to what I had to do here. There was no room for doubt anymore.

I straightened my spine, peering at the trees around me. Where were Howie and Laura stationed? And Mike? Would they get to me in time? But their loyalty was to the Guild first and foremost, a fact that was made clear by Ellowen. Best not to count on anyone other than myself in this mess. I'd gotten Maren into it, and it was up to me to get her out.

The only one who had given me assurance that he'd find Maren had been Rax. When I'd returned from the parley at Howie's, Rax was still gone. I banged on the door to his Boler but no answer.

I was able to make out the large tree which marked the entrance to the clearing where we had met everyone the night before. Well, according to the plan laid this afternoon, it was now time to call attention to myself. I drew a deep breath. "Maren! Where are you? You've had your fun with the Fae, but it's time to come back! I'm not going anywhere until you come out!" I stepped from the path, pushing aside tree branches to get to that clearing.

Well, time to put some light on the subject. I took my phone and, holding it high, I flashed its light in a full sweep of the trees. If my voice hadn't called attention to me being there, then surely the light slicing through the darkness would do the trick.

"Maren? If you don't return in the next ten minutes, I'm going to go to the police. They're going to think I'm crazy when I tell them you went chasing after some fairies, and that's why you're missing. The whole world is going to know about us, but what choice do I have?" I looked all around and above me. Nothing. "That's right! I wanted to go to the media and tell them about you and your powers, and I'm going to! The whole world will know about the Fae folk once again!"

Hopefully, Tien would take the bait. He'd better! Just bring Maren back, and things would be cool on my end. The Fae could figure their own way of dealing with their power struggle. Leave us out of it.

Yeah. The Guild had their priorities keeping Linette's leadership, but I had mine as well.

I stepped into the clearing and shone the light in an arc. "Come out, come out, wherever you are! C'mon, Maren. This isn't funny." I wasn't sure how much longer I could keep up this charade, pretending that Tien wasn't involved. But Linette had said it was important, so I had to trust her. She knew Tien better than I did. Besides, the element of surprise might be the only advantage I had. That and Tien being overconfident.

It seemed like forever that I stood in the glade of trees, calling out to my sister. Finally, I felt a brush of air on my face, heard the rustle of leaves above me. This was it. My mouth went dry and every muscle in my body tensed. I didn't dare to move, let alone try to see if Howie or the others were around—not that I'd see the Fae anyways.

"Your sister is fine…for now."

At Tien's voice behind me, I swung around. Couldn't see him at all, of course, but still… "You have her! Bring her back now, and I promise we'll never tell anyone about you or that veil that separates you guys from humans or anything. Please. We don't want to harm you. Just let us go."

The wind became stronger against my skin, and when Tien spoke next, his voice was harsher. "I know you won't tell anyone. I'm going to ensure that doesn't happen."

"No, please—"

"Take her!"

Suddenly the area between my shoulder blades tingled. I darted to the side, swinging my arm out! It had to be Tien's Fae. "Help! Help me! They're—" Oof. The air whooshed from my chest, folding me in half. A band of steel dug into my ribcage. My feet left the ground and my cell phone dropped.

I could see the light on the screen become smaller and smaller as the pressure tightened on my ribcage. I was airborne! My hands went to my middle, but all I could feel was my sweater. But something had me! The crushing pressure in my ribs was proof of that.

I screamed my lungs out in terror. The one thing that really petrified me was heights! I couldn't even climb a stepladder without freaking out! Now here I was skimming over treetops, being held up by God only knew what. It might have helped if I could see my captor. To know that whatever Fae creature had me wasn't going to let me slip!

I watched the world pass below me. I could see the lights of Virginia Beach and the ribbon of car lights on the highway. Shit! Shit! Shit! It took every ounce of self-control to keep from peeing myself. Don't drop me. Please!

Where was Linette? Where were all the good Fae who were supposed to rescue me? Hell! I'd even take a sprite to come to my aid. I struggled to suck in a breath of air. It wasn't just the pressure on my ribs making it hard to breathe, it was the airspeed. It was a wall pushing against me.

The lights below faded. My body went limp. Everything went black.

***

I came to from the sharp pains piercing my sides. I was lying on damp grass, no longer airborne, thank goodness.

Every breath I took felt like I was being stuck with a knitting needle as I sat up. God, whatever they bound me with was gone now, but man oh man did they tie me up tight when they took me up into the air. I ran my hands up and down my torso, feeling a series of bruises.

Looking around, I could see that I was on the edge of another glade, a clear grassy circle surrounded by tall trees. I looked up at the sky; the clouds were breaking up, and I could see the moon on the horizon. I called out, "Anybody here? Tien? Maren?"

I gasped, seeing a huddled figure opposite me by the farthest tree. Even with the covering of vines holding her arms tight to her body and the cloth shrouding her head, I knew it was Maren.

"Maren!" Ignoring the shooting aches, I scrambled across the grass. But before I reached it, I ran into an invisible wall. It was perfectly transparent, but as solid as steel. After bouncing off it—ow!—I pressed my hands against the perfectly smooth surface, calling out to Maren. When there was no response, I started beating my fists against it. It didn't do a damn thing to get me closer, but it did startle Maren awake.

"Kara? Is that you?" The covering on her head puffed out and she squirmed, fighting against the restraints on her arms and legs. "Kara!" She let out a heart-wrenching cry.

It tore through me like a knife. I pummeled the energy field harder. "I'm here, Maren! What have they done to you? I'm gonna kill that son of a bitch when I get my hands on him!" I even kicked at that invisible wall; fat lot of good that did. Ow!

"It's Tien, Kara! He blindsided me and brought me here. I can't even fight back with the tele-thingy! He's got my hands all wrapped up!" She coughed. "Be careful! He can also make himself invisible!"

Like that mattered? I couldn't see any of the Fae folk! Vampires? Sure! Werewolves? No problem! But the bastards that kidnapped me and my sister? Nope. Some things are just sooo unfair. I pressed my hands against the force field. "Did he hurt you? Aside from being tied up and—"

"He's never going to let us go, Kara!" The agony in her voice was heartbreaking. "After he kills Linette, he's the boss. Then he's gonna put us away on some island or something! We're going to be imprisoned till the day we die! We have to get out of here before he comes back!"

"He won't kill you," a young voice cried out right next me. "He only wants to kill Linette! And he doesn't even want to do that!"

"Pia? Is that you?" Maren twisted and rolled on her side to get closer to me. "Help us, Pia! We have to get away from here. I've got children, a new granddaughter. You don't want to hurt us. Please. You're our only hope."

The wall of energy fell back a few inches when Pia wailed, "I can't! I'm sorry, Maren, but if I help you, Tien will kill Dool. I should have left when he did. I waited too long."

"No, Pia!" I pressed into the energy field that was Pia. Maren was only a few feet away from me. If I could convince Pia to join forces with us, we could get out of there. "Pia, Dool told Linette about his secret meeting and the new power he's got now. But Linette is going to defeat Tien. She has the Guild backing her."

The whirring outside the glade became louder. I could even make out the sounds of blows and shouted voices. Holy shit! The Guild was here? I pressed into Pia again, "Listen! Linette and the rest of the Fae are here! We're going to be rescued."

"Dool? He's here?" Again, the energy field moved.

Suddenly there was a vacuum and I lurched forward! In a flash I was in front of Maren, tugging the cloth sack from her head.

Her eyes were round, jerking back. But when she saw my face, she let out a grinning yelp. "Kara! Thank God!" Her gaze flitted to the side. "Quick, before she has a change of heart! We have to get out of here."

She held her hands up to me and I tore off the fabric wrappings. They held each of her fingers, then her entire hand was swaddled tightly. With her hands finally free, Maren grimaced and grunted as she flexed her fingers.

I bent over to tear at the vines that were wrapped around her body like a fisherman's net. These were tough to break!

"I got this," Maren said to me, moving me away. My fingers tore at the thick vines, but Maren was already doing her thing—untying the binds on her hands. One end of the thick vine rose and twirled around Maren's hands, freeing her. This time instead of just levitation, she was making the binds do her will! We were going to be all right! Her power was stronger and it was now unleashed.

"We've got to get out of this glade while they're distracted fighting each other. I hope Linette wins, but I'm more concerned with us surviving." I stepped closer to the opening, listening hard. The battle was louder with more whirring vibrations and thuds. With any luck, it would be the end of Tien and his band of rebels.

When Maren stumbled trying to get to her feet, I grabbed her arm to help her up. "C'mon, Mare! You can do this!"

"My legs and feet are numb, Kara. Help me."

I grabbed her arm and looped it over my shoulders, practically lifting her so we could get to the wall of trees. There had to be some way of getting through. But the gaps between the thick trunks were too narrow to squeeze through. Damn!

"Can you levitate us out of here? You put me in the air

in the RV, so maybe if—"

"That's far enough."

My heart lurched, hearing the male voice behind us. I knew that voice. Tien was back. Back from the battle, which meant he'd beaten Linette. Oh shit. Maren and I were goners.

Twenty Eight

Kara

While I was frozen in place at the sound of Tien's voice, Maren spun around to face him. "We're leaving! I don't give a damn about you with your stupid paranoia. Get the hell out of our way or…"

"Or what?" Tien's voice replied. I couldn't see the bastard, but Maren was staring at a space in the field.

"I'll…I'll hurt you!" she sputtered, raising her hands like talons.

"I doubt that."

As if she had been hit by a cannonball, Maren flew back through the air and thudded against the trunk of a tree, falling to the ground like a rag doll.

"Maren!" I screamed, rushing to her still form. "Oh no!"

I rolled her onto her back. Thank God, she was breathing, but she was out cold. That son of a bitch could have killed her!

From behind me, Tien's voice rasped, "She's not dead. If I wanted her death, she would be a bloody pulp before you." I turned to where his voice was, but as usual, saw squat. He wheezed and said, "You are two fools. You don't deserve the powers gifted you. You're like children with a priceless violin and are treating it like a plaything..." His voice trailed off in a sharp gasp.

I squinted into the air in front of me, but I couldn't make him out at all. "You're hurt, aren't you?" I said.

He took a deep, rattling breath. "As is Linette. She's as ferocious in battle as I. She's wounded me as badly as I did her. My group is smaller, so we fled the battle." His voice grew closer, and I flinched when I felt his breath on my face. "The battle caused by the presence of you both." I could feel the rage in his voice.

"We didn't do a damn thing to you, nor your people, Tien. We were just on vacation when all this —"

"Enough!"

I flinched. Maybe it's wimpy, but give me a freaking break. The invisible fairy man just coldcocked my sister and was pissed off as hell. I pressed my lips together.

His voice sounded like gravel. "You are two unnatural beings. You were not born into magic like the rest of us; neither were you imbued with it like those werewolves or even the vampires. Even so, they at least came into their state through natural causes. But you two..." He began to gasp again for a moment or two before continuing. "You should be eradicated like the mistakes you are."

"So you're gonna kill us, huh?"

"No. Taking a life is anathema for the Fae. My kind only does that as a last resort."

"Sure didn't stop you from going after Linette, you hypocrite. Your own flesh and blood, at that!" Yeah, I have the habit of shooting my mouth off at inopportune moments, but this guy was planning on killing me, so what did I have to lose anyway?

"Fool. I was not looking to take Linette's life! When I

overcome her, she'll be banished. That was my intent for you and your grotesque sister as well!"

"Banished? What's that—some fairy form of grounding or something?" I did air quotes. "Go to your room, young lady; you've been baaad." Just like what Mom and Dad would say to us when we were kids and acting up.

"Something like that. It's a place of exile for our people." He took a breath. "I intended to have you two, along with Linette and any followers loyal to her, be sent there, but things have changed." He started coughing again.

"Yeah, you didn't expect the ass-kicking she gave you, huh?" That small voice in my head—the one I usually ignore—was saying, Great, Kara. Just keep digging that hole deeper, why don't ya! And as usual, I ignored it.

"You'll be happy to know that I'm taking you away from this place. You don't belong with my kind."

"What? You're not killing us?"

"No, I'm not. There are others who wish to deal with the two of you."

He let out a grunt, and suddenly Maren's body was torn from my arms. In the next moment I was snatched around my ribs. Tien had us both in his grasp, like he was carrying two sacks of rice, and we flew up above the treetops before I could scream.

"I'm getting you two away from my people," Tien said. "You won't be my problem anymore."

I started to beat at his arm. I couldn't see it, but I could sure feel it; it felt like a steel cable.

"Do you want me to drop you, you fool?" he grunted. He twisted me around until again I felt his breath on my face. "Now, sleep…"

The whirring of his wings was the last sound I felt as I tumbled into darkness.

Twenty Nine

Maren

My eyes sprang open and I was wide awake. The last thing I remembered was Tien's gesture that flung me into that damn tree, seeing stars for a split second before everything went black.

And now, instead of blackness, I was in a room of glowing white. Was I dead? Was this heaven? And why was I lying on my back?

I went to sit up and immediately learned that I was tied up! My arms, legs, and chest were all pinned down! I lifted my head to see.

I was on some kind of silver table. A gleaming silver table. But it wasn't cold. In fact, it was molded to my body like a memory-foam mattress. The bands that held me down grew from the table's surface and wrapped me. There wasn't any tightness to them. I tried to slip my hand out, but when I did, the straps gently pressed back at my effort as hard as I pulled. When I stopped pulling, the tension also ceased. Damn it.

I looked over to the side. About four feet away, Kara was in pretty much the same predicament as me—lying atop a silver cube that rose from the floor, bound in the same way I was.

"Kara!" I called to her. She didn't move. "KARA!" Oh man, she was out cold too!

Wait.

The realization shot through my mind. I've been here before!

And it was true. We had been in this room before!

I looked around. This is where it happened.

My memory was as spotty as trying to recall a dream I had. We were in the RV, and the maps app on Kara's phone had gone wonky. We were driving slowly along the mountain road when the entire world became bathed in that brilliant white light.

Then my memory of being here came to me, and this was as crystal clear as a YouTube video.

I had come to on a table just like this one. But I was naked. Across from me was Kara, also in her birthday suit. But floating about six inches above her torso was a silver box, the size of a large Domino's pizza. It was the same gleaming silver as the cubes we were lying on, and a low hum came from it. It moved back and forth over her, from her waist up to the center of her ribcage and back down.

I hissed out to her, but she didn't respond.

But from behind me, I heard a man's voice. "You ought not be awake. Sleep now."

And the next thing I knew, Kara and I woke up screaming in the RV.

Wearing each other's clothes.

Shit.

Shit. Shit. SHIT! Kara was right, dammit!

We *had* been abducted.

**

Well, nobody told me to go back to sleep, so I figured we were alone. And not naked this time, so that was a plus.

I looked around the room. It was circular and pretty large, about the size of a round skating rink. The walls glowed in white, arching up to a ceiling about fifteen feet above me. The walls blended into the floor at the bottom, which was the same silvery color as the cubes that held both me and Kara.

I let out a snort. Of course, the stupid thing would be round. We were in a flying saucer, weren't we?

It was brightly lit because the walls and ceiling themselves glowed. Not like they had lights behind them like in an office, no; they glowed themselves. Not too brightly, either, but it was well lit.

I put my head back down. Yeah, I sure as hell knew this place.

I jerked my head back up and stared at the surface I was on. Oh yeah. And just to be sure, I looked over at Kara. Same deal there.

I could get out of these bindings, no problem!

I turned back to my table and squinted a little. Yup. It had an aura.

It was the first time I ever saw a "thing" having an aura. People? Sure! Even animals and plants had auras! But cars? Houses? Furniture? Nope. But this table had one.

This table was alive. Not alive the same way a person or animal was—more like how a small plant was or even my Fae ring. It was organic or something, whatever the hell that meant. But…it was alive.

I closed my eyes and reached out with my mind to it, searching for anything that could give me a sense of this object's 'table-ness' or whatever.

I had tried yoga—not for long, but that was another story—and the instructor had gone on at the end of a class about how all living things were connected in some "cosmic consciousness" kind of way.

Of course, that was all bunk and bullshit.

Until I woke up one day seeing auras and moving stuff with just a thought.

So, with my eyes closed, I tried to sense the presence of this table's essence or whatever.

Oh! I gave a little start when I felt something in my mind. It was the feeling I got when I just knew I was being watched. Or that there was someone right behind me about to go "boo!" That split second when I'd sense the presence of someone else...

I felt this table's table-ness in my mind.

'Release my bonds', I commanded it in my head, and felt a sense of a reply. It wasn't any "Oh, okayyyy..." kind of thing. It was more along the line of a quick nod. I opened my eyes and lifted my head to see my restraints flowing off me back into the table as if they had melted. There wasn't any sign on the table they had been there; the surface was pristine.

I hopped off, and as soon as I did, the table melted back into the floor the same way my bonds just did, and again, the floor was perfectly smooth.

"Could sure do some wicked interior designs with this kind of stuff," I said out loud.

"Marennnnnn!"

I spun around to see Kara, now wide awake and wide eyed.

"It's okay," I said, coming up to her side. "I'll get you out of there toots-sweet."

"What the hell is going on? Where are weeee?" The poor girl was terrified. Her eyes were huge and her face was taut with fear.

I patted her leg. "We're back where this all started, sis." I waved my hand at our surroundings. "You were right. We were abducted somehow. And this is where they took us! I just remembered a snippet of being here before."

She pulled and yanked her arms and legs. "I can't get out, Maren! Why are you free and not me?"

"Relax, hon. Stop pulling at these straps; that doesn't

work."

"How would you know! You're standing there!"

"I was tied up just like you until a second ago. If you listen to me for a damn second, I'll have you out of there, no problem."

"Promise?" God, she was scared. She sounded like she was just five years old.

"Cross my heart." Geez I hoped it would work. "Now, close your eyes and try to calm down, okay?"

"What are you going to do?"

"I'm going to mind-meld with this table like I'm Mr. Spock!"

"What?"

I laid my hands on the table, and looked at it up and down. It had the same faint, blue aura my own table had. "Shh…" I said to Kara. "Just calm down for just a few seconds, okay?"

She closed her eyes, and I closed mine.

Again, I reached out for this table's essence or whatever, and boom—there it was. *'Release this person,'* I thought in my mind. *'Release her now'.* Again, I got that fleeting sense of compliance, and I opened my eyes to see Kara's bindings melt back into the table's surface.

"You can get up now."

Kara's eyes opened and she sat right up. I took her hand, and she hopped down onto the floor. "How did you—" She stopped and stared as the table flowed back into the floor. "What the hell?"

I nudged her with my elbow. "As much as I hate to admit it, you were right. We were abducted, and I'm pretty damn sure it's by aliens. Either that, or Elon Musk is doing some really, really wild shit!"

"No way! You believe me?"

I gave her a quick hug. "Let's figure out where the hell we are, okay?" I pointed at the porthole that was set into the wall. "Let's take a look. I hope to hell we're not in orbit or something."

"We're not in orbit, Maren. We'd be floating if we were in orbit."

"Oh yeah? Do they float around on the USS Enterprise?" I said over my shoulder as I strode to the small window.

"Uh-oh, that's true." She came right up behind me.

We both peered out the window.

"WHAT THE HELL?" we both said in unison.

Thirty

Kara

Holy shit, Maren," I said. "This is the last thing I expected to see!"

She let out a sigh and leaned against the wall. "Me neither."

Outside the portal wasn't any alien planet. Neither were we orbiting over the planet Earth like in the space station. Nope. I was looking out the porthole at a pretty damn familiar site.

We were right in the camper park that Maren and I pulled into just the other day. In fact, I could look in one direction and see Howie and Laura's behemoth of a camper, and in the other direction was...well, my camper. Yup. The Magical Mystery Tour rig was right next door.

"We're inside Boler Guy's rig, Maren," I said.

She lurched off the wall and came back to the porthole. "Shit, I think you're right! His camper does have the small window right by the door! But…" She grabbed my arm and turned me around to face the cavernous chamber we were in. "How the hell is this able to exist, then? Look at the size of this! It's the size of an auditorium, for God's sake, and his Boler could barely hold a single bed!"

"I guess it's some inter-dimensional thingamajig."

She yanked me around to face me. "What the hell does that mean?"

I rolled my eyes at her. She'd never, not once, watched any of the documentaries and shows I've seen. Such an ignoramus. With a sigh, I said, "It means that this room can be trans-dimensional, silly."

Maren shook her head like I just cuffed her upside. "Trans-dimensional, huh?"

I nodded. "Yup."

"What's trans-dimensional?"

"It's…uh…it's a…oh, for God's sake!" I waved my hands at her. "I don't know!"

She smirked. Yeah. Here we were, trapped in some flying saucer or something, and she's smirking because she caught me out. Sisters could be such bitches at times!

I crossed my arms and stared at her smirking puss. "Let's just say that it's super high-tech stuff, okay?"

"Okay. Now I know as much as you. Which is nothing!" She smirked. "Just sticking a label on something doesn't mean you understand it, Kara."

"Whatever." I went back to the window. "Looks like there's another meeting at Howie and Laura's. There's Mike the vampire heading up to their place."

"Oh yeah?" Maren joined me at the window. "Oh wow! Does he clean up niiiice."

She had a point. It was the same guy from the other night who was the drunken sot she'd flung across the road, no doubt about it. But he must have showered or something. He was wearing a navy-blue, button-down shirt and black slacks. They must have been tailored, because they fit him like a glove. His silver, almost white hair was neatly coiffed against his head. He was striding purposefully toward Howie's rig.

"Mmmm…" Maren said. "He could be a stand-in for David Bowie." She started banging on the porthole. "Hey! Mike!" she yelled. "Mike!"

He stopped and looked around.

"Over here, Mike! In the Boler!"

He had a puzzled expression. His eyebrows were tight and his lips were thin. He turned around in a circle slowly as Maren continued to yell to him. He tilted his head to one side like a confused puppy, swinging his head from side to side.

"I got his attention, but he can't figure out where we are!" Maren exclaimed. She pushed me away from the porthole. "Let me break this stupid window." She pointed her hand at it and gritted her teeth.

Nothing. It didn't crack or anything.

"You getting anywhere with this?"

"No. I tried to tell it to open, the same way I told those tables to let us go, but there's no sense of it in my head." She rose both hands. "I'll try to break it, then!" She gestured at it with both hands, her fingers sticking out like talons, her face all twisted with effort.

After about a minute, she let out a long whoosh of air. "I guess the dimensional whozis is stronger than my tele-thingamajig-ness."

I looked out the window. Mike was gone. He was probably inside with Howie and Laura.

Wait a second.

I started tapping and rubbing the wall beside the porthole.

"What are you doing?" Maren asked.

"When we looked at Boler Guy's camper from the outside, the door to it was right next to this window, right? So there's got to be some kind of door in this wall." I ran my hand all along the smooth, white surface, feeling for some sort of crack or seam. Damn it, there wasn't anything at all! "Nothing," I said.

"Maybe I can get the walls to obey my thoughts, Kara?" Maren spread her arms facing the wall beside the window. "Open sesame!" she said.

Nothing.

"I don't get it," she said, dropping her arms. "When I woke up, I told the table to let me go, and it did right away. Then it basically melted into the floor. And then the same thing happened with you. But now…" She shook her head and went over to the spots where we had been tied down. "Maybe it only works on the floor or something?" She stared at the floor. "Open sesame!" she said.

I went over to her. "I don't think that's going to—"

With a pop, the wall beside the porthole split open like a sliding door. We looked over to see that bitch from the beach, who had been hanging around us, waltz in from the campground.

She tilted her head at us and made a quick gesture with her finger, causing the wall to seal up. Her eyes flashed at us. "How did you escape your bonds?" she asked in an even voice.

Maren lifted her hands at the woman, her fingers like claws. "Magic, you bitch!" She shot her hands out.

And nothing. The woman made a pointing gesture with her index finger. "Be still now," she said.

And Maren froze solid as a statue.

"Maren!" I cried. I grabbed at her. "What the hell did you do to her!"

"She was about to attack me with her mind and I stopped her."

"You're Anjou, aren't you?"

She was wearing the same outfit we saw her in at the beach the other day: the silver headscarf and the lustrous gray harem pants. Her face was unlined, but I could tell she was as old as us at least. "So," she replied, "Rax told you my name, did he?"

"Yes! Now stop whatever you're doing to my sister!"

She stepped up to us and looked into Maren's eyes. "I'm going to release you. But mark my words—if you attempt to attack me again, you'll be very, very sorry, do you understand?" Making a fist with her pinky jutting out, she held it up to Maren. "You may nod or shake your head. Will you refrain from attacking me?"

Maren's head slowly nodded.

"Very well." Anjou opened her hand, spreading her fingers wide.

Maren came back to life immediately. "Wow. That was weird," she said. She rubbed her arms. "Any chance you can teach me that trick? All I know is how to shove people around."

"Silly human." She turned away from us to stand in the center of the chamber. She looked up to the ceiling. "I thirst."

Immediately the floor next to her shimmered and a pedestal popped up with a clear glass of liquid. Anjou picked up the glass, drained it and put it back on the pedestal. As soon as she did, the whole shebang melted into the floor just like that table thing I had been on.

My mouth dropped. "Some kitchen you got going in this joint," I said.

Anjou turned to me, puzzled. She looked off. "Kitchen…kitch—oh yes, your sustenance preparation area." She blew out a breath. "My people dispensed with that primitive nonsense thousands of cycles ago."

Show-off. "What the hell do you want with us?" I snapped at her. "You took us when we were driving, and now you took us again!"

She dropped her head at me. "I took you to prevent that Fae from murdering you. I had to reveal myself to Tien in order to convince him to not slaughter the two of you during his dispute with his leader." She put her hands behind her back. "In exchange, I gave him the power to cloak himself from other Fae. In other words, Earther, I bought your silly lives. You're welcome, by the way."

"Yeah, well…" Did she do that?

Maren stepped up. "You're expecting gratitude? Are you kidding me? What's your problem? Why did you guys mess with us in the first place? If it wasn't for you, none of this would have happened!"

Anjou nodded slowly. "You have a point. My people are baffled by your species."

"What does that mean?"

Anjou turned and gestured at the wall. Immediately, it shimmered into the world's largest curved television set. Before us was an ocean of stars. "This doesn't look familiar to you," she said. She gestured with her hand and the screen zoomed in on one of the stars.

But it wasn't a star. It was the shape of one of those hurricanes you see on The Weather Network. It was a swirling cloud of bright pinpoints of light, surrounding a bright center. "This is your galaxy," Anjou said.

"We call it the Milky Way," I replied.

With a small indulgent smile, she nodded. "Of course you do. It is a poetic name, I suppose." She gestured again, and the screen zoomed in so fast I was almost dizzy. She stepped up to the wall and pointed. "This is your star—"

"The Sun."

"Whatever." With another gesture, the screen changed again, shifting perspectives, and we could see the Sun and a pale-blue dot. "And this is your home. It teems with life. But not just life…organisms have evolved on millions of planets, just in your galaxy." She turned to us with an arched eyebrow. "Life is present across your galaxy and among many others."

"So? That sounds pretty reasonable from what I've learned," I replied.

"Yes, I suppose you Earthers have achieved that much in mathematical reasoning." She gave a phony series of claps. "Good for you; you can count!" What a smug bitch. "But the problem is that your kind have left out one important part."

"Oh yeah?" Maren asked. She stood there with her arms crossed and feet apart. I've seen the Pissed-Off Maren enough times to know she's steaming mad. "Like what, smart-ass?"

Anjou responded to Maren's barb with a confused expression. "I'm primarily what you would call a biologist. I'm not familiar enough with your language to understand your meaning. Smart? Yes, I'm intelligent, of course. Ass? Isn't that an insult? How can you have a compliment and insult in the same expression?"

Maren waved at her dismissively. "I'm not going to do a remedial English class, lady. What's your point?"

Anjou shrugged. "Very well. The important part your kind have failed to see is how..." Her face twisted. I swear to God, she looked like she was about to burst into tears. "How..." She knotted her hands together, and began to wring them. "You fools! You don't see how precious you are!"

"Huh?" I said. That's all I could get out.

Anjou strode back and forth in front of that space display. She flicked her hand, and I almost got dizzy watching the image zoom back out. She stabbed a finger at one of the galaxies again. "This is your Milky Way! In the entire vastness of billions of stars and billions and billions of planets—"

Maren giggled. "You sound like Carl Sagan. He used to say 'billions and billions' all the time!"

Anjou dropped her head. "Where do you think he got that phrase from?" She made a sharp gesture with her hand. "Of all the planets in just your galaxy, there are very, very few that have sentient life, you fool. You want multicellular organisms? There are thousands of planets with that. Do you want vegetation? Even small animals? Thousands of planets. But"—and she pointed at both of us—"my people have been exploring this galaxy for untold generations, and of all those planets, only yours has evolved a species that is capable of thinking to the degree your kind have. In your entire galaxy, your species is the only one with music, or art, song, or poetry." She stepped up to us. "Yours is the only planet where its inhabitants dream."

"What, so you expect us to high-five you or something? Do we get an A plus or something?"

Anjou barked a laugh. "Not at all! You're the highest-evolved sentient beings in your entire galaxy! And you know what you do more than any other life form? In your entire galaxy?"

Maren's eyes rolled. "What?"

"YOU SLAUGHTER ONE ANOTHER!" Anjou roared. It was so freaking loud Maren and I almost jumped right out of our skin! "You...you fools!"

"Now wait a minute! We're just trying to get by!" I snapped at her.

"You are such fools. You don't have the slightest idea how...how precious each and every one of you are! Instead, you exploit one another—your strong make virtual slaves of those who are weaker. Your history is drenched in lakes, no, oceans of sweat, pain—and so, so much of that fluid... 'blood,' is it?"

"Yeah, it's blood. You got that word right," I said.

"You murder one another in so very many ways, so...casually you snuff out intelligent life. And for what? Why are you so cruel to each other? So...so casually cruel. Your information systems vomit up tales every day celebrating this aspect of yourselves.

"We call that 'the news.' It's what happens and we want to know."

Anjou burst out laughing. "You revel in it! You shake your head in some superior moralistic manner and think 'those people'... You bathe in these tales of bloodshed! Your so-called 'news' is a daily record of your failing as a species."

Shit. I never looked at it that way.

But Anjou wasn't finished. Not by a long shot. She pointed a finger at Maren, then at me and said, "You have no idea how precious you are! Well, you foolish, stupid, stupid human; you should know that there are other species who do know how precious you are...who know what you can become."

"Oh yeah? By kidnapping us? By holding us prisoner?"

"That was Rax's fault entirely. We needed to understand your reproductive characteristics a little better. This...process the female of your species undergoes baffles us."

"Whaddya mean? Don't you guys have kids?"

"Yes! Of course we do! But not when we're children ourselves! We breed after we mature! Your species breed far too early, and then your reproductive systems...fail." She shook her head. "Just when you're actually prepared to fill your offspring with actual wisdom, your bodies cease the ability to reproduce. Why is that?"

"I dunno...human nature?"

She scoffed. "Your scientists are spending more time trying to cure baldness in men than trying to improve your breeding cycle." She shook her head again. "Such a foolish people."

"Well, do you people know why, then?" I asked.

She shook her head. "We do not. That's why we took you. We've been examining the females of your species for some time now trying to understand why you are so genetically disposed to this. Your entire planet's life forms appear to be bent on reproducing too early, and we are trying to understand this biology. But then... That stupid Rax!"

"What? What did he do?"

Anjou let out another huff of frustration and gestured at the screen on the wall. It disappeared and returned to its glowing normal state. She pointed a finger at me. "He learned immediately that you were dying, and decided— without authorization I might add—to perform that genetic alteration upon you." She shook her head. "Upon both of you, because your sibling had the precursors to your own illness."

"What illness?" Maren gasped.

"I'll fill you in later, hon," I said.

Anjou continued without missing a beat. "But then he got carried away and inserted some of our own genetic material within you, giving you these powers." She stomped her feet. "That is not to be done on this planet, but he did it anyway! Those procedures were forbidden for your kind by us centuries ago!"

"Why?"

She sighed. "While they worked, they also didn't. The subjects became outcasts when their powers were discovered. They called them 'witches' and at best shunned them, and at worst, killed them." She pursed her lips. "Your race is very good at murdering what it does not understand, isn't it? What it does not understand, it fears. And what it fears...it kills."

"Wait a minute. What about the Fae? The werewolves? Vampires? Sprites?"

"They occurred naturally—just other branches of your evolution. Well...the vampires and wolf people were mutations, but the Fae and sprites as well as the others—"

"Others?"

"Never mind. But not you and your ilk. You...are an interference by us that went wrong. Stupid Rax. He wanted to save your life, but instead, made you..."

"Made us what?"

From behind us, at the porthole, a deep voice rumbled. "I made you witches."

Thirty One

Maren

I watched Kara slowly turn around to look at the guy. "You...you did what?" she asked.

Rax nodded. "It wasn't entirely intentional, but..." He nodded. "You are now witches." He looked from Kara and then to me. "Both of you."

I jabbed a finger at him. "This is ridiculous! You can't go around and just 'make' witches! Everybody knows that!"

Kara turned her head and looked at me, her jaw pulled to the side. "Since when did you become an expert on witchcraft, Maren?"

"Oh come on! It's one damn thing to say that there's aliens! But now witches? For God's sake, Kara!" Yeah, I was becoming unglued. I just didn't realize at the time.

Kara scoffed. "And werewolves, and fairies, and sprites, and"—she eyed me—"some pretty hot-looking vampires..."

235

"Stop that, Kara!" I shot a look over at this Rax dude. He was standing by the porthole, probably right in front of the entranceway to this weird craft. Such a tiny thing from the outside, but inside it was the size of a freaking hockey rink. I put my hands up to the side of my head and grabbed fistfuls of hair. This was all coming at me too fast. My head started to spin, so I yanked my hair. The shot of pain kept me from passing out. Hey, it works; I learned that the hard way years and years ago.

I let go of my hair and stared at Rax. "So how the hell do aliens make witches?" I gave my head a shake. "This will be the cover story of next week's National Enquirer, I'm sure."

"Except even they wouldn't believe it, sis," Kara said. "Still...how did you do that, Rax?"

He hung his head and mumbled something.

"What?" I asked. "Speak up, spaceman!"

He lifted his head. "Programming error. And the moon was full."

"What the hell is that supposed to mean? 'Programming error'?"

He nodded. He stepped toward us and waved his hand around. "This craft is extremely complex. When we culled you from your planet—"

I huffed. "Culled? That's what we do to herd animals, buster."

"I'm sorry, my ability with your linguistics is still developing...when we brought you to our craft...our intent was to simply study your reproductive systems and how they interact with your neural development. Your species breeds too early as far as we're concerned, and we wanted to learn why."

"Yeah, yeah," I waved my hand at him. "Your partner in crime already told us that. So, what was this programming error? And what the hell does it have to do with the damn moon?"

From behind me, Anjou said, "I told him not to do it! But no! You're headstrong, Rax!"

"DO WHAT?"

Rax replied. "In the course of the examination, we found that you had precursors to a deadly illness for your kind."

Kara spoke up. "Pancreatic cancer, right?"

Rax nodded. "You would know, because your condition was much, much worse."

"WHAT?" I blurted. "Kara, do you have cancer?" I turned to her.

"No, she doesn't," Anjou said. "No longer, that is."

Kara's eyes filled with tears. "I wanted to keep it a secret, take this once-in-a-lifetime trip with you, and then I'd tell you. When it was all over..." She held her arms out to me. "Oh, Maren, I'm so scared!"

I grabbed her in my arms and held her as she burst into tears.

Rax came up behind us. "It took a few days for your system to recover, Kara. We were able to stop the illness in Maren quickly because it was so early in its development with her. It was caused by your genetic makeup."

I sniffed. "It's what killed our mother," I said.

Kara, her face buried in my shoulder, also nodded. "That's why I held off from telling you. I knew I was a goner." She was right; I couldn't blame her. Mom was dead within just a few months of finding out. It was brutal.

I just held her tighter. I looked over at Rax. "So you fixed us up, is that it?"

He nodded. "Yes. We used our systems to implement genetic changes within you at the level of your nucleotides...but then...it went a little"—he fumbled with his hands— "Ca-ca?"

Anjou chimed in. "He means it all went to shit."

I looked over at her. "How so? You cured us, right?"

"Yes," she said. "But your moon was on the very cusp of becoming a full moon that night. And it released an unknown type of energy just as we were doing the procedure..." she held her hands out, palms up. "We don't understand what happened, but the genetic alterations became somewhat…enhanced." She shook her head. "In ways we are not able to understand. But as a result"—she gestured at us—"you have the powers of the ones you call witches on your planet."

Kara lifted her head from my shoulder. "I don't have any power."

"Yes, you do, Kara," Rax said. "That power remained dormant while your body was repairing your cancer. It was quite widespread and took some time, but yes, you are also a witch."

"Bullshit."

"And also cured of the cancer," he added with a small smile.

"I. Call. Bullshit. Total bullshit."

Anjou let out a huffy sigh and said something in a language I couldn't understand. But the floor at her feet shimmered for a second, and a soccer ball—yeah, a soccer ball—took form in front of her there.

Anjou picked it up. "This is a common plaything on your planet, is it not?" she asked.

"Yeah, it is," I said.

She bounced it on the floor. "We're still trying to understand your preoccupation with these rites your people participate in."

"It's called 'playing,' you know. We play because it's fun."

She made a small shrug and dropped it onto the floor. It bounced a couple of times and went still. "Could you move it, Maren?"

"Yeah, I guess so."

"Please do."

I pulled a little away from Kara and pointed at it. I'll be honest, I was sorely tempted—sooo tempted—to bounce it off that woman's face just for the sake of principle—but I didn't. I just waved a finger at it and it rolled across the floor. I flicked my finger in another direction and it shot to the other side of the room. "Is that enough for you? I know how to do telekinesis."

Anjou nodded. "And now Kara...would you please move the ball? Do just as your sister did, please."

"Wha-? I tried to do this the other day." She shook her head. "I can't."

"Please try."

Kara rolled her eyes. "Ohhhkaaaaay..." She snapped her hand at the ball.

It rocketed across the room, slammed into the opposite wall and bounced back to the other side.

"Holy Toledo!" Kara gasped. "Did I do that?" She waved at the ball again, and it floated up about four feet off the ground. "Maren! Can you see this? Is this for real?" She whiffed her hand from side to side, and the ball mirrored her gesture, flinging itself back and forth from one side of the room to the other. "Holy shit!"

She dropped her hand and bent her head. "Whoa...this does take a lot out of you, doesn't it?" She grasped my shoulder. "I'm feeling a little woozy..."

I put my arm around her waist. "I know how you feel, sis," I said. "That first time at the river took a lot out of me."

She let out a gasp. "Look at me, all tele-thingy and stuff, huh?"

She gave me a sly smile and I stuck my tongue out at her. "That's my line."

Anjou barked something out in her weird language and a big ol' soft, comfy chair popped up from the floor just as Kara's knees buckled, planting itself right under her butt.

"Wait a minute!" I said, pointing at the comfy chair Kara was sitting in. "That's Nana's big chair!" And it was as clear as I could remember. Light-green gingham upholstery, right down to the throw pillow at the back and the cotton doilies Nana had crocheted on each of the arm rests.

I turned to Anjou. "You guys scanned our memories!"

"Standard procedure," she replied.

"Oh, Maren..." Kara sighed. "It's Nana's big chair..."

She was still a little woozy, and boy could I relate. She'd be starving in a couple of minutes, if my own experience had any similarity. Right now she was toying with the doilies on the armrest. "It even has the stains where you spilled that ice cream when we were kids…"

I dropped onto the arm of the chair and hugged her. "You bitch," I said. "Why didn't you tell me about the cancer?"

She laid her head on my arm. "That's what I went to your place to tell you, but you had all of Wayne's clothes on fire, remember? I knew my goose was cooked, so I figured I'd just back you up." She buried her face in my arm. "I was so grateful you came with me on this trip…"

We sat there for a few minutes, and then I heard Kara's stomach rumble. "Hey," I said to Anjou. "Any chance of you guys having some bacon cheeseburgers kicking around this dump? My sister's starving, aren't you Kara?" I got a slight nod in reply.

"As you wish," Anjou said.

She mumbled something else, and just like that, the floor shimmered and right in front of us two square pedestals rose from the floor. On top of each one were two perfect, steaming bacon cheeseburgers in front of us. I lifted the top of the bun. Yep. Mine had relish and mustard. I lifted the top of Kara's bun. Just mayo and ketchup.

I looked over to Anjou. "Doc's Diner, right?"

She made a small smile. "Your childhood memories said they were 'The best burgs around' I believe?" Her eyes widened for a second. "Oh! I forgot!" She said some more stuff I couldn't understand, and once more, just like that, there were two milkshakes, one chocolate and one strawberry, in those old-time heavy glasses in front of us on another pedestal that had popped up from the floor.

This is like an episode of Sabrina or something, I swear to God. The upside of alien brain scans.

Kara sat right up and grabbed her burger. "Look! She even got the napkins right, Maren!" she said. She took a bite.

"Ohmygod! Ohmygod!" she said.

Which was as good an endorsement as anyone could ask for. I didn't think twice about it. If these two were going to do us in, they didn't need to poison our food. I'd bet you a million bucks they could just zap us or something and we'd be gone. I dug in. And yeah, it was heaven. Piping hot, just juicy enough, and the toasted bun was absolute perfection.

What's better than meeting aliens and having your favorite dish from childhood appear out of thin air?

Total yum.

Thirty Two

Kara

Polishing my burger off, I sat back in that beautiful comfy chair and let out a Maren-sized belch. I stretched out in it and let loose a jaw-creaking yawn.

"You'll never be the same, Kara. The first time is a real doozy," Maren said.

I snorted.

"What's so funny?"

"Remember when you told me about you 'doing it' for the first time?" I laughed out loud. "I told you you'd never be the same!" I cackled a laugh. "And then you said it was a real doozy!"

Maren's jaw dropped. "Shit. You're right!"

We both had a chuckle over that. I yawned again, and looked over at Rax and Anjou. "Are we about done here, then? I could really use a nap." I watched them for a reaction. They were going to let us go, weren't they?

Rax's face fell. "You were never our prisoners, Kara. You're free to leave any time you wish." I shot a look over at Anjou to see her nodding in agreement.

Maren had been sitting on the arm of my chair. She hopped up. "Then let's blow this pop stand!"

I grabbed her arm. "Hang on for a second." I looked over to Rax and Anjou. "Are there any ground rules for letting us go?"

"Should there be?" Anjou asked with a small smile.

"Well...I don't know..."

Maren huffed. "Yeah! You don't get to grab us without warning!"

"That's a good one," I said. I looked at Rax. "Well?"

"Very well. We won't transport you without notice."

Anjou held up a hand. "Unless it's an emergency."

"Wait, what sort of thing would be an 'emergency' to you guys?"

She shrugged. "I don't have any idea, but I don't want to give you our word and then be bound by it."

I looked from one to the other. "Well, what if we decide to tell the world about you?"

Anjou burst out laughing. "Go right ahead! You'll be labeled as mentally defective at best, and confined by your government at worst."

"Does anyone else know about you guys?"

Anjou was about to answer, but Rax cut her off with a wave of his hand. "Why does that concern you?"

Maren snorted. "Maybe we want to make a Facebook group." We both laughed at their baffled expressions. "I'm kidding. But it would be nice to know we're not the only ones."

Rax held my eyes. "Perhaps you're special." We stared at each other for a long moment. Being "special" was a real ego stroke. And to be told by visitors from another planet I was special? And this guy does "research" all around the entire planet? Now that was a shot to the ego.

I cleared my throat, still holding Rax's gaze. His eyes,

those gold discs, were warm as he looked at me. They didn't waver the way guys sometimes do, darting up and down over your body when they're coming on to you; he just held my gaze...what the hell was that all about?

I mean, don't get me wrong; he's really good looking. His dark, almost mocha complexion, and his trim physique—not David Bowie skinny, but nicely trim like a British film star—stirred an attraction in me, I won't lie.

I cleared my throat again. "Do you think I'm special?" I asked.

But before Rax could tell me the stuff I'd love to hear, Anjou chimed in. "There's no doubt you and your sister are unique, Kara."

And that broke whatever was going on. Damn...

I looked over to her. "You're not going to give me a straight answer about other people that know about you guys, are you?"

"Our kind have been observing your species for untold ages," Anjou said. "I'm sure in the past, there have been instances, despite the precautions we take."

"If it means anything, Kara"—Rax said, and I turned to look at him—"you're my first."

Again, there was that silence between us as we stared at each other. I wondered what he looked like in swim trunks. Coming out of the surf, in swim trunks...oh man.

Now it was Maren's turn to break the spell. "Well, fine, I guess," she said. She tilted her head at them both. "Okay, me and my sister are 'special' or something; thanks for the compliment. But I'd like to know one thing."

"Go on," Anjou replied. Her eyes narrowed. "If I can answer, I shall."

"What's so special about Earth? Why are you so interested in us if we're so bloodthirsty? I mean, compared to you guys, we're still in the Stone Age or something, right?"

Anjou smiled. "You flatter yourselves thinking your kind are that technically advanced to make that sort of comparison. The difference is more like you're primates in the trees and we're Elon Musk." Her lip curled. "And I'm being generous to say you're even primates."

That barb didn't bother Maren in the slightest, but Anjou's superior attitude got under my skin. "Oh yeah?" I said. "You guys came here you know. If we're so backward, then why are you here?"

Anjou's mouth slammed shut and she looked over to Rax.

He gave her a quick nod, and she turned back to us. "Because of Santa Claus."

"WHAT? Santa Claus? You're kidding me, right?"

She made that small smile again, and Rax replied. "Yes. But not just Santa Claus...your entire world is filled with such legends of innocence. Your species possess something my people lack."

"Not lack, Rax," Anjou said. "It was no longer needed and became redundant." She gestured at us. "Just like how their ancient ancestors once had tails but no longer do."

"But yet we're fascinated by it, Anjou," he replied. He looked over at me. "It's your species' ability to see the wonder in life. Your kind of do it all the time, but it's most prevalent in children. You experience that sense of wonder, that awe..."

"Like a kid on Christmas Eve watching for Santa Claus," I said.

"Yes!" he said, his eyes lighting up even more. "You, for example! As a small child, one summer afternoon, you spent a long time lying in the grass watching a mere ant go about its work! You saw it pick up a breadcrumb and then struggle to bring it to its anthill..."

Oh my God. That memory came rushing back to me as soon as he said it. It was at Nana's one summer. Maren was still a very little, and Nana was looking after her and I was left to my own devices in the backyard. I noticed that ant and spent forever watching it as it worked with that breadcrumb! I had watched that movie Honey I Shrunk The

Kids and felt like I was in the movie as I hovered over that tiny creature for what felt like hours.

"You sure got a lot out of scanning our brains, huh?" I said in a soft voice.

He nodded. "You were but a small child, and yet that memory of that…wonder stays with you. There are so many other examples! The first pleasure you felt at mating—"

I cut the air with my hand. No way I was going to discuss my sex life with a guy I just met! "TMI!"

"Very well…" he looked at me, then Maren. "The wonder you felt the first time you whelped an offspring, then."

"Ewww! That's harsh! We call it 'giving birth,' Einstein!" Maren snapped. "Whelped! You make us sound like dogs!"

Poor Rax. The more he opened his mouth, the deeper he put his foot in it. He huffed a sigh and looked over at Anjou.

"What my colleague is trying to say is that these aspects of your kind fascinate us. Your thoughts of your 'Santa Claus' legend is a mere flight of fancy. Your watching that ant as a child is a burgeoning scientific inquiry. Your mating rituals…oh how complex a process just to breed! Your experiences when you whelp—"

Maren's teeth gritted. "It's giving birth hon…"

"Very well. My point is that your kind don't approach experiences like these for the simple things they are…you attach an emotional context to them."

"That's because they mean something. Don't you guys do that?" I asked.

They both shook their heads. "We do not," Anjou said. "Your kind though? You do it constantly! Some words scrawled on a piece of…paper…you call those 'love letters' and treasure them for lifetimes. You attach this meaning to such mundane things! A piece of molded metal becomes a testament of your love for each other you display on your hands."

"You mean wedding rings, right?" Maren asked.

"Doesn't work out all that shit-hot every time you know."

"And even that separation becomes important to you."

"Well, duh! We were married you know."

Rax held up a hand. "You asked why we watch over your kind and ache in frustration for the tragedies your kind so readily visits upon one another. You have tremendous power to destroy." He shrugged. "My people also possess powerfully advanced technologies. We are a much, much older people than your kind. But…in our growth, we lost something that your people have in great measure."

"What's that?"

"That"—he gestured with his hands, groping for words—"that meaning you mentioned. That meaning, and that sense of wonder and joy." He shook his head. "My people no longer have that. It evolved out of us, I believe."

"Well, that kinda sucks," Maren said.

"As you would say, 'Ya think?'" Anjou said. "It is impossible for us to experience. Hence we study your kind in the hope to revive that from something vestigial to becoming atavistic once more."

I wasn't sure what those words meant, but I got their point. "You guys want to feel again, is that it?"

"We experience emotions, Kara," Rax said. Again, giving me those golden eyes. "But not as brightly as your kind does. Your species center your lives around these feelings."

Maren snickered. "Sounds like you guys 'bred' it out of yourselves, huh?" I shot her a look and she held her hands up in surrender. "Sorry, couldn't resist."

I sighed. "Well, I hope your observations work out for you guys." I crossed my arms. "I think it's in you still."

Anjou's face became puzzled. "Why would you think so?"

"Because you miss it, silly! Because you know it's important! If it didn't matter to you, you wouldn't be doing this stuff, right?"

"No! It's merely an investigation into past aspects of our people! We're not all that interested! How could you—"

Rax cut her off with a wave of his hand and stepped over to me. "Kara's right, I think. Why would we be doing this work if it wasn't important to us in some fashion or another?" He held my eyes again. "You have deep wisdom, Kara."

I felt the blush rise from my neck, which made me blush more. Or was it a hot flash? Oh man, I don't know.

"Why, Kara!" Maren said. "That's the nicest thing any alien's ever said to you!"

Talk about breaking up a moment.

I got up out of that chair. "Well...I think we'll head back to our place," I said and headed to the porthole window. I looked out, and yeah, there's the campground. It was daytime. "How do you make this place so big, but look so small from the outside?"

"Our craft is quite vast," Anjou said, with a touch of pride in her voice. "What you see here is but a small fraction of its size. In fact, we're not physically at the campground. That camper you see parked there is just a portal that takes you to our craft."

"Really? Where are we then?"

"Right now we're on the other side of your moon. We're well hidden there from the instruments of detection your world has pointed skyward." She gestured at the wall by us. "When you pass through the passageway portal, you're immediately back on your home planet."

I was still staring out the window. "How the hell do you do that?"

"Do you really want to learn about trans-dimensional travel right now, Kara?" Anjou said.

"You're right. Never mind." Maren was right at my side. "Let's get back to our place, what do you say?"

And we just stepped through the wall and back to our campground.

One that had werewolves, vampires, and probably Fae and sprites hanging around, sure.

But it was home.

Thirty Three

Maren

We stepped out into a beautiful late summer afternoon. The air was crisp, but not chilly. I could sense the ending of the season; in just a matter of days the leaves would begin to turn. The driving over the next couple of weeks would be a sight with all the fall foliage.

I took a deep breath. I was back on my home planet, from the dark side of the moon if Rax and Anjou were telling the truth. "Y'know something Kara? It feels good to be home, doesn't it?"

"I was thinking the same thing. Sure, it was just stepping through a portal, but we were at the moon, weren't we?"

I nodded. Yes, we were sisters—seeing this the same way. "No splashdowns, though. No ticker-tape parades, huh?"

She gave me a side-eye. "Would you really want that?"

"Hell no! My head's still spinning from what just happened. I'll be perfectly happy to go to our rig and take a nap." I yawned.

Kara pointed over my shoulder. "Uh-oh, gonna have to put that on the back burner." She gestured. "Howie just saw us."

I turned to see our neighbor Howie at the door of his rig the size of a bus standing there with his mouth hanging open. He gave his head a shake and started barreling toward us, waving. "You're back! Where the hell have you been? Are you two okay?" he rattled off as he pulled up to where we were standing. "We've been looking all over for you two! Tien said he never harmed you, but couldn't tell us who it was that took you guys!"

"So you beat Tien?" I asked. "Is Linette okay? Was anyone hurt?"

"There were a few bumps and bruises, but everyone's fine," he said. "Michael was a demon; the Fae couldn't lay a finger on him, and he dropped that Tien fairy like a ton of bricks, let me tell you. And"—he shrugged—"when he did, the rest of Tien's group gave up right away."

"Michael did that?" I said. "That drunken vampire?"

"Yeah. He was pretty motivated. He was going to tear Tien limb from limb until Linette called him off." Howie shook his head and looked at me with a glint in his eye. "I've known Mike since the nineteen sixties, Maren; I've never seen him so worked up." He snickered. "He's even sobered up! He hasn't had a drink in days! Ever since you knocked him on his ass, he's been on the wagon!"

"Wait a minute. What do you mean 'days'? That just happened the other night!"

Howie blinked at me. "What you been smokin'? You guys have been gone the last three days."

"Oh shit!" Kara muttered. "Not again!"

We both turned and looked at the Boler. "Something about those guys messes time up for us," she said to me.

"When they first took us, we were gone for three days, and now again. I wonder what's up with that?"

"Well..." I plucked at my top. "At least we're wearing the right clothes this time."

"Yeah," Howie said, "Who did take you? Was it that Rax guy from the Boler? No way the three of you could hide in there for three days." He was right, of course. The damn thing was tiny.

"Well..." I hedged.

Kara took over. "It was kind of weird, Howie. We're not exactly sure where we were." She gave me a quick arch of an eyebrow, the same gesture she'd use when we were fibbing to Mom and Dad growing up. Then her face brightened. "But whatever the hell happened to us, we're really happy we made it back!"

Howie's face clouded for a moment. He didn't have to be Sherlock Holmes to see we were dodging him. Then he shrugged and said, "Well, I hope one day to hear the tale. I'll let Laura know you guys are safe and sound and she'll get word to Linette and the sprites." He turned to head back to his rig.

"And Mike too," I added.

"Don't have to," he said. He pointed up the roadway. "I think he knows."

I turned to see Mike running at us full speed.

"Maren! You're okay!" he yelled, grabbing me around the waist and spinning me around. "I was so worried about you!" He set me back on the ground.

Kara let out a harumph and said, "I'm fine too, Mike, thanks for askin'."

"Oh! Hi Kara! It's good to see you!" he said over his shoulder without taking his eyes off me.

The guy had sure gone through some changes the last few days, that was for sure. That drunken lout who'd accosted me just the other night was nowhere in sight. His clothes were cleaned and pressed, his eyes were clear, and that sallow pallor to his face was gone. He was still pretty pale, but looked more Scandinavian than cadaverous now.

His voice grew quiet, almost hesitant as he looked me in the eyes. "I was so scared when we couldn't find you," he said. "I've been looking day and night for you." A quick smile quirked his lips. "I don't know what it is, but there's something between you and me, Maren."

I scoffed. "Yeah, right!"

He held my eyes. "And you feel it too, doll," he said. He stroked the side of my cheek with his index finger.

And a chill went right the hell right up my spine. What the hell? It took all my self control to keep from quivering.

"That's stupid!" I snapped at him. I didn't step back though.

"And you feel it too," he said. "Can't explain it, but it's there. Am I right?"

Now I shook, but it was as much from frustration as hormones. "That's crazy! We don't know each other! In fact, the first time I met you, I flung you across the road!"

His voice was steady, but oozed over me anyway. "Haven't had a drink since then, either. You really caught me off guard with that," he added smiling.

I stood my ground. I wasn't scared of the guy, despite his come-on. It actually felt pretty good. He looked about fifty or so—not all that much older than me... Stop that, Maren!echoed in my brain. This guy's a freaking vampire! but I didn't care. Still, for appearance's sake, I snapped at him. "Yeah, well, keep getting out of line and I'll do it again, how about that?"

He shrugged. "Go ahead, no big deal."

"Oh yeah?"

"Yeah!"

Yes, we were arguing like a couple of kids in the schoolyard, but he had so gotten under my skin! So I popped both my hands up and splayed them at him.

And yeah, he flew back about thirty feet.

But instead of hitting the pavement like the last time, he stopped in mid air. Then did a little pirouette and landed lightly on his feet. "I was on guard that time, see?" he called over to me. "And sober!" he added with a grin.

My eyebrows shot up in surprise. How the hell did he do that?

He held up a finger. "Now check this out!"

In a blur, he shot from where he was across the roadway and was right in front of me again. He smiled brightly. "We can do this all night if you want. We vamps are really fast when we want to be. Until"—he lifted his hand and did that thing with his finger down my cheek—"we decide to go real slowww."

Oh God. I felt that one right down to the soles of my feet. I gasped. Dammit.

Finally, common sense arrived. I held my hands up and took a step back. "No, no, no, buddy. I'm not doing this."

Now he grinned like the cat about to swallow the canary. "I can be patient," he said. And then he batted his eyes at me.

You've never really had a guy come on to you in the most surreal of ways until you've had a freaking vampire bat his eyes at you. Especially a freaking vampire with curly eyelashes and the brightest of blue eyes. They were almost grey, they were such a pale blue, glinting like a frozen stream on a mountainside.

"What the hell is with you?" I snarked at him.

Again, that shrug. And that gaze… "Beats me! This is a new one for me too, Maren. I have no idea what's 'with' me. But I do know it's also 'with' you. And"—now his smile became as warm as the noon sun on a beach in Mexico—"I'm sure willing to find out just what this 'with' is all about."

"Now stop that!" Wait a minute. I saw some of those movies. I tilted my head at him. "Are you doing some kind of vampire voodoo like in the movies? Where they have this power of seduction?"

He shook his head. "That part's just legend and myth." He waved a hand at the sky. "It's a beautiful sunny day, and

I'm not burning up, am I? No, that's a legend too. No, we don't have any 'hypnotic power.' And for what it's worth, I've never felt this way before. And for me, 'never' is a really, really long time."

"How old are you anyway?" I asked. Hey, it's a reasonable question with a guy, right?

He reached out and tapped the tip of my nose. "Old enough not to answer a prying question. I'm not asking you your bra size, am I?"

I sighed. "Guys and boobs, some things never change…"

"Look, we'll talk later. I think Howie got word to the Fae."

I looked away from the pale blue glacier which were his eyes over to Howie and Laura's rig. Yep. He was right. Linette and her advisor, Sebille, along with a couple of other Fae, were descending from the air. Along with darting balls of light that I knew were a group of sprites.

There were other people milling around the campground, but none of them took any notice of the light show going on at the entrance of Howie's rig. The Fae that arrived all had an ethereal glow to them, and the sprites were tiny orbs of light, like floating Christmas tree lights, darting here and there as Howie and Laura held the door open for them to enter.

And it seemed that they couldn't see Mike either. His antics of floating in the air and then zooming back to me didn't register with a single person. When I gave him that blast with my mind that sent him flying, he wound up right next to a camper that had four people sitting in lawn chairs chatting. They didn't bat an eye when he floated back to the ground.

"Nobody in the campground can see them," I said. "And they don't see you either, do they?"

"I decide who can see me and who can't, doll," he replied. He flashed me a cheesy grin. "And you're one of the lucky ones!"

I rolled my eyes at him, then gestured back to Howie's rig. "I guess I'm not getting a nap then, am I?"

"They're going to be curious about where you two have been," he said in a quiet voice.

I looked over at Kara. "What are we going to tell them?" I asked.

Thirty Four

Kara

I decided to tell this group everything. After all, they worked hard to find Maren; the least I could do was just tell them the truth no matter how weird it was.

Ha! I was sitting in a trailer campground telling mythical people that aliens exist!

When I finished, I looked around the room at each one of them, and it was wonderful. Like Maren, I could see the Fae and sprites now. Her description didn't do them justice. I felt like my eyes were round as golf balls, ogling them.

And…my cancer was all gone. I mean, if I was able to use telekinesis, and now see mythical beings, then I was healed right? I squinted and looked over at Linette from the corner of my eye to see her aura. Yep, I got that too.

"So, they're aliens…" Howie said, letting the question hang in the air. When I slowly nodded, he added, "Where are they from?"

I pointed up. "Out there somewhere. Right now, they have a ship sitting on the other side of the moon."

"No, I mean, where 'out there' are they from?"

I shrugged. "I don't even think they're from this galaxy, to tell you the truth. They told Maren and me that Earth is the only planet in our entire galaxy with sentient life." My lips pulled to the side in irony. "In fact, Anjou was yelling at me about that. As if it was my fault that there are wars going on over in Syria." I held my hands up, palms facing upward. "What does she expect me to do? Run for President of the UN or something?"

Mike piped up. "Don't think that would help much if you ask me."

I faked a laugh. "Damn it. A new lease on life and I don't get to rule the world."

Howie leaned over from his seat on the sofa and patted my knee. "Well, you're right about the cancer; there's no sign of sickness on you that I can see." He looked at Laura beside him. "You see anything, dear?" When she shook her head no, I felt another weight lift from my shoulders that I didn't even know was there.

It sure had been one hell of a time the last few weeks. From being told my days were numbered with a Stage 4 cancer diagnosis, to waking up to find out my sister had magical powers, to being kidnapped as a pawn in a Fae civil war, and here I was sitting in a motor home and hanging out with my newest friends who were fairies, werewolves, and a vampire.

Some vacation, huh?

"Why are you shaking your head, dear?" Linette asked. The Fae folk were in a small group at the other end of the room. Linette was in Howie's easy chair with Sebille standing behind her on the right. On the left were a few sprites, just floating in the air at eye level. They had stayed silent throughout my tale of aliens and magic.

I scoffed. "Can you blame me? This has been some ride these last few days for this 'mere mortal' to handle, y'know?"

Mike barked a laugh from beside Maren. "Well, you're no mere mortal now, doll, you're a witch!" They weren't cuddled up on the sofa beside me, but Maren looked dangerously comfortable with that bloodsucker.

"Nay! Ye not be a witch!" I shot a look over at the sprites. It was Ellowen speaking. "Ye were nae born to it! Ye be some mutant made by those other-worlders!" She was buzzing about furiously. Ye be a miscreation by them!" She darted from Linette to Maren and me, hovering in front of us like a hummingbird. "Ye said they put their blood into ye!"

"Not 'blood,' Ellowen—DNA. They added some molecules, that's all."

"Bah! Blood from a strange creature!" She gestured over to Mike. "Like his evil kind!"

Mike bristled. "Now wait a damn minute!"

"I never cared for the vampires to be part of our Guild. Evil, bloodsuckers...more leeches than Mythics..."

Howie leaned forward. "Now Ellowen, we settled all that decades ago. Mike can't help what was done to him, and he's not fed on a human for years."

Mike jumped to his feet. "And they deserved to die! I did the world a favor every time I took one of 'em!" He paced around. "And ever since I swore off killin', anytime I've ever took blood from the living, I never—not once—took their lives." He marched over to where Ellowen was hovering. "Don't look down on me, sprite. Your kind have their own sordid history too."

"Everyone be still!" Linette rose to her feet. "Ellowen, I certainly understand your misgivings about Maren and Kara. 'Tis a strange event. But don't let the mystery of it cause you to lash out. You're much wiser than that." She tilted her head at Mike. "I apologize on behalf of our Guild, Michael. Of all of us, you've worked the hardest to control your appetites, and it's been at a great cost to yourself." She raised a hand at him. "But to recall the sprite's fascination with fire is also unfair, is it not? Those days are long gone now."

She turned to Kara and me. "But you two need to understand our dilemma here. Neither of you were born witches, but now here you be, witches in full, and brought about by other-worldly beings." She shook her head. "Can you not see the puzzle you are to us?"

I sighed. "We're a puzzle to you? Can you imagine how it feels to be us? I was just trying to go on a once-in-a-lifetime road trip with my sister!"

Maren put her hand on my arm. "No, you guys are wrong. We are witches."

"Ha!" Ellowen snapped.

"I'm serious." She looked around the room. "Isn't it part of the legend that the origin of witches came about from the effect of a full moon? I mean, one thing I know about witches is that they really get their jam on when it's a full moon." She looked at Linette, Howie, and Laura. "Just like you guys."

"I get a kick out of full moons too, y'know; just sayin'," Mike added with a grin.

Maren looked over at him and they both smiled for a second. What the hell? She was enjoying his attention? Yikes.

"Okay, Mike," she said, "point taken." Turning to the rest of the group, Maren continued. "We were told that they did their procedure on us—"

"Not 'they,' Maren," I said. "It was Rax. Anjou was against the idea. Give credit where it's due."

She nodded. "He told us that it was done just as the moon was on the cusp of becoming full, right?" When I nodded, she said, "So we, too, are 'children of the moon' just as some of you guys are."

"Not so fast! The witches spend years learning how to ply their craft!" Ellowen said. "And the two of ye, just like that, be doing magical things!"

Maren shrugged. "Maybe there's dormant genes in us

from an ancestor who was a witch. I don't know. But I believe that we're genuine witches."

Sebille finally spoke. She had been watching all the goings-on in silence since the meeting began and we told what had happened to us. "Children of the moon..." she said quietly. She nodded to me. "And in a way, you were brought to life during that. You were dying and now you are healed, is that not so?"

I closed my eyes and nodded. I was still getting my head around the idea that I wasn't dying. Just a few days ago I thought that Maren and I playing in the ocean was going to be for the last time. I had believed in my heart and soul that everything I did was going to be for the last time. Didn't matter to me whether or not I was a witch. My eyes filled with tears of gratitude at the gift I received from Rax. The gift of life. I just nodded in response to Sebille's question.

Sebille came over to where Maren and I were seated. She put her hands on each of our heads. I felt a pulsing sensation at her touch, like a low-pitched hum. She murmured something in a language I didn't understand, and took her hands away.

She turned to the rest of the group. "Hear me now, all of you," she shot a side-eye to Ellowen. As the counselor to the Fae, and as counselor to this Guild Of Mythics, I declare these two women to be full- and true-blooded witches, to be accepted by us as such, and invite them to become members of our Guild." She leaned forward to be face-to-face with the still-hovering Ellowen. "We must put our fears aside, my friend and accept them. Can you trust in my judgment?"

Ellowen remained hovering in the air and folded her arms across her chest with ahumpf! She looked like a ticked-off Tinkerbell.

"By your judgment, this Guild has flourished for ages, Sebille. I do not like your decision. At all." She turned to the group. "But hear me now, all of you; I shall abide. Sebille be the wisest of us. And thus I abide." She turned back to Maren and me and quick as a flash, darted to each of our cheeks and lightly kissed each of us. With another sigh, she said, "I give thee the kiss of welcome to our Guild."

The rest of the group stood, and one by one, came over to us and each of them kissed our cheeks, each saying the same words: "I give thee the kiss of welcome to our Guild." When each one did, a thrill shot through me. Exactly why, I don't know; but I was part of "the cool kids" now.

Mike had positioned himself to be the last in line. As he drew nearer, he kept his eyes glued to Maren, with the smartest of smart-assed smiles on his face. He quickly gave me a light buss; it felt like a cousin's kiss or something.

But when he leaned over to Maren, he said the words in a heartfelt way. "I welcome you to the Guild and to my life, Maren from far away…"

When he leaned in to kiss her cheek, she put her hands on each side of his face and kissed him on the lips. Whoa!

"I accept your welcome, Vampire," she said lightly as she released him.

Mike's eyes rolled up in his head for a second. "Wow!" was all he said as he staggered back to his seat.

I looked over to Maren. What the hell was that about? She gave me an impish look and shimmied her shoulders. Oh boy, I'd get it out of her when we were back in our rig, believe me.

So, I turned to the group and asked, "Thank you for your welcome. We'll try to be worthy of it. Now I have a question." I looked over to Sebille.

"Speak, witch," she said. "I'm listening."

"What the hell do we do now?"

Thirty Five

Kara

Looks like we're on our own, finally," I said to Maren as I pulled the rig from our spot the next morning. Howie and Laura's rig was gone, the Boler that Rax had used as a portal to his craft was gone, and even the minivan that Maren's crush Mike had, was missing.

"Well, unlike you and me, they have lives to get back to."

I shot a look over at her. "Hey, we got lives too, y'know."

She shook her head. "No, not really. What Sebille said yesterday really hit home with me."

"She said a lot. Which part?" I wheeled my rig through the entrance gates and onto the main road. It would be just a short hop to get to the interstate. We'd follow that and be at Maren's daughter's house by nightfall so Maren could see her brand-new grandchild. Damn it, she's too young to be a grandma! And I'm older than her!

Maren snuggled into her seat, her head rocking from side to side.

"C'mon!" I said. "Spit it out already!"

"Sebille told you that basically you were reborn the first time we were on Rax and Anjou's ship, right? You were at death's door, and now you're cured." She spread her arms. "You have a new life in front of you, Kara."

She turned in her seat to face me. "And isn't it just sooo serendipitous that at exactly the same time you learned your old life was ending, my old life had blown up in my face?" She gave a sharp nod. "Both of us, at the same time, had our old lives swept away. If you think about it, we were as ready as we could ever hope to be for what just happened."

I drove in silence, absorbing her words. She was absolutely right. Both of us, at the same time, had our lives yanked out from under us. My son had just fledged, and I had been given the cancer news. Maren's kids were already grown and gone, but the future with Wayne had ended like someone just snapped their fingers. There wasn't any pressing reason to get our butts back to Auburn NY anytime soon.

"Rax couldn't pick better people than us to scoop up, you know that?" I said quietly.

"Well, the universe is supposed to unfold as it's meant to…" Then Maren laughed lightly. "This world is sure as hell different now, huh? Stuff we both believed turned out not to be the case at all! You thought you would just keep working at the diner, and I thought Wayne and I would become even bigger shots in the real estate biz."

"It's more than that. Way more."

When Maren looked at me with her eyebrows knitted, I continued. "Look, you never believed in aliens or magic, and now we've met aliens and can do magic."

"Yeah, but you always bought into that stuff."

"No! Not really. There's a difference between wanting to believe something and actually believing it to be true. I really, really wanted aliens to be real, Maren. But I didn't believe in their existence until now. I had to have it front and center for me. And"—I shrugged my shoulders—"It's pretty much the same with the magical powers we have now. I wished there was real magic in the world, but I never saw it before."

Maren burst out laughing. "We've overloaded on this stuff! Not just meeting aliens, but finding out fairies and werewolves and sprites are real! You kidding me?"

I took my eyes off the road for a second to shoot her a look. "Y'know something, you not mentioning Mike says a hell of a lot more about you and him than if you mentioned us meeting vampires, hon."

"Grrrr…" Maren mumbled. "Busted."

"So, you're hot for him, huh? Gonna take him for a little trip to 'Maren Country' huh?"

She held up both hands. "Slow down. He's in my head, that's for sure. Just where it goes between us—if anywhere—I don't know. I mean,"—she held up one finger—"I'm on the rebound, aren't I? My marriage just broke up and I'm the dumpee."

"Well, a sexy vampire being warm for your form has to help the ego, right?"

Her face brightened. "You think he's sexy too?" When I gave her a shrug-nod, she squeaked. "He's sooo hot!" She reached across and patted my thigh. "The fantasies I've been having about him! Whoaaaa…."

"What about your attractive lawyer, Maren? Last time you were in touch with him, you were pretty…ummm…" I paused.

"Yeah, I was. And Derek Scott's a great guy. But c'mon, Kara! I'm a witch now! How the hell could I let anything start up with him now? He's trying to build his practice and all that everyday normal stuff."

"And Mike's a hell of a lot more interesting, right?" I eyed her.

"Yeah!"

"Maren, messing around with a vampire? That could be really dangerous you know."

"That's part of the thrill! Come on, Kara! You dated a

member of the Hell's Angels for God's sake!"

She had me there. I had to work through my "bad boy" phase. But my bad boy didn't have the craving to suck my blood. Sure we did some kinky stuff in the bedroom, but nothing like that. "At least Corey Caymen was human," I tried.

"Barely. He was a lowlife and you know it. You always had to pick up the check when you two went out, he'd disappear for days at a time without explanation, and"—she shuddered—"his friends! Ugh."

In my defense I was only twenty years old at the time. And we only lasted a couple of months. I held up my hand. "Okay, maybe you have a point. If anything, Corey turned out to be a perfect loser and I dumped him. But you and Mike? Well, he's got a steady job, even if it's at a funeral home. But Maren! A vampire?"

She grinned at me. "First-time bad boy for me!"

"You're not worried he'd…you know…kill you?"

She shook her head. "Nope."

"Well, I hope that's not going to be your famous last word. Just be careful, okay?"

"Look, I don't know if I'll see him again, okay?"

"He's got your phone number, though. I'll bet he calls you or sends a text."

"Too late!" She pulled out her phone and held it up. "I already have three!"

"Oh brother."

"Want me to read them to you? They're really romantic!"

"Do I have a choice?"

And no, I didn't. I drove onto the interstate listening to my middle-aged kid sister read me her high-tech love notes. And yeah, they were as cheesy as a high school kid's. But Maren was as excited as a high school kid. I kept my snark to myself and let her run with it, happy that she was all worked up over a guy.

To be honest, I never saw her get this excited over a guy. Well, not since we were kids anyway. It was refreshing, to tell the truth. Well, new life and all that, right?

After she finished all her mushy stuff, she put her phone away and said, "Okay, so we going to do what Sebille and the others suggested?"

"I can't see how we can. Sure, it's a great idea to find other witches and learn more about the craft or whatever, but how the hell do we do that? Put an ad in Craigslist?" I could picture the ad:

> *Two middle-aged women seeking others*
> *for fellowship and friendship.*
>
> *Must be practicing witches with*
> *knowledge of spells, potions, and herbal*
> *lore. Ability to fly with a broom a plus.*

You gotta be kidding me. How the hell are we supposed to do that?

"Look Maren, how about we visit your new granddaughter and take it from there, okay?"

"We'll keep our eyes peeled though?"

"Sure." Whatever that means. "If we come across a witch, or even a coven, we'll introduce ourselves, how about that?"

"I'll be there's lots of stuff we can learn. Maybe love potions, huh?"

"I think you're covered in that department!"

"Not me, silly! For you!"

I rolled my eyes. "My love life's fine."

"C'mon, Kara! The last time you were nekkid with a guy, he was doing some alien medical procedure on you! And you weren't even awake! And furthermore, he's not even a 'guy'! He's an alien!"

Maybe. And a good looking one at that. But that's as silly an idea as Maren's idea of getting together with a vampire.

But then…we're witches for crying out loud! The idea of hooking up with a regular, everyday sort of guy like Maren's lawyer Derek Scott was just as ridiculous if you think about it. I could see a first date or whatever: "So, tell me about yourself, Kara. What sort of things are you into?" Ha. "Well, I'm a brand-new witch, created by aliens, and I'm trying to figure out how to cast a great cooking spell." Yeah…I'd like to see them write about this situation in the Modern Love section of The New York Times!

I put my nonexistent love life out of my head. "So, we're not going to head right back home after visiting with your family, right?"

"Nahhh…you got money from your lottery winnings, right?"

"Oh! So you're gonna freeload off me, huh?"

"Don't worry, I can pay my own way. And if we start getting short, maybe a trip to Vegas might not be such a bad idea, what do you think?"

"We'll jump off that bridge when we get to it."

I set the cruise control and put on some music.

As we travelled down the highway, I still couldn't believe what happened to us in this past week.

This was one hell of a Magical Mystery Tour, that was for sure.

The End

Author's Note:

I've been writing for years now, but when I wrote my first book in the Paranormal Women's Fiction genre (The Witching Well) I felt like a kid again. It was so much fun, and the ideas and characters came to me fully formed.

I jumped into writing about Kara and Maren right away. Like them, I have a sister, and we're just two years apart in age.

Back in 2019, my only sibling almost died. She spent a week in the ICU in an induced coma. It was harrowing. I had never been so afraid in my life, and I wasn't the sick one! The monitors softly beeping, the hiss of the ventilator and tubes running into her were electronic emblems of just how dire things were. And my big sister looked so, so small in that bed.

As hard as it was, looking back, I feel blessed.

Blessed because we live in the same city (Kingston), and I could sit at her bedside every night in the hospital. As she floated in her sleep, I told her stories from our childhood; tales of our parents, and reminisced about our ice skating on the lake. "Skate, Corliss, skate back to me!" I said over and over, leaning in past the tubes, hoses and wires keeping her alive.

I said blessed, and I mean it. I was there with her in the night when her eyelids fluttered and I felt her hand grasp my own. Watching her eyes open is one of my most deeply cherished memories.

I've always had the dream of getting an RV camper and bombing across country. One of the great things about being a writer is that I can indulge my dreams as I put them on a page.

Kara and Maren are not Shelley and Corliss. For starters, we're a (cough, cough) a tad older! And neither of us had ever been hit on by a Vampire, okay?

I truly hope you enjoyed this book. If you could leave a review, I'd appreciate it.

I'm deep into Book 2 of Witch Way, it's title is 'Hex Appeal' and will be out shortly. All of my works are exclusive to Amazon.

As always, thank you for your readership. I'm deeply grateful.

Warmly,

Shelley Dorey

ABOUT THE AUTHOR

Michelle Dorey, writing as 'Shelley Dorey' is the author of more than a dozen spine-chilling novels featuring ghosts, haunted houses and the supernatural. She has been on the Amazon best seller list many times throughout her career.

A voracious reader of the masters like Stephen King and Dean Koontz, she decided to try her hand at writing after going on a Ghost Walk in the enigmatic city of Kingston, Ontario, Canada where she lives. Her first book, Crawley House was inspired by a true tale of a family's nightmare, living in a home owned by Queen's University.

"Expect the supernatural when the bedrock of a city is limestone. Throw in the fact it is bordered on three sides by the mighty St. Lawrence River, The Rideau River and Lake Ontario and you are in for some thrills and chills of the paranormal variety--which of course is my cup of tea."

Does she love Kingston? You bet! Her husband Jim, a transplanted native New Yorker born and raised in the Bronx, agrees. Michelle and Jim like nothing better than spoiling their two pugs with treats and long walks in their neighborhood. Funny, but the slightly neurotic dogs always refuse to go for a stroll in the cemetery nearby.

OTHER WORKS

All of Michelle Dorey and Shelley Dorey books are exclusively available on Amazon

Women's Paranormal Fantasy By Shelley Dorey
The Mystical Veil Series
Hex After 40 Series
Celtic Knot Series

Ghosts And Hauntings By Michelle Dorey
The Hauntings Of Kingston Series
The Haunted Ones Series
The Haunted Cabin